Blood of Discovery

D.M. Wyatt
Maggie Valley Publishing

ISBN: 978-1-7351339-0-4 (Paperback)

First printing edition 2020

Maggie Valley Publishing
Rolla, Missouri

For Amanda
Oops was never a mistake

D.M. Wyatt

Blood of Discovery

D.M. Wyatt

Chapter One

A box of Danishes glistened on the break-room table. Alexa scanned the treats and asked, "Where'd these come from?"

"Your boyfriend," Tamara said without looking up from People magazine.

Alexa shook her head and sighed as she sat down.

Carly hovered, finally plucking a cheese Danish. "Oh, come on, he's not dropping off treats to any other office."

"No other office has as many possessed copiers as we do," Alexa said. "I'm sure his company is getting so much business from our repairs they're sending over food in sheer gratitude."

"That's bullshit," Tamara said, looking up from her magazine. "Maintenance is covered in our copier contract. We pay a flat rate no matter how many times they come out."

"How do you know that?" Carly asked.

Tamara said, "It's how that shit works! Uh... Everywhere." She speared a steamed broccoli floret with her plastic fork, waving it toward Alexa. "There's no denying," she said, "he has the hots for you."

Alexa glared at Tamara.

"Admit it, you like him," Tamara said.

Alexa continued to glare.

"Toss the poor boy a bone. You should go out with him some time."

"Should I?" Alexa asked. "I mean I don't exactly have the best track record with men."

Tamara rolled her eyes. "You're young. Anyone you've dated up to this point has been a mere boy."

"It's time you take up with a real man," Carly said.

Alexa groaned.

"He's made it clear he likes you, just short of stalking you..." Tamara paused to meet Alexa's glare. "Just thank him for the danishes and see where that takes you."

As Alexa stepped out of the kitchen she caught his cologne, the repairman was still in the office. The scent was the oddest mixture. She couldn't quite identify the tones, but nothing like bottles at the cologne counter - it was very peppery but not spicy, more like a well-seasoned steak. He walked to the exit, but turned around and scanned the office. She grinned in his direction and continued toward her desk hoping he didn't overhear her lunch conversation.

She rubbed her cheekbone, hoping to alleviate the pain that had been coming and going all summer. Alexa thought possibly she was suffering from a sinus infection if it weren't for being able to smell, and yet the center of her face ached all of the time. Maybe it was a toothache? Crap, did she need to go to the dentist?

As she sat down, Alexa continued to rub her cheekbone with no relief. She dug through a drawer for a bottle of Tylenol knowing two white pills were not going to cut through the pain.

She leaned her head back with her eyes closed unable to clear her mind. Instead, the throbbing sinuses or tooth or whatever it was, seemed hell-bent on killing her. She opened her mouth and stretched her jaw, offering only a momentary release from pain. And then the throbbing returned. Alexa sucked on an ice cube from her glass of water, holding the melting cube against the roof of her mouth. Ah, that helped.

"You should get those headaches checked out," Tamara said as she returned to her desk.

"Nah, I'll be fine," Alexa said, rolling her head to look at Tamara.

The wash of concern on Tamara's face was quickly erased by a wink. Tamara settled into her chair and the click-click-click of her fingers hitting the keyboard filled the air.

Alexa winced as the sounds of a busy hospital room rose in her mind. A man and two women in frantic conversation along with beeping monitors drowned out the keyboard strokes next to her. Someone in green was pressed against the bedrails, leaning over her and a cold stethoscope pushed against her breast as she gasped for air. The screaming oxygen sensor began to fade, the green scrubs were blurring, and her head became heavy until darkness consumed her.

Alexa pushed Tamara's death scene to the back of her mind with the jumble of her other coworkers' final moments crowding her head. Her throbbing face didn't distract her from the constant slew of death scenes, nor did the death scenes abate her pain. Combined, they scattered her focus and she wondered how she would make it through yet another day.

Chapter Two

The smell was nauseating, a mix of filth and death. The hall was too dark to see what was on the floor, but Alexa suspected she didn't want to know. She couldn't get her feet under her as she was dragged along the muck. Men on either side pulled her toward the high-pitched screaming. The screaming, oh the screaming, she wished the screaming would stop!

Alexa struggled against the men dragging her. They ignored her attempts to break free and squeezed tighter to maintain their holds. The man on her right yanked her arm sideways as he moved, his hand sliding down her arm, resting on her wrist, shooting an incredible pain through her body.

A thick wooden door flung open and sunlight blinded her as she was pulled inside. The stench of the room overwhelmed her, even worse than the hallway. She slammed her eyes shut as all of her senses were assaulted – the tight grip on her arms, the wretched smell so strong it filled her mouth, the intense light, and the screams... the echoing screams...

Shaking with fear, Alexa opened her eyes and she was alone. The room was black. And silent. And... no stench. Her heart was pounding as she looked around realizing she was in her bed. It was a dream. Just a damn dream.

She took several calming breaths, happy to not be in a dank hallway. She rolled to her side, her eyes adjusting to the dark forms on her bookshelf bringing comfort from her childhood days. Her heart rate calmed and she rolled over to stare at the opposite wall. Alexa tossed and turned until she decided sleep was impossible. She got out of bed and changed into a t-shirt and shorts.

She never felt any insecurity jogging, even in the pre-dawn hours, but something was different — the park was abnormally vacant. No other joggers on the path, dog walkers nowhere to be seen, even the birds were quiet. And that sense, that uneasy sense someone, several someones, was watching her. She shook off the vibe as a carryover from her nightmare.

Trotting past the playground Alexa hoped to put the unnerving feeling of being watched behind her. She put her focus back onto the path knowing she was about to enter the most isolated portion of the park where the trail turned and faded out of view from the playground. Trees formed a thick canopy where even in daylight the area was shaded and dark. Without light she focused on the ground to ensure she didn't veer off the path or trip over fallen branches or rocks.

Hair prickled on her neck. She still held the feeling of being watched.

Alexa stopped running. From the middle of the path she peered around to assess her surroundings. She couldn't see beyond the lawn, but knew not much further away was a bramble of trees and vines hiding a shallow creek where teenagers were known to hang out. A slight rustle in the bushes caught her attention. Without questioning her intuition she knew she was about to be attacked. She held no urge to run, but to stand. And... fight?

Alexa's eyes scanned the area, but she couldn't cut through the darkness. Then she smelled it, a very distinct scent of pepper. The odor was getting stronger as they neared. They were moving slow, almost silent, getting closer.

Another rustle.

Ten dark forms burst from the bushes running towards her. Alexa stood still as an inner drive took over, converting her fear into anger. She adjusted her stance for better balance.

The men spread out into a line, prepared for her to run away. Alexa scanned the line of men and locked eyes with the one second from the center. She maintained her focus on that particular man as a surge of warmth bubbled up within her and the air began to stir around her feet. Alexa felt an inner-warmth explode and the air pushed outward, dropping the other nine men to the ground.

The tenth man, the one she had chosen, lunged at her. Alexa grabbed onto him, holding him close. She could hear his heartbeat and the blood coursing through his veins inches away from her mouth. His cheek was right there – how she wanted to sink her teeth into his soft flesh. In a fluid movement Alexa stretched her mouth open and sunk her teeth into his cheek. The bite was insufficient; she wanted more. The instinct to pull caused her to rip her teeth downward. Screaming and cracking bones filled the air as blood pooled in her mouth. The blood was intoxicating and kept her latched to his face. When his body went slack she dropped him to the ground, but she knew he was not yet dead.

Nine sets of yellow eyes were staring at her and the men had fangs. She had never seen anything like that except in the movies. They looked terrified of her, but she was much more scared.

Alexa looked down to her victim, covered in blood, his jaw nearly ripped off his face. He also had fangs.

Did she do that? Rip his face off?

The pool of blood was enormous; he was bleeding to death. From his perspective, his last moments of life, she could see herself – a brunette jogger in shorts and a t-shirt. Covered in blood on her face, neck, arms, and all down her front... in her sea of red only two white fangs stood out.

She had fangs.

A jittery hand, covered in blood, reached toward her mouth. She ran a nervous finger along a tooth extending over her lower lip.

The men were crawling to a stand and backing away from her. One reached out to the man lying on the ground, pulling his dead body from the scene. Another joined his efforts, no one taking their wary eyes off Alexa.

She growled. They gathered the limp body and bolted back to the bushes.

Alexa looked back to the sidewalk, blood splattered and smeared. Blood. Blood everywhere. It pooled at her feet and was splattered on her shoes, her legs, shorts... A dead man's blood was covering her head to toe. Terror filled her and she was shaking.

Tears welled in her eyes, confusion pounded in her head. She took in the blood-filled sidewalk again. Alexa needed to leave immediately; she could hear a jogger in the distance.

Wiping her feet in the grass, Alexa blindly made her way back to her parents' home. Beyond the rooftops she could see the sky brightening to a light blue. The sun had not yet broken the horizon, but was coming. She stood on the sidewalk, tears streaming down her face. She wondered how to explain to her parents about the blood, the teeth, the dying man, the... the bad dream. This was all a dream. Just another one of her bad dreams.

Chapter Three

She stood in front of her house unsure what to do. Alexa knew she needed to go inside yet she continued to stand frozen. She watched, as if detached from the scene, as her mother opened the front door. Alexa couldn't hear her mother's words but she was saying something. And running. Her mother was running towards her, wearing a nightgown, looking terrified.

An arm wrapped around her. It was her mother's arm and she was guiding Alexa to the house, repeatedly looking over their shoulders. Once inside, Alexa watched her mother fumble with the locks and then to pat-down Alexa's body. She was looking for something but kept glancing at Alexa's face.

"Alexa," she said. Her voice was distant, like in a fog. "I need you to retract your teeth."

Mom saw her teeth? Her fangs? They're exposed? She didn't know how to retract them. She tried to shake her head, but her whole body felt like it was vibrating.

"Okay, okay," her mother said. "Let's just go in the bathroom where you can sit down."

Alexa blinked and tried to focus, shaking as she was guided to the bathroom, her legs sluggish. She stood on the white tile, staring at the floor, making sure not to step on the blue rug in front of the tub with her blood soaked feet. A bustle behind her as her mother grabbed towels and a washcloth from the rod. She could hear the water in the sink running, then her mother was in front of her with movements that were chaotic, first wiping Alexa's face, then her arms. Alexa watched the blue washcloth turn red and redder and redder, until hardly any blue showed. She looked at her arms where the washcloth left red streaks. There was still so much blood. The movement stopped and Alexa looked up.

"Are you injured?" her mom asked.

Alexa shook her head "no" and pushed toward the toilet. As she vomited she felt her teeth retract.

Then she vomited again.

So much blood. The toilet was a sea of red and Alexa was gasping for air. Her mother flushed the toilet and put the lid down. She helped Alexa sit then continued wiping blood off her face.

"Were you bit?"

"Um..." Alexa looked toward her right shoulder and back to her mother. In a quiet rasp she said, "I don't know." Her shirt was pulled up and over her head. Her mother inspected her shoulder and ran a finger over the surface.

Alexa mustered the strength to say "mom." She wasn't heard as her mother continued wiping and inspecting her shoulders and arms. Alexa repeated, "mom." She still wasn't heard.

"MOM!" Alexa's scream broke her mother's inspection. "Mom," Alexa cried, "I killed a man."

Her mother froze.

Alexa repeated, "I killed a man. Wh... Wh... What am... am I going to do?" She gulped. "This is... his blood. Mom..."

Her mother knelt down, her eyes darting and scared. She tried to wipe Alexa's tears as her own began to well. "Crap," she muttered and sighed. Assessing Alexa, still covered in blood, she took a deep breath and said, "I think you need to tell me what happened."

Alexa gulped and stared at the floor, avoiding eye contact. "I was, um, in the park and it didn't feel right. And I just knew they were there and when they got closer I could smell them and knew there were ten of them. And then they came rushing out of the bushes and, um..." She paused, coming up for air. "And, um, I'm pretty sure I growled at them? I think that's when my teeth popped out." Her mother nodded, wide-eyed. "Then I felt this... uh... surge? And I was able to push the men back, like with the air."

Her mother's eyebrows shot up. "You were able to levitate *ten* men?"

"Well, no, they didn't go up. It was more like a cloud, or a, a, a force field and it knocked them down. Well... all but one. It was like I *wanted* to fight him. So he ran into me and I... I guess I caught him and my focus was on his cheek..."

"He didn't knock you down?"

"No, I just grabbed him and held onto him. And I... I bit him." She gulped and noticed the blood had soaked her shorts. All of this was from her bite. She began to shake again.

Her mother stroked her arm in reassurance, but her face showed alarm. "What happened after that?" she asked in soothing tones.

Alexa took a deep breath. "So, um, after he fell to the ground the others grabbed him and ran back into the bushes."

"They took the body with them?"

Alexa nodded and asked, "Do I have to turn myself in or something?"

"I don't think this qualifies as a crime."

"What do you mean?"

Her mother sat quiet for a moment. "Honey, I don't think there is anything to do. They don't know who you are and.... There's no body, no proof, no..."

"But he died!"

"I understand, but the rules are different with vampires."

Alexa sat on the toilet staring at her mother. Vampire? Did

she say vampire?

"Mom, am I a vampire?"

"Yes, Alexa, you are."

Tears welled again as she hyperventilated. "Why? How did I become a vampire?"

Her mother stroked her face. "Nothing happened, it's in your blood. Your father is a vampire."

"What?" Alexa's eyes darted back and forth and blinked rapidly as she tried to understand. "Are you a vampire?"

Her mother shook her head. "No, honey, I'm a witch."

Alexa had to looked away and let her eyes roam the light blue walls of the tiny bathroom. Feeling like the air had been sucked from her lungs Alexa returned her focus to her mother. "You... you knew? You knew this was going to happen?"

Her mother shook her head. "No, I didn't know this was going to happen. I'm actually quite surprised. We thought you had very few vampire traits at all, that you were mostly a witch."

"I'm a witch?"

"Yes. I'm a witch and your father is a vampire. That makes you what people call a hybrid - half witch, half vampire."

Alexa's chin began to tremble again. She was being stroked; her mom was trying to comfort her. She pushed her mother's hand away and stood up. "I need to take a shower."

Her mother left the bathroom as Alexa turned the knobs for the shower. In slow, mechanical steps she removed her bloodied shoes and the rest of her blood-soaked clothing before stepping in the tub. Confused tears poured as the water rained over her head. The blood washed away, but the confusion and fear remained.

Her mother returned and bustled around the room. "Watch your step," she warned. "I took the rug, so the floor is slippery.

There are towels here for you."

Alexa heard the door close. Why? Why was this happening? Why did no one tell her? Vampires? Vampires were real? And witches? What the hell? How was any of this possible? How did she not know? Why? And the dead man. She couldn't erase his disfigured, bloodied face. She did that to him. With her teeth. She killed a man with her teeth. Her vampire teeth. She was a vampire. A killer. She was a killer. Who else was she going to kill?

She turned off the water and slumped to the floor of the tub. She stared at the showerhead, focusing on the circular designs of the nozzle. No answers came from the circles, no clarity. Again she questioned if she was in a dream. When at last Alexa exited the shower, she wrapped towels around her hair and her torso, and went to her bedroom.

"Alexa," her mother said softly from the end of the hall.

Alexa turned around in her doorway, staring at the beige carpet. She wondered why she had never noticed the brown specks in the weave. They were everywhere, and yet for years she had walked over them never noticing the carpet was anything but beige.

"I called your office. I left a message you were sick."

"Thanks, mom." Alexa closed the door, dropping the towel to the floor as she walked to her bed where she had left her nightshirt and shorts earlier. Was that an hour ago? More? It seemed a lifetime since she had changed into her jogging clothes, now soaked in blood, soaked in the blood of a man she killed.

She slid into her nightclothes and crawled into bed. When she closed her eyes she saw his limp body on the ground and the sets of yellow eyes glaring at her. She saw his disfigured face, and again she was crying.

Chapter Four

Alexa opened her eyes to the blissful realization she was in her room, safely tucked in her bed. She took a deep breath, exhausted from the crazy jumble of dreams still hanging in her memory.

She remembered the faces in her dream, which was odd because she never sees faces, and her mom was there. She couldn't remember her mom ever being in her dreams, but this time she was – cleaning her off and talking. She even said she was a witch! This counted as possibly the craziest dream she ever had!

The sun was full and bright, as if it were late morning, maybe even noon? Shouldn't she be at work? She flipped on her side, wrestling the pillow as she remembered the last thing she heard in her dream - her mother reported calling Alexa's office to say she was sick. With the pillow out of the way she saw the clock, red numbers flashing eleven a.m.

A sickening feeling swept over her, a knot built in her stomach.

Alexa rolled to her back and ran her tongue along the roof of her mouth. The flesh was tender, like she had eaten scalding hot pizza. She discovered new ridges that didn't exist the day before.

Panic was settling in, what if that wasn't a dream? Could she really *be* a vampire? Was her mother really a witch?

If she in fact had fangs, she had no idea how to bring them out. She scrunched her face, and grinned, and performed a variety of exercises, yet nothing caused any movement. Maybe they only came out when the sun was down?

Maybe she needed to forget that stupid dream?

She sat up and looked around her room, everything seemed the same... except she was either scared of a freaky dream or she was a murderer. That man's face — It was so vivid with the flesh ripped away exposing his teeth and a broken bone held in place by visible tendons. And all of the blood. Ugh, the blood – the signature of all her nightmares.

She stood up and walked to her bookshelf, running her hand along the spines. The top of the bookshelf sat at eye-level holding more books and a few knick-knacks from her childhood. Running her finger along the edge Alexa saw she ought to dust.

She stared at the doll resting on the top of the bookshelf. The doll vibrated then slumped to the side. Alexa had been making that doll rattle and fall over since she was a little girl.

Holy crap, she was a witch.

And that wasn't a dream.

Shaking as she stared at the doll, the previous hours played through her head. Shouldn't she be able to do more than make a doll twitch if she could blast nine men to the ground? She focused on the doll again. It convulsed on its side.

Up. She wanted it to go up, or fly off the shelf. It vibrated again.

Dammit.

She took a deep and stabilizing breath to calm her nerves, then glared at the stupid doll. Fly dammit, fly! Squinting her eyes she remembered the swoosh of air when she was in the park, how it felt like a heat from her gut expanded outward and forward. She glared at the doll again and focused where she remembered the heat while concentrating on the little bit of space between the doll and the wall... And... push.

The doll came flying at her face, Alexa yelped, and her fangs came out.

She froze. And started trembling again.

Tears flowed as she hobbled back to bed. She sat on the edge, clutching a pillow, sobbing. Alexa wanted nothing more than to curl up and go to sleep, or wake up, or whatever. She rubbed her face dry as she continued to sniffle. She needed to get her fangs back in her mouth, but she didn't know how.

Tentative and cautious, she probed the fangs with her tongue. The upper fangs rested easily over her lower lip. Crap, there were lower fangs too. As she tried to run her tongue along the back of the top fangs she had to continue opening her mouth. Alexa stretched her mouth further and felt a sensation, a pull. She opened her mouth just a little more and her teeth folded back into her mouth.

Alexa craned her mouth open again, further, further, until her teeth came out then she retracted them.

She pulled the pillowcase off the pillow and wiped her nose, dropping the soiled fabric to the floor. Tucking the naked pillow to her chest, Alexa curled onto her side staring at the wall as fairytales and stories of vampires and witches ran through her head. What was truth? What was fiction? She had no idea. What she did know is that she killed a man. The gruesome scene continually running through her head was a mess *she* created.

Chapter Five

Knowing her mother had gone outside, likely to work in the garden, Alexa left her bedroom in search of something to eat. Her stomach had been rumbling for hours, but she was too upset to face her mother. Rummaging through the cabinets Alexa found a box of chocolate covered peanut-butter bars. She opened a package and walked around the kitchen with the chocolate bar hanging out of her mouth like a cigar.

She opened and closed cabinet doors with no surprises. Boxes neatly lined a top shelf, rows of canned vegetables on the next. Spices, dishes, cookbooks all appeared as they did every time she had rummaged through the kitchen in search of a snack. Yet, she was determined to find a meal. A box mix for brownies lured her for quite some time, but she really needed something substantial and definitely more immediate than a twenty-minute bake time. Almost with disdain, she settled on a red can of chicken noodle soup. It fit the bill – filling and quick to prepare.

She wondered if vampires ate soup? Aren't they supposed to dine on blood? Yet, soup sounded good and was the best as the cabinet had to offer. Hunting down prey would surely take longer than the twenty-minute brownies or the two-minute soup. Was she supposed to hunt for prey? Crap, did *dad* hunt for prey?

Waiting for the microwave Alexa poured Coke into a glass with ice. The kitchen door opened as she was removing the bowl of soup from the microwave. She considered abandoning the bowl to escape to her bedroom without confrontation.

"Alexa, please sit down," her mother said.

Alexa ignored her mother, carefully balancing the bowl of soup with one hand and grabbing the glass of Coke with the other.

A stool from the kitchen counter scooted across the floor. By itself.

Alexa froze.

Slowly she looked from the stool to her mother. "Sit," her mother said, pointing at the stool.

Alexa stared at her mother. She wanted nothing more than to forget the world of witches and vampires - the men in the park were just a bad dream. Again, she looked at the stool and back to her mother. Her mother's finger was still pointing at the stool and her expression had not changed. Obediently, Alexa returned the glass and bowl to the counter of the kitchen peninsula and pulled the stool back its original position. She sat down where she had eaten breakfast almost every day for twenty years.

Her mother moved further into the kitchen behind the peninsula, facing Alexa. "Eat," she said. "You haven't had anything all day." She pulled a box of crackers from a cabinet and set them in front of Alexa.

"Thanks," Alexa mumbled as she reached for the crackers. She extracted a sleeve of crackers from the box and removed seven crackers. She smashed them between her hands, dropping a mound of cracker crumbs onto her soup. She stirred the crumbs into the soup and fished out a spoonful of noodles, chicken broth, and soggy crumbs. Her mother watched with a look of encouragement from under a red bandana.

Alexa put the spoon in her mouth trying to ignore that she was being watched. The soft contents didn't quite hit the mark, but she was hungry and loaded the spoon again. With a shrug she said, "I can't figure out what witches and vampires even *do*."

Her mother tilted her head and said, "Just live life. Everything you have been doing."

She sat with another loaded spoon hovering over the bowl. "Why wasn't I told?"

Her mother sighed and leaned on the counter with both arms. "Alexa, there is so much more to this than not telling you. And it's gut wrenching that you found out the way you did. We had hoped to tell you last year and the year before and many many, times before that, but permission never came through. There are very strict rules about dealing with hybrids and we really want to do this properly, but both sides, the witches and the vampires, cannot agree how you are to be recognized. I talked to your father earlier, and I want you to know he's really upset about what happened to you. But anyways, he believes, especially since your teeth came in you will be acknowledged by the vampires, it's just going to take some time. There are some other political issues that need to be resolved that, well, quite honestly I don't even understand." She tilted her head again, a softness filled her expression. "You should know I never had high hopes that the witches would come around on this subject, but especially now with your teeth..." She shook her head. "Anyway, your father is going to try to get home tomorrow and we'll talk more then."

Alexa dropped her spoon into the bowl. "I don't give a shit about being acknowledged, I mean if they do or they don't, whatever. Why couldn't I have at least *known* witches and vampires were real? I mean, you could have, should have, told me at some point. But not telling me at all, *ever*? That's bullshit!"

"Honey..."

"NO!" Alexa said. "Don't sooth this over with 'honey.' Mom, that was the scariest fucking thing in my entire life. Those men intended to rape me and leave me for dead. That alone is terrifying, I mean, rattles me to the bone..."

"I know..."

"No, you don't..."

"Yes, Alexa, I do."

Alexa was ready to continue her rant, but was cut short by the severe expression on her mother's face.

"I know only too well that terror, Alexa Marie. We have bent over backwards to keep you safe so you would never know that horror."

Alexa wanted to crawl into a shell and hide away. She looked at the bowl in front of her - her appetite disappeared. She looked up to her mother unable to be angry, but she was. No, she wanted to cry.

"Your father is beside himself that anyone got that close to you. When he comes home I am hoping he will be permitted to tell you more. I know you have a million questions, and I understand you're upset, but I really need your patience."

"I can't eat," Alexa said and left the kitchen. By the time she reached the hallway she heard her mother sniffling and tears filled Alexa's eyes.

Chapter Six

She sat on the floor with headphones blaring, her back to the bed and feet propped on the wall just as she had done as a pissed off teenager. She had cried herself to sleep the previous night after avoiding dinner with her mother. She woke up angry, mystified how or better yet why, her parents had hidden her identity. Nothing made sense and the more she thought about it, the angrier she became.

As she tapped her foot on the wall to Stone Temple Pilots she sensed the energy change in the house, her father had returned from his trip. She also recognized when he was moving down the hall toward her room.

The bedroom door opened, the floor creaked, then the bed shifted as he sat down next to her. He lifted the headphones to get her attention, but she continued to stare at the wall. "I understand you are upset," he said in his Austrian accent.

"Of course I am," she said turning to look at him. She didn't need much imagination to picture him wearing a black cape and sporting long white fangs. With jet-black hair and dark brown eyes, her father could easily pull-off being a vampire, his accent only adding to the illusion.

"You are not injured?"

She shook her head.

"You were able to overpower this man?"

She nodded.

"That is good," he said, nodding in approval. He leaned forward and planted a soft kiss on top of her head, lingering enough that Alexa wanted to jump into his lap and cry like she did as a little girl. Instead her anger kept her planted on the floor, wedged between the bed and the wall.

"I cannot fathom a single reason this was kept from me," she said.

"We are shielding you."

"From what?"

A wistful grin swept his face. "I can tell you, warn you, there are many that wish to eradicate hybrids, they may hunt witches for sport, but eliminating hybrids from vampire bloodlines is truly their goal."

Alexa huffed. "That was for sport?"

"The man who attacked you?"

"Men," she corrected. "There were ten men running at me."

His face was veiled; she couldn't read his emotion, but knew he was holding something back. After some thought, he nodded. "I will ask for the matter to be investigated."

"Fine, but that doesn't explain why all of this was hidden from me."

"Sometimes," he said, "knowing is more dangerous than ignorance."

"That's ridiculous," she said.

"Ach, it may seem so, I would imagine. Alexa, you were born into an unfortunate situation and for that I am deeply sorry. My only goal is to protect you and your mother. You must trust me. Ignorance of your lineage, disregarding that you are witch or vampire, will keep you safe."

"You're not telling me something."

"Again I must ask you trust me. When the time is right you will be told everything, but you must be patient. "

Alexa shook her head. "Okay, fine. Mom said there were rules or something around this. I don't get it, but whatever."

"Alexa, this is for your protection."

"Not telling me is for my protection? DAD! Vampires

attacked me! Maybe someone should tell *them* I don't know shit so stay away!"

"You were alone in a park, where there were no humans. No one can attack with humans around. Stay near humans," he ordered, "they are your shield."

"That's it? Stay around humans? How do I even know who's human and who isn't?" She shrugged in confusion.

He looked at her as if she were missing the obvious signs. "Their scent," he said simply.

"What scent?"

He tilted his head, a look of concern crossing his face. "Do you note any scents on me now?"

Alexa nodded. "You've come from a restaurant."

"What of your mother?"

She rolled a shoulder and asked, "You mean her perfume?"

"Describe her perfume."

"It's floral, like roses and another flower."

"Does your mother have any jars of perfume?"

Alexa stared at her father as she ran a quick mental inventory her mother's vanity and dresser.

"Do you wear any perfume?" he asked.

"No, the dryer sheets..."

"Alexa you do not smell like a dryer sheet."

"I smell like mom..."

With a faint grin, he conceded, "You do smell very much like your mother, but there is a difference. Are you able to discern it?"

Yes, there was a subtle variance between her and her mother. She couldn't say specifically the difference, but something carried on Alexa that her mom was lacking.

She nodded unsure and her father raised his eyebrows. "You are a much stronger vampire than we suspected. An acute sense of smell will serve you well."

"Stay near humans and be happy I've got a strong nose? What the hell am I sniffing?"

He took a deep breath. "Witches smell of growing things... plants, flowers, trees, as you and your mother smell of roses. A vampire carries the scent of flesh, of meat, as I do." He bowed slightly with a soft smile and said, "yes, I did recently dine in a restaurant, but it is the scent of flesh that defines me as a vampire and it is the subtle scent which carries on you. It is soft and nearly undetectable, even to most vampires. Now a human, a human smells of minerals and rocks and of... uh, metal."

"So... stick around people who smell like metal?" she asked sarcastically.

"Alexa, I hear your frustration. You must understand this is not my decision. I promise to appeal on your behalf."

"Appeal to whom?"

He stood up and left the room leaving Alexa looking mystified at the empty space in his wake. That was it? Did he just tell her to ignore she was a vampire? And to keep pretending she's a human? What was that crap?

She leaned her head on the bed and stared at the ceiling as tiny drums pounded from headphones looped around her neck. She wasn't sure what she expected with her father's arrival, but it sure as hell wasn't advice to stay around humans. No, she wanted more. She wanted excitement, or surprise, or... well *anything* other than *that*! Shock, sorrow, maybe dismay? Where was his concern? Maybe someone could sit down and talk about the murder she had committed? Why did they act like it was no big deal? Both of her parents were surprised she was a vampire, but not very. Could someone help *her* cope with the discovery? It was sort of a big deal to her.

Tears welled in her eyes, yet again. Angry with the tears, angrier at the situation, downright pissed at the lack of information, Alexa grabbed the shoe sitting next to her and threw it across the room, hitting the wall.

Chapter Seven

Standing in the bathroom Alexa could hear the telephone ring. Her mother rapped on the door. "Tess is on the phone."

Alexa had refused Tess's phone call the night before, asking her mother to say she was sick. She couldn't avoid Tess for much longer before the troops were rallied and her six closest standing around her bed worried she was on death's doorstep. "I'm coming," she grumbled.

"Hey," Alexa said into the phone receiver as she stood in the kitchen.

"How ya doin'?" Tess asked.

"Feel like shit."

"Did you break down and see a doctor?"

"Yeah, I'm on antibiotics for a few more days, hopefully it will be cleared up by then," Alexa said.

"Guess you're not up for going out tonight, are you?"

"Oh hell no," Alexa groaned. "I'll be crawling in bed by eight."

"Shame, should be a good time."

"I'm sure it will be. You can tell me all about it later."

"Damn, you really *are* feeling crappy," Tess said. "Guess you won't make it to softball either?"

"No, sorry. I, uh, forgot to tell the girls at work about it too."

"That's okay, I think we have enough people. Listen, Jess got the clubhouse for Meg's party. Think you'll be alive by then?"

Alexa chuckled. "Yeah, I will. I already mailed my contribution to Jess. Seems sorta lame to just send a check and let her do all the work."

"But she's so brilliant at it."

"That bitch can shit miracles."

"That she can, that she can," Tess said. "Okay, well get yourself healthy, and I'll see you around."

"Will do." She hung up the phone and turned around to find her mother watching her. She knew her father also heard her conversation from his perch in the living room, hiding behind a newspaper. "She wanted me to go out tonight," Alexa explained.

"You should go," her mother said.

Alexa sighed. "Mom, do you have any idea how terrified I am of going out in public? What do I do when I realize there's another vampire in the area? Or smell someone and finally understand 'oh that's what a witch smells like?' I don't know how to function with this knowledge. *You didn't prepare me for any of this.*" Alexa's eyes filled with tears and she stormed past her mother to her bedroom.

She flung herself onto the bed, sobbing. The door opened and her parents entered. Her mother crawled on the bed and sat next to Alexa, stroking her head. Alexa pushed her hand away.

"Alexa, you don't need to change your behavior. In fact, you shouldn't change anything at all. Just go about your day and your interactions as though nothing has changed."

"But everything *has* changed!"

"No it hasn't," her mother said. "You still carry the scent of a witch and the people around you who are able to identify that, have always known you're a witch."

Alexa rolled over to face her mother and sniffled. She hadn't thought that her own scent revealed her in any way - this was a surprise. "What about being a vampire?"

"There is no reason to let anyone know about that," her mother said.

Looking between her parents, Alexa was confused. "But dad

says I have a subtle vampire scent."

Her mother shrugged. "To me, you and I smell the same. I have never picked up this other scent."

"But *I* can smell it," Alexa said.

"Vampires have a much stronger sense of smell. None of the witches I know ever picked up on it. Everyone marvels how much you *don't* have the mixed scent of a hybrid," her mother said.

"Is that a good thing?"

"Yes. There's a lot of people who look down on hybrids. You're a witch who easily walks among humans – you're almost transparent. There's no reason to reveal yourself," her mother said.

Her father stepped closer. "Why did you lie to Tess and say you were sick?"

Alexa stared at him. He knew why, but was waiting to hear her say it. She continued to glare at her father.

He said, "Telling your friend such a bold lie shows you understand at a… a… subconscious level that to reveal what has happened may be troubling to others around you."

"Uh, yeah, I'm not sure how to announce that I'm a killer."

With a dismissive sigh and a shake of his head, her father squatted next to the bed. "You are not a killer, nor do you have the drive to be a killer. Any instinct to track and hunt that carries with some vampires would have displayed early in your childhood. You have never given any hint of being a vampire and there is no reason to reveal it now."

"But that dead man…"

"Is dead because you defended yourself. As for encountering vampires, they would have no reason to suspect you are one as well. You only present as a witch and your teeth will not drop unless you are provoked."

"And what if somebody provokes me in public?"

"The type of provocation causing a vampire to bare his teeth is another vampire baring his teeth. Had the man who attacked you only thrown you to the ground you would have used other means to fight back," he said. "That he displayed his teeth triggered an instinctual response in you, one he initiated. There are severe repercussions for displaying any non-human behaviors in public."

"Like what?"

"Execution."

Alexa considered the severity of her father's words. "Who patrols that? I mean, what if someone saw what happened in the park?"

He furrowed his eyebrows. "Well," he said with a contemplative sigh. "The attacker would have been immediately addressed. As for you, there are extenuating circumstances with defending yourself as well as ignorance of your lineage... any tribunal held would be a formality." He rocked his head with a dismissive shrug.

"Tribunal?" Alexa asked with alarm.

"As I said, a mere formality."

"Who conducts them?"

"Alexa, those are details I cannot discuss."

"What the hell?" she asked. Her mother reached to stoke her face but Alexa pushed the hand away. "What is with all of this secrecy?"

Alexa rolled over and stared at the opposite wall. After an uncomfortable silence her parents left the room. The wall was proving to be as soothing and informative as the people she most trusted.

Chapter Eight

Alexa followed the sound of clanging dishes in the kitchen. She wasn't surprised to find her father seated at the counter and her mother buzzing around putting dishes away. She had sensed their presence when she was in her bedroom and smelled them as she entered the hallway.

She was, however, surprised to see the mess of papers surrounding her father. He was head-down, writing on one piece of paper with quick glances at another with a several numbers scribbled across it. He usually did this sort of work at the dining room table.

Alexa looked between her parents astonished. Her mother closed a cabinet door and turned with an expression like she was ready to ask a question, but Alexa narrowed her eyes then glanced over at her father. "You guys knew I was walking in here before I got here," she said. "You've always known where I am. You can sense me and smell when I'm approaching."

Her mother smiled and said, "Yes, but you have managed to elude us quite a bit over the years."

Her father laid down his pen and looked between his wife and daughter. "We knew when you left the house and when you returned," he said.

"Oh my God, you *knew* when I snuck out of the house?" Alexa asked with horror.

His face brightened with amusement. "Every time, Alexa. I attempted to follow you, although often you were much too quick." He shook his head and smirked. "That ought to have been my first hint of your vampire abilities. Fortunately, you would go to Brie or Tess's house. Those were safe locations for you. It was the times you girls ventured away from their homes that I worried."

Alexa rocked back as if she had been struck. "Ah geez, you *followed* me?" She grappled for words as she looked between her parents. "I feel so... *violated!*"

Her father waved a dismissive hand. "You have a strong instinct to avoid danger, the likes of which I have never witnessed in another person. And your friends offer a secure barrier. Even as an adult you continue to seek their companionship. The times you eluded me," he said with a nod then lowered his voice in disapproval, "to do things of which I did not approve, I knew you were safe. It is your safety that has been my concern."

She thought of all of the wild and stupid things she and her friends had done over the years – just how much had he seen? Alexa pushed the worry out of her mind to wrestle at a later time. "Speaking of my friends, exactly what do I tell them?" she asked.

"Why would you talk to your friends about any of this?" he asked.

"Because we tell each other everything. I can't keep a secret like this."

"Honey," her mother said, "you would be surprised at the secrets your friends have kept from you over the years. Telling humans about your identity can be very dangerous – to you and to them. There is no reason to say anything at all."

"How is it dangerous to *them*?"

"People go missing quite a bit," her mom said.

"You mean like, they're abducted?"

Her mom nodded yes.

"And *murdered*?"

Her mom nodded yes again.

"Just for knowing witches and vampires are *real*?"

"Well," her mom said. "If a human finds out and doesn't make a scene, they're typically okay. But, like you're feeling right now, there's the urge to tell someone. That's when everything goes downhill."

"But I've heard about people practicing witchcraft."

"Mmmhmm," her mom said nodding. "Honey, I know you have a lot of questions, but we really need to stop this conversation right here."

"Why? Is somebody listening?" Alexa looked along the tops of the cabinets wondering where microphones would be placed.

Alexa looked between her parents. The stoic fronts they presented conveyed nothing else would be discussed other than plans for dinner. She wondered what question had pulled her into the kitchen in the first place, she couldn't remember. Alexa heaved a deep sigh and returned to her bedroom.

Chapter Nine

Alexa walked into the Human Resource office after missing three days of work, handing over a forged doctor's note. Where her father got the damned thing was as elusive as everything else in her new world.

The HR assistant, Connie Markenson, tilted her head with a sympathetic smile. "I hope you're feeling better," she said. Darkness would be Connie's last moments with her eyes closed accompanied by the steady sounds of a beeping monitor. Alexa now attached a new identifier, "human" as Connie smelled like a coin purse. Alexa assumed coins qualified as mineral scented?

At her desk, Alexa flipped through the receipts someone else had entered while she was out. Yellow post-its flagged the anomalies, but experience had proven to check all of the entries. In monotonous motion Alexa checked each sheet against the computer entries until her eye caught the time. Usually her stomach alerted her, but today her lunch break snuck up her. She secured her computer and headed to the elevators mystified why her coworkers didn't mention they were headed for lunch.

With a deep sigh Alexa stared at the crowd of people in front of the elevators. She considered returning to her desk but then she caught a familiar peppery, steak scent. She turned in time to see the copier repairman's uniform disappear in the stairwell. The good-looking repairman was a vampire?

With curiosity eating at her, Alexa opted to escape the crowd waiting for the elevators and headed for the stairs. As she reached the door under the exit sign she wondered if she was making a stupid move... and opened the door. Footsteps ascending the stairs pounded above her as she entered the stairwell. She heard him stop. The door closed behind her echoing through the stairwell canyon. She couldn't decide what to do – head down to the sandwich shop, return to the office, or follow the repairman? She stepped away from the door and leaned her head back on the wall with her mind in a cloud, unable to decide.

Slow footsteps above her turned and she saw him peek over the handrail. Alexa closed her eyes, chastising herself for wanting to meet this man. Her heart pounded, she had no idea what to say. He walked slowly down the stairs and she could not force herself to move away from the wall. He stopped on the landing and stood still, keeping his distance. At his death, something hit his neck, yet his eyes remained fixed on an old woman in front of him lying in a pool of blood. Alexa felt his heartache and flinched as she pushed the vision and its accompanying pain to the back of her mind.

"Are you okay?"

Alexa locked eyes with the repairman; her lower lip trembled. She wanted so much to say she was okay, but she was not. "Um," she said with a gulp, "I don't think so."

"Are you hiding from someone?"

She shook her head. "No. I just, um..."

"What's wrong? What happened?"

"I... encountered someone... that uh... wears the same, um, cologne? As you."

"Cologne? Could you be more specific?"

"Like, pepper."

"Oh shit." His face went white and he sat down on the top step. "Did someone attack you?"

She nodded.

"Are you hurt?"

"No," she said softly. "Just confused. I... I... I didn't know any of this existed."

"Is that when you found out?" he asked.

She nodded.

"Yeah, I sort of had the impression you didn't know. You never seemed bothered by me being around and, actually, you were a little oblivious to other people that came in your office." He continued to watch her and his concern seemed genuine. She decided she liked his eyes.

"You know, we're not all like that," he said.

No, she didn't know that. She looked away as tears began to roll. She shook her head. "No, I don't know anything." Alexa dragged a hand across her face to wipe the tears. She rolled her eyes as they welled again. With a sniffle she said, "I appreciate you keeping your distance. I don't know what I was thinking coming in here."

He nodded. Worry filled his face as he leaned forward as if he wanted to launch to her side and take her in his arms. Alexa would have liked someone to hug her, but no, the vampire ought stay right where he was.

"I promise, I have no thoughts of attacking you," he said.

She shrugged. "I have no idea how to judge you, or anything. I don't know who is good or bad, or what's right or wrong. I mean none of this makes any sense." She wiped another tear, mad she was crying in front of him.

"I'm really sorry this happened to you," he said. "May I ask... how did you get away?"

She tipped her head, wondering how to explain that morning. "I emitted some kind of energy – I don't even know what to call it. And when I fought back it was just an awful mess. I'm having a hard time dealing with what I saw... and what I did."

"Damn. I don't know what to say. That has to be one hell of a way to find out."

She sniffled and nodded. "The bigger problem I'm wrestling is trying to find out why I was never told. My mom and dad aren't divulging much. I just don't get it."

He shrugged his shoulders. "Yeah, that seems like something important to teach you at some point."

"Teaching me. Hmm yeah, that would be awesome." She paused and took a hard look at him - he was average height with a slender build, almost skinny. Her survey roamed up to his hair, sandy blond with a touch of curl. She returned her attention to his eyes, brown and mystified. Mystified? Why was *he* confused? Alexa wondered if he knew she was a hybrid? Did he think she was a full-blooded witch? What would happen if he discovered her to be a hybrid? Did she have to be careful what she revealed?

She gulped and said, "I mean I don't even know what to do or how much I can do. There's just a lot I don't know."

They exchanged uncomfortable glances and their eyes darted around the stairwell. He cleared his throat, breaking the silence. "I don't even know your name."

Alexa stiffened, contemplating her escape through the door next to her.

"My name is Eric."

She remained quiet.

"I thought I heard someone call you 'Lexi' so maybe it's short for Alexis?"

"Alexa," she said. "Some of my friends call me Lex."

"Not exactly how I had hoped our introductions would take place," he said. "I had actually been trying to find the right time to ask you on a date." Her face drained. "There's nothing to read into that. I literally meant going to a restaurant for dinner."

"Was, um... was my, um, perfume..."

"Yes, I admit your scent caught my attention."

"Is that the only..."

"No!" He seemed to startle himself and softened his voice, "no, it might have been what turned my head, but, ahem, you, ah... I find you interesting, I mean beyond the basics of being pretty and smelling good, there's something about the way you carry yourself. Your coworkers seem to like you and from what I've seen you seem like a hard worker, probably smart." He appeared uncomfortable and shifted positions on the stairs.

Alexa blushed, but kept a wary eye on the vampire. Again anger bubbled into her mix of emotions – how was pretending to be a human protecting her in this situation?

"I've never had any desire to attack you," he said earnestly. "If anything, I would protect you."

She remained quiet.

"Let me ask you this," he said, raising an eyebrow, "you sensed the danger with that other guy?" She nodded her head. "Good. Call it intuition or whatever, but it's real and a valid way to judge people." She saw his concern never wavered while he maintained his distance. A door slammed on an upper floor and voices floated through the stairwell. He cleared his throat. "This probably isn't the best place for us to continue talking."

Alexa's eyes drifted away from the vampire and she took closer notice of their surroundings, the bare cement and the chipped paint on the handrail. She felt a headache building and rubbed her temple. "I need to get back to work."

"Me too. I really want to take you out some time... public, someplace pubic," he said. "But someplace safe where you can talk about this more in depth if you wanted." He dug into a chest pocket, extracting a business card and ink pen. He flipped the card over and wrote on the back, then carefully placed the card on the step. "This is my number and I'll leave it here. If I never hear from you, I completely understand. I will keep my distance when I come into your office." With a weak grin and a nod, he returned up the stairs.

Alexa watched the vampire depart. When he left the stairwell she ascended the steps toward the card lying on the floor. The group from the upper floors passed as she held her foot on the vampire's business card, waiting until they were out of sight. Alexa picked up his card, "Palmer Copier Services – Finest in Metro Brentwood – Eric Lange, Service and Repair." She turned over the card and saw where he had written his personal number. Feeling unsure if she wanted this man's information, she shoved the card in her purse, and returned to her office without lunch.

She sat quietly at her desk with the repairman's card staring up at her. As people trickled in from lunch Alexa put the card in her wallet and leaned back in her chair, closing the bottom drawer of the desk with her foot, hiding the wallet and the card.

"You didn't go to lunch?" Tamara asked as she sat down.

"No, I'm not really hungry."

Tamara pulled a tube of lipstick from her purse and said, "Sounds like you needed to stay home another day to recuperate." She applied the lipstick, returned the tube to the purse, and put the purse in a desk drawer.

"Probably." The urge to cry bubbled up. She wasn't being productive at work, but at least she wasn't listening to her parents bustle around the house as if nothing ever happened. Taking a deep breath, she was able to subdue the tears. She pulled out the folder of receipts and returned to her computer screen, burying herself in work for the remainder of the day.

Chapter Ten

Standing on the sidewalk after work, Alexa watched throngs of people making their way to parking garages: human, human, witch, human, vampire, human, witch, witch, vampire... She couldn't keep count, everyone was intermingled. Did the witches and vampires mind they were so close to each other? Were they ignoring each other? Surely they weren't blind to the people passing them? How had all of these people existed and she never knew the difference?

She took a timid step away from the wall and joined the herd. With the crowd thinning she didn't want to be left standing alone without the human shield her father insisted she needed. As she made her way to her car Alexa decided she needed a distraction when she got home. Remembering a newsstand around the corner Alexa turned away from the parking garage, crossed the street, passed three witches, and walked into the small shop.

Two humans stood behind at the counter, deep in conversation. One nodded acknowledging her arrival and returned to his discussion. Five male witches walked out of the store empty-handed, leaving one customer, a woman, in the far corner.

Alexa fixated on the woman. She would to die soon, in a matter of hours, from a man strangling her. As much as Alexa wanted to escape the shop, she hated being near people who were about to die, but she was curious about the woman's scents. There were two, one with marigolds and grass, and another almost like fajitas. Was that what hybrids are supposed to smell like?

She approached the woman. "I'm sorry," Alexa said softly so the clerks couldn't hear. "Are you a hybrid?"

The woman turned around, annoyed. "What's your point?"

Alexa waved her hands. "No, no, that's not what I mean. My teeth came in, but I don't carry the scent like I'm supposed to or whatever. Honestly, I didn't know about any of this because I was raised *human*."

"You're so full of shit," the woman whispered as she turned away.

"What the hell? I was asking for help."

The woman spun on her heel, her brown hair swinging over her shoulder. She eyed the two clerks snickering over a magazine. "Your teeth came in? Prove it."

"What? Here?" Seeing the woman's serious glare, Alexa looked around the store. She scanned the ceiling for cameras then the large window with people passing on the sidewalk. In an audible voice she said, "oh you mean this one down here?" She dropped to a squat in front of the bottom row of magazines, picking up a crafting guide with a smiling child holding a cross-stitched sign. Alexa held the magazine between her and the clerks, and looked up to the woman as she dropped her teeth.

"Holy shit," the woman gasped. She stared at Alexa's mouth and whispered, "How is that possible?"

Alexa retracted her teeth and stood up, still holding the craft guide.

"That's so weird," the woman said. "You have the slightest scent change when your teeth come out and now it's gone. But those are full-fledged, definitely not hybrid teeth."

"What's the difference?"

"Mine are super short. Listen, I don't know what you wanted to ask, but forget it. Be happy you pass as a witch and don't ever let anyone know you're a hybrid."

"But that's the problem. I don't even know how to pass as a witch. I was raised human, I have no idea what I'm doing."

The woman shook her head. "Yeah, the witch's council doesn't want hybrids practicing, not even basic spells. If they can't kill us then the least we can do is to act like humans." She cast a wary eye toward the door. "It's not safe to be a hybrid. Get out of here, go home, lock your doors, and be happy you can pass for full-blood."

The woman walked out of the shop leaving Alexa in the corner. The clerks looked up making eye contact with Alexa. She grinned and quickly turned back to the rack of magazines. She dropped the craft guide into a random slot and walked up to the counter. "Where's Newsweek?"

The guy on the left nudged his chin as he said, "behind you."

She grabbed the magazine, paid for it, and left. Across the street stood the five witches that had left the store when she entered. They began to step off the curb in her direction when a black car revved its engine and rolled forward. Alexa watched the car cruise past and looked back to the witches. With a half-hearted smile she turned toward her parking garage, hoping enough people were still on the street to give her cover. She passed the woman she had been talking to, but the woman ignored her and continued her conversation with another hybrid, a man with a strong scent of coffee and steak. He too would die in the coming hours. Alexa quickly shook his death scene and fixated on his scent. She mused coffee would be an incredible scent to carry.

Her internal radar remained focused on the witches making their way across the street. She turned the corner happy to see crowds stream into her garage. As she stepped off the curb she realized the witches behind her stopped walking and probably reached where the hybrids were standing. Alexa didn't want to speculate if the men played a part in the deaths. Instead, she took a deep breath as she hurried to her car. Guilt washed over her wishing she had said something to the couple as warning.

Chapter Eleven

Sitting at the dinner table, Alexa stared at her plate as she mindlessly pushed mashed potatoes back and forth creating a valley. Her mother's attempts at conversation were met with shrugs and silence. Alexa didn't want to talk about work, her friends, her friends' relationships, or the weather. The one event that had been weighing heavily on her mind continued to be still avoided by her parents and she didn't know how to approach the topic of the soon-to-be-murdered hybrids. Would her psychic abilities be called into question? She had learned as a child to avoid that conversation – her friends thought it was weird and her mother skirted the subject and changed topics.

She assumed the death scenes were a psychic ability. Wouldn't that be a witch's power? Ugh, again, no one to talk to, no one to answer basic questions.

As Alexa pushed the mashed potatoes around her plate she wondered about the couple in front of the newsstand. How were they lured away from the street corner? Had they been followed for long? Were the witches across the street were the attackers? Did the woman know the witches? If anyone else had seen Alexa's teeth she could have been a target as well. Holy crap, what if the woman said something to the witches?

She took a deep breath and tried to find something else to occupy her mind - the copier repairman. She grinned. Surely he would be an unwelcome topic for dinner conversation. Alexa felt the restraints of living with her parents caving in on her. She contemplated if she had the resources to move out of the house. She probably had enough in savings to pay first and last month's rent as well as any necessary deposits for utilities, but she had nothing as far as furnishings. She was sure her friends would help out with a variety of household items. Ah, her friends. Her beloved "Circle of Seven," the name she and her six closest friends had called themselves since eighth grade. How many times had each of them offered to let her move into one of their apartments until she found her own place? Maybe it was time to take someone up on the offer?

"Alexa!" She raised her head to find her mother frowning at her. "You haven't eaten and your food is cold."

"I'm not really hungry," Alexa said.

"You've barely eaten in nearly a week."

"I have a lot weighing on my mind."

"Would you like to talk about it?" her mother asked.

"Yes I would, but every time I ask a question I'm shut down with stupid answers like 'stay around humans.' So, yeah, I've got to figure out how to come to terms with killing a man and what to do with these new fangs I've sprouted, not to mention that I can levitate things or whatever that power is called. I'm pretty sure I have other powers, but we can't talk about that either, can we? Since neither of you are very forthcoming with answers..." She glanced at her mother then scanned the opposite wall, avoiding eye contact with her father. She could sense his frustration and knew if she kept needling the subject he would get angry and storm out of the room. With an unenthusiastic shrug she said, "I know you told me to continue on as nothing happened, but something *did* happen and I'm upset by it and brushing it under the rug isn't helping me cope." She quietly stood up and left the room.

At work Alexa tried to push the previous week out of her head. She had ignored the office chatter about the murders so close to the office. Her encounter with the murdered hybrid couple had rattled her sense of security even more than that of her jittery officemates. Between the murder she had committed and meeting a woman about to be murdered Alexa floundered in making sense of anything.

She focused, instead, on the papers in front of her and the data she was entering into her computer. She ate a sack lunch at her desk and kept to herself.

A woman named Mary brought a folder of copied receipts to Alexa's desk. Mary's death would be several years away as she sat at a kitchen table, choking on something. Alexa startled with the realization that Mary was a witch – she smelled like petunias and tea. She thanked Mary for the folder and watched her walk away. Alexa tried to recall when she started working at Stokes Butler Insurance how she met Mary. Alexa had befriended the women seated near her cubicle, but Mary worked at the opposite end of the office and only came by once a week to drop off receipts. Mary never talked to Alexa, never joined in any of the office banter, and always ate lunch at her desk.

Surely Mary knew Alexa was a witch? Why didn't she say something? Did Alexa say or do something to offend her? Alexa worried she had violated some form of witch courtesy. Again she was frustrated with her lack of information.

Opening the folder of copied receipts Alexa's mind drifted to the repairman. He seemed earnest in his concern for her and recalling their interactions over the past year he never came across as threatening. She found him attractive, both in looks and scent. Alexa leaned back in her chair, shaking her head at herself. She found a vampire attractive.

She reached down to the bottom drawer where she stored her purse and dug around until she found his business card. She flipped the card between her fingers a few times before picking up the phone and dialing.

"Is Eric Lange available?" she asked the receptionist. "This is Alexa Cressing at Stokes Butler... no I don't want to submit a service request." Alexa was put on hold and she contemplated hanging up as Marvin Gaye sang about the grapevine.

"This is Eric." His voice boomed through the receiver.

"Um, hi, this is Alexa."

He paused for a moment then said, "Hi! Are you where you can talk?"

"No, not really."

"Can you call me after work?"

"No," she said, losing her resolve to continue the conversation.

"I hope you're not calling to tell me to kiss off."

With a faint laugh she smiled and said, "No."

"Can I take you out to dinner?"

"I guess so."

He chuckled. "I suppose picking you up is out of the question?"

"It is."

"Do you like steak?"

"Yes."

"Then why don't you meet me at Sullivan's Steak House on Third Street? Friday? Seven p.m.?"

"Yes, I can do that."

"Okay, I'll meet you there."

After she hung up the phone Tamara leaned back in her seat to catch Alexa's attention. "I don't think you have ever used the telephone since you started working here. Who was that?" she asked. Alexa blushed, but remained silent. "Was that the copier repairman?" Alexa smiled without response and turned away, pretending to work.

Chapter Twelve

When Friday arrived, Alexa obeyed all of the rules of caution: meeting at the restaurant, making sure to park in a crowded, well-lit area. She obeyed all of the rules except telling her parents about her date. She lied and said she was meeting her friend, Brie.

A black car circled the lot as she parked. There were plenty of spaces available and she wondered if the driver was looking for someone. As she crossed the lot the car exited and cruised at a slow pace in front of the restaurant. She spotted Eric standing by the door and dismissed the car as it turned into another lot on the opposite side of the building.

Eric beamed when she arrived. "I wasn't sure if you would actually show up," he said.

She shrugged and said, "Well, I'm still not sure if this was a very wise move for me."

"We're in public, you're fine. I am glad you're here."

They walked inside and Eric gave his name to the hostess. While they waited they stared at the Sullivan family photos adorning the walls. The hostess called Eric's name and they stepped forward.

Meandering through the tables Alexa noticed several vampires in the room. Their heads all jerked in her direction and she felt self conscious. Two witches sitting at a corner table also watched her arrival. The room, however, was filled with plenty of humans eating and chatting, completely unaware a witch and vampire had just entered the dining room together. The witches and vampires returned their attentions to their own tables and Alexa took her seat, contemplating her fastest escape route.

Eric said, "It's been ages since I've been here."

"Oh yeah?" she said distracted, glancing around the room.

"It's one of my parents' favorite places to eat."

With a pounding heart, Alexa took a deep breath recalling her father's frequent admonishments for expressing fear. "Distract your thoughts," he would say. She relaxed her shoulders as she listened to the noises of death flooding her head. Alexa mused this may have been the first time she found comfort in other peoples' deaths. Her eyes rested on Eric patiently waiting for her to settle down. Alexa scrambled to recall the last thing he said.

"Are you close with your parents?" she asked.

"Yeah, they're pretty cool."

"Do you have any brothers or sisters?"

"One sister, Therese," he said. "She's four years older than me and lives in Houston."

"Is she married?" She took another deep breath, grateful for the idle chatter.

"Yeah, like six... no seven years and they have two kids."

"Really? What are their names?"

"Brynn and Noah," he said. "They just visited last month."

"I bet your parents lapped that up."

"Oh yeah, I don't think they even noticed me and Therese and her husband were in the house."

She laughed. "Do you and your sister get along well?"

"Yeah, she's the typical bossy, over-protective, oldest child, but we're good. I used to accuse her of pretending to be mom and that always pissed her off. What about you? Do you have any brothers or sisters?"

She shook her head. "Nope, I'm an only child."

The waitress arrived with two glasses of water and took

their drink orders.

Eric asked, "How long have to been at Stokes?"

"I started working there about two years ago. What about you? When did you start your job?"

"I've been doing copier repair almost since I got out of high school. Helped pay for college," he said. "But I've been with PCS not quite a year. I had a hell of a time last year when I was laid off from my previous company. I had to get a second roommate to avoid moving back with my parents."

"I can't really judge," Alexa said. "I haven't even left home yet."

Eric grinned. "Really?"

"Yeah, after college I just couldn't pull the money together. My friends have offered several times to let me move in with them, but I've heard horrible things about friends being roommates and really, when I move out I want to go solo."

"Hmm, yeah, Ryan and I have had a few bouts living together. It's threatened our friendship on a couple of occasions."

"And yet you managed to make it work?"

"Well, you know guys just work it out with their fists and then it's over," he said. "But it's helped having a third person present - either as a buffer or a mediator."

The waitress returned with their glasses of wine and was ready to take their orders. Flipping through the menu Alexa toyed with ordering chicken, but the steaks in the room smelled incredible. With the waitress hovering, Alexa was torn between chicken and steak. Chicken or steak? Chicken or steak? Chicken or... "I'll take a rib eye, rare, and a baked potato with the butter on the side."

Eric looked up at the waitress, handing her the menu, "I'll have the same." He looked back at Alexa as she handed off her menu. "I read you as a salad and grilled chicken type of girl."

"I almost ordered that. It was a tough decision."

"So, where did you go to college?"

"Meyers downtown," she said.

"I guess your parents encouraged keeping you close to home?"

She tilted her head. "You know I tried going away, but you're right, they really did work hard to keep me at home. They also haven't urged me to move out since I finished school either."

"I can't believe they never told you anything."

"I'm so pissed I can barely stand to be in the same room with them right now. They keep telling me how they have been protecting me, but I don't understand how that works when they were sending me out to school, to work, and walk around without knowing anything? It's like..." She searched for the words and sighed. "I don't know what it is, but it's not right. I mean... doing so when you know the risks is one thing, but your parents sending you out and not saying a damn thing? That's just stupid."

"I agree, it was shortsighted not to lay all of the cards on the table."

"Not just shortsighted," she said, "but dangerous."

Eric nodded in agreement.

"And now that I'm aware, I'm noticing so much stuff. Most immediately I feel stupid, because you know, like, damn that's been there all along, why didn't I see it? But then, who do I talk to about it? I can't exactly pull my friend, Chloe, to the side and tell her about the woman I met at the store the other day, or tell her about what happened at the park. My friends Tess and Lindsay would *love* to hear about you, but I can't start that conversation. As soon as I omit details, their super-sniffers come out. They always know when someone is hiding something and good luck, because they will latch on and squeeze it out of you." Alexa heaved an exhausted sigh as she shook her head at the ceiling. "You know the one person I've told everything to, has been my mom. I've told her about the nights I've snuck out of the house and even the time I tried pot. I don't know what's worse – that she's hid this from me my entire life or that I can't talk to her about it now." As tears welled in her eyes, she looked away from Eric. "It's that I can't talk to her," she whispered.

They sat in silence as she tried to recompose herself, yet again. Alexa glanced around the room taking closer notice of the witches and vampires dining nearby. They dressed, talked, ate, laughed just like all of the humans in the room. Their only distinguishing features were their scents. They were even behaving like humans. She looked over to Eric, his face filled with concern. She offered a small smile.

When the meal arrived Alexa carefully carved the fat away from the meat then took the first bite, savoring the juices as they filled her mouth.

A loud cough across the room grabbed both Eric and Alexa's attention at the same time. One of the vampires was growling at the other, but masking the sound as a cough.

Alexa leaned in and whispered, "are we safe sitting here?"

Eric rested his arm on the table. "Yes, this is the safest place possible. No one here is a threat to either of us."

She smiled and said, "I can see why your family likes eating here, it's really good."

"I'm happy you like it," he grinned and continued staring at her. She averted her attention to the napkin in her lap as he spoke. "I wish I knew how to help you through this. I don't know how much assistance I can be, but I can listen."

"I don't know. Some things are starting to make sense. What I thought were old dreams might actually be memories.

Questions I've had for years finally have a logical answer, well as logical as any of this can be."

"But you have questions."

"Oh I have a million questions. And as soon as I think of one question, five more pop up. It's gotten to where it's almost impossible to sleep with my mind running nonstop."

Eric chuckled.

"And you," she said, "you're only complicating things."

He raised his eyebrows, "Me?"

Alexa looked at him squarely. "I don't know what to think about you. I can't imagine my parents would approve of you. You're definitely a distraction from the other crap that has happened, but am I walking into more trouble talking to you?"

"To be honest, I've never approached anyone like you. I tend to keep my distance, or maybe they keep their distance? I don't know. I can't explain what it is, but I'm drawn to you – all I want to do is talk to you and learn more about you. Nothing would make me happier than to sit here until dawn, just talking. But the moment you tell me to bug off, I will. I don't want to hurt you or jeopardize your safety."

After dinner Eric escorted Alexa to her car. Another couple walked nearby, slow, huddled in quiet conversation.

Eric nudged her with an elbow. "What's an ideal date for you?"

Alexa wrinkled her eyebrows. "This has been nice."

"No," he said. "This is mandatory for a first date. What should we do for a second date?"

Alexa laughed. "You presume I'd even want a second date. I guess it depends on what you suggest."

Eric wagged a finger at her. "No, you don't get to pull circular arguments with me. If anyone were to score a second date with you, what would you like to do."

She offered him a conciliatory grin. "Eric, I like you and I would definitely like to go on a second date. Honestly, anything where we got to be together would be fine in my book. I've heard that going to the movies is a horrible date because you don't get to talk. I don't know... I like being outside. Nothing fancy. If we had a beach nearby, that would be cool." she shrugged. "But really any chance to hang out."

With a slow, contemplative nod, he grinned. "You didn't give me any concrete ideas, but I like being outside too. I'll come up with something. Of course if you come up with an idea you're more than welcome to give me a call."

At the driver's door Alexa fumbled through her purse, pulling out a set of keys. Eric stepped closer so when she turned to face him they were mere inches apart. They stood quiet, looking at each other.

"I would like to take you out again," he said.

"I'd like that."

His eyes traveled her face. "You complicate my thoughts too."

Alexa continued looking at Eric, assessing him. His intent was clear, but he offered her an out – just turn and get in the car. She didn't want to leave. She should go. She didn't want to leave...

He leaned in and pressed a light kiss on her lips. He jolted back, "you're a hybrid!"

Unsure if the discovery was an unwelcome surprise, she nodded. "What gave it away?"

"Your scent changed."

Her usual strong floral tones had faded to only a hint of rose. A meatier scent similar to her father's came to the forefront, but quickly fading.

He leaned in and when he brushed her lips a second time the

scent stopped fading. He murmured, "I think I'm triggering it." Moving to her ear, he exhaled on the nape of her neck, flaring her vampire scent even stronger. He ran his lips along her jaw and took possession of her mouth. She responded, encouraging him. Eric pulled back and looked into her eyes. "I was wrong. Now I want to attack you."

Alexa smiled and blushed.

Eric searched her face and broke from his reverie. He stared at her with his eyebrows wrinkled. "Being a vampire is what upset you so much."

"It is."

He lifted her chin and turned her face toward the light. "Your teeth have only recently come in - Your lip isn't scarred yet from retracting them. Is that how you found out? When your teeth came in?"

Alexa's eyes dropped to his mouth where she spotted two faint scars on his lower lip. Her eyes shot up to his. "My teeth came in when I was attacked," she said.

He shook his head. "You don't even know how to use them, do you? It was a good thing you were able to do some witchcraft to run him off."

She looked away. The vision that most haunted her, bubbled back to the surface. With her eyes slammed shut she confessed, "Eric, I killed that man." Sheepish, Alexa looked up to Eric.

His eyebrows peaked. "With your teeth?"

She nodded.

"Without any training? On your first day? While being attacked?"

"I didn't *try* to kill him, I mean, that wasn't my plan. Well, there wasn't a plan... it just..."

"You defended yourself," he said. "That's all there is to it. He provoked you and you fought back."

She shrugged.

"But, you feel guilty about it, don't you?"

She nodded.

"Don't. He's not worth it. He could very well have killed you instead. Besides, if he hadn't been stopped he definitely would have attacked other women. You did a very noble thing."

"It doesn't feel like it."

He stroked her cheek. "Trust me, you did the world a favor." He chuckled. "Now I understand why your family is hiding you." He dropped his hand and stepped back. "A child of a mixed union, a hybrid, you're in great danger. There are groups hunting people like yourself. But damn, if you can knock out a kill on your first day, they might be in for a rude surprise."

"Are you upset I hid it?"

He shook his head. "No, not all. You're lucky that you can hide it so thoroughly."

"Until someone kisses me." She grinned.

Eric stepped forward and kissed her again.

Chapter Thirteen

Alexa headed home, leaving Eric standing in the parking lot. During her drive she inventoried his every nuance. He had always been attractive in his repairman jumpsuit, but the white shirt, tie, and dress slacks melted her resistance. He had a sweet smile making him easy to trust. She hoped it wasn't a mask. If anything were to ever give away Eric's true intent, it was his eyebrows. She found their various expressions amusing. And his kiss - like nothing she had ever felt before, not the sloppy wet kisses of the boys in high school, not the lusty kisses of her last boyfriend, Jack. No, this was different. Very different. It was raw and drew up her energy and ignited her passion.

Her mind had been so busy replaying the date she was surprised when she pulled onto her street. The lights in the house were on meaning her parents were still up. Alexa stepped through the front door prepared with a full account of joining Brie for happy hour at Big Jimmies.

Her mother launched off the couch. "Oh my God, Alexa! Are you okay?" She grabbed Alexa patting her over, looking for injuries.

"What?" Alexa ran a quick assessment - crap she smelled like Eric. "Mom, I'm fine," she said pushing her mother's hands away.

Her father followed, his face filled with concern. "Alexa, you must to tell us what happened."

"Nothing happened! I went on a date."

"With a vampire?"

"Yes." Alexa met her father's eyes in challenge.

"But he is a *hunter*," he said in disgust.

"So?"

"Alexa!" her father yelled. "You do not understand..."

"No, Dad, I don't understand!" she yelled back. "You know why? Because you didn't tell me a damn thing. Alllll of this was a bigass secret." She flung her arms out. "He's a hunter? Is that a type of vampire? What other types are out there? What am I, Dad? What are you?"

"You are a witch," he said in a stern, even tone.

"Oh, no, Dad. I am very much a vampire! Remember? I killed some guy in the park. That wasn't with witchcraft but these pointy things in my mouth you failed to warn me I would sprout one day."

Her father exhaled, heavy in exasperation.

"Please don't repeat that you didn't expect me to have any fangs," Alexa said. "Because I have them, I've used them, and they're lethal."

"I dare say your tongue is the sharpest thing in your mouth."

"Fuck this shit!" she said and marched out the front door.

Her father followed her into the yard. "Alexa! You cannot be out here without other people about."

Alexa continued walking.

Her father followed. When she reached the end of the block she turned to face him. "I've been doing this my entire life. What's changed?"

He stood quiet as he wrinkled his forehead in thought. "There was a murder earlier this week and the perpetrators have not been captured. Protecting you is difficult. I do wish you would heed my advice and stay near humans."

Alexa was surprised he didn't give a more evasive answer. "Can you tell me about the murder and why it impacts my ability to walk around the block or take a jog in the park?"

"You were not headed toward the park."

She sighed at her father's perceptiveness.

"There was a man and a woman found dead in an alley, not far from your office building," he said. "They were decapitated, it was a brutal, but odd attack, very odd. My concern for you is that not only was it close to your work, but that they were hybrids."

She cocked her head. "When did this happen?"

"Tuesday."

"Possibly Monday evening?"

"Yes, that is possible. Why do you ask?

"I spoke to that woman when she was inside the newsstand." She told her father about the witches when she entered the store and how they were lingering on the street afterwards. When asked, she gave descriptions of them as best as possible. After recounting her visit to the newsstand, her father confirmed the bodies were found in the alley was behind the shop. Alexa began to tremble.

"Alexa, your fear," her father said.

She took deep breaths, slowed her heart rate, and stabilized the trembling.

"Your information will be very helpful. I will ensure appropriate parties receive this and we can hope those witches will be brought to justice."

"Do I need to give a statement to anyone?"

"No. You do not need your name to be associated with this attack. Please, come back to the house."

Alexa walked quietly next to her father. How many times had they walked this way chattering about anything that crossed their minds? Now, dead silence. She wanted to ask him so many things, things not even related to being a vampire, but of course she had plenty of vampire questions as well.

Instead she stayed silent - it wasn't worth the trouble.

Her mind returned to the hybrid couple. She mourned them. The lady seemed nice; killing her was senseless. Likely the same could said about the man as well.

What did her dad mean by "protecting" her? How on Earth was she difficult to protect? Again, a question that would receive a vague response.

She tossed a forced smile to their neighbor and waved as he parked his car, then she followed her father into the house.

Chapter Fourteen

Alexa curled into her cozy reading chair and stared at the drawer containing her diary. She recalled the various entries she had made during high school, but she wasn't sure when she had last written anything. Tonight was definitely worthy of a new entry, but really, did adults keep journals of their first dates?

"Dear Diary," she thought, "I went on a date with the dreamiest guy I've ever met. And guess what? He's a vampire!" Alexa giggled to herself. No, writing in her diary was not what she wanted to do.

Her mother came into her room and plopped onto the bed as she had done a million times before.

"Do you want to tell me about this date?" her mother asked in her normal, casual tone after all of Alexa's outings.

"No, not really," Alexa said.

"Where did you go?"

"Steakhouse"

Her mother grinned and shook her head. "Rather traditional vampire meal."

"Is it?"

"Rare steaks, I'd say so."

Alexa glared at her mother. Was this her attempt to share information? Vampires eat rare steaks? She glanced at the doorway as her father approached. He leaned on the wall, looking between his wife and daughter.

"So vampires like rare steaks, huh?" Alexa asked.

"Or raw," her father said.

She thought about the possibility of eating an uncooked

steak and tilted her head and raised her eyebrows, "Probably wouldn't be too bad."

Her mother rolled her eyes.

"What do witches eat?" Alexa asked.

"Lawn clippings and weeds," her father said, staring at her mother.

Her mother smiled and shook her head. "Your father has eaten plenty of salads and managed not to wither away."

"Yeah, I know, I've seen him eat salad."

"Who is this man you saw tonight?" her father asked.

"I'd rather not discuss him. Even if we were all human it would be too early to say anything. I met a guy, I like him, he seems to like me and I have no reason not to trust him at this point."

"You are not at a stage where you are able to judge a man's intentions," her father said.

Alexa scowled. "I was pretty sure of the intentions of the men in the park, they were looking to rape somebody – and not just one do it while the rest watched, but each one planned on getting a turn. And those witches the other day seemed like they were out for blood. Even when I thought everyone was human, they would have looked like trouble." She watched her father's face change as he tried to control his anger. "But the guy I met up with tonight? He was a complete gentleman and had you and I been on solid ground I would have gladly asked him here to meet you first. But no, everything is a secret. So no, you don't get to meet him and we're not going to discuss him."

"This is a dangerous path, Alexa."

"Really? Exactly how did you and mom meet? Did grandpa approve?"

Exhaling evenly, her father snarled, glanced at her mother,

and then turned down the hall.

"Alexa," her mother said, "that's a rather sensitive subject."

"What the hell? You can't even tell me how you two met? I never did believe your story about a blind date, what the hell is the big deal?" She looked to the empty doorway and back to her mother in disbelief. "The secrecy is killing me. This is absolute bullshit." Fuming, Alexa pulled her tennis shoes on.

"Alexa, you cannot go to the park," her mother said in a panic.

"I'm just going to go for a drive."

With the radio blasting and the windows rolled down, Alexa drove through town. She contemplated cruising through the back roads, but with one sharp turn she found herself on a meandering street she hadn't visited in three years. She parked in the middle of an empty lot at her old college, in front of the arts building. She walked up to the public phone ready to call Brie or one of her other friends, but instead fished the business card out of her purse.

Chapter Fifteen

A half hour later a silver Toyota drove onto the lot and headed straight for her car. Alexa sat on the wall with her ankles crossed, watching him search for her. When he spotted her, he put the car into gear and pulled up to the building.

Eric got out of the car, looking up at her - she was easily ten feet off the ground. The slam of the car door boomed through the empty lot. "Are you coming down, or should I climb up there?" Alexa shrugged, but otherwise didn't move. From the corner of her eyes she watched him stalk to the end of the wall and pull himself up as she had done, then walk along the ascending slope. He sat beside her, quiet for a long time.

Finally he asked, "Did you hang out here a lot in college?"

"Nah, they were pretty strict about us getting up here. Security guards were always running someone off."

"I guess the roof was completely off limits?" he asked, eyeing the roofline.

"mmhmm." She nodded.

"But you've been up there, right?"

She finally cracked a grin. "Of course."

He tipped his head toward the roof. "C'mon." Eric pulled Alexa to her feet and they walked further up the wall until the roofline was waist high. Eric hoisted himself onto the roof then extended a hand down to Alexa.

The view was even better than from the wall. Tall buildings surrounding the campus seemed like they were sleeping. Traffic in the distance offering white noise broken only by the crunching of the gravel as the couple walked. A beer bottle and broken glass showed this wasn't undiscovered territory.

Eric stood across from Alexa as she leaned against a large air conditioning unit. "What happened?"

"They smelled you."

"Of course," he said. "I'm sorry about that. I should have kept my distance."

"It's not your fault. Tension has been building since I was attacked." She shrugged. "He said you are a hunter?"

"I am. Did he say what type you are?"

Alexa shook her head. "No. Not a word. So you're a hunter by birth? Meaning your parents are hunters and their parents are hunters?" He nodded. She asked, "Is that the pepper scent? That's what hunters have in common?"

"That's right."

"My dad doesn't carry that type of scent, but the man that attacked me, the one I killed, he did. I guess he was a hunter too?"

"Sounds like it."

Alexa closed her eyes. When was urge to cry going to stop? "There's so much I don't know."

"I guess the witch part isn't stumping you?"

"No. Finding out I'm a witch answered more questions than it raised."

"You know, we can't turn into bats?"

She smirked, appreciating his efforts to lighten her mood. Alexa dropped her attention to her hands and began fiddling with her thumbnail. "Do you drink blood?"

"Not exactly. I mean we're built to do it and actually we can live off blood alone. But for me I drank it once, some do it a lot, but mostly it's just getting a taste. A little goes a long way."

"Why did you only have it once?"

"It was a ceremony, a becoming a man thing. I was fourteen and my dad's friends gave me a fancy goblet of wi..." Eric cut himself short.

"Witch's blood?"

With hesitation he said, "Yeah."

"Is that... is that what attracts vampires to witches?"

"Yeah, it is. It's powerful stuff. It's like the best glass of wine you've had in your life times a hundred. With witches, the blood is energizing. I guess some think it gives a youthful glow? I don't know about that, but it is intoxicating. Actually," he said, "any blood does that, but witch's blood is the gold standard."

"Vampires drink each other's blood?"

"They do, especially when fighting. Actually, going after another vampire is a way to build your own strength."

"But you said you have only had blood once?"

"I don't hunt, I don't fight... there's no reason or really, opportunity, to put my teeth in someone else. And it's just no big deal." He shrugged.

"But others do?"

"Yeah. Usually unsavory characters trying to stir up trouble. The guy who attacked you, he was probably hunting witches... and boy did he pick the wrong one!" Alexa offered a weak smile. "Of course there are guards who protect areas and they regularly engage in fights, so they would have plenty of opportunities."

"And they get stronger as a result?"

"I guess so, that's what they say. I don't know why it's needed, we're already stronger than witches and humans."

"Really? Huh. My friends have accused me of being 'freakishly strong.'"

"I imagine you and I could probably lift one of our cars together without any problem."

She craned her head around the A/C unit to peer at the two

cars in the parking lot. Alexa turned back to Eric. "Have you done that before?"

His face lit up. "Yeah. A friend and I did our own senior prank in high school. We moved the principal's car from his driveway to the playground across from his house. We stayed up all night so we could watch the expression on his face. It was funny as hell – he thought it was stolen. We had to take off before the police showed up, but I would have loved to have been there when they discovered it. No tire marks, no way to explain how it got there. We had lifted it over a low barricade. I have no idea how they got it out of there. It was pretty awesome."

Alexa laughed trying to imagine the scene. The laughter made her feel better and she walked toward another air conditioner unit.

"So what about human blood?" she asked. "Does it do anything?"

"Eh, I guess it fills the need, especially for those addicted to drinking blood, but I heard it doesn't taste that great. A good steak is far superior to human blood,"

"So people taste different?"

"Hmm," he thought for a moment, "Blood is supposed to taste however the person smells."

Alexa scrunched up her face. "So humans taste like metal and body odor?"

"Pretty much."

"Oh yeah, I would much rather have a steak." Alexa swirled her foot in the pea gravel. "If you haven't fought, I guess you haven't killed anyone?"

"No." He shook his head. "I've lived a pretty sheltered life here, a nice quiet human existence. My father has, though. He's been in several fights, like most of the men in my family."

"Just instigating trouble?"

"Nah, they were in the army."

Alexa cocked her head. "The US army?"

"No, a vampire army."

She waved her hands in the air. "I'm... I'm going to table that one for a bit. I don't think I can process what it means to be in a vampire army. I swear at some point I'm going to wake up from this chaos." She began walking again. "My favorite spot is over here." Eric joined her as she headed to the south end of the building. "Why is it that my dad insists that I stay around humans?"

"Humans, first and foremost offer you security in numbers," he said. "But the real reason is that if a witch or a vampire reveal themselves, the humans panic. They can destroy us in that state. They *have* destroyed us in the past. It's universally understood not to attack or reveal in public."

"Do you like jumping off buildings?" she asked.

Eric looked over the edge, then at Alexa. He raised his eyebrows and tilted his head. "I do, but never one this high."

"It's a soft landing." She nodded toward the lawn below.

Eric tilted his head again, took a step back, and leapt from the roof. When he hit the ground he rolled forward. Quick to gain his footing he turned around to watch Alexa. She stood right at the edge, took a step into the air and as she dropped close to the building she kicked a foot to the wall launching herself over Eric's head. She dropped to the ground, landing in a squat.

"How long have you been jumping off buildings?" Suspicion was laced in his voice.

She looked back to the roof. "I was probably ten or eleven when I finally worked my way up to jumping off our house."

"Clearly this isn't the first time you've jumped here."

"No it's not."

"How did you know I wouldn't break my neck doing that?"

"I've always known I could do things other people couldn't," she said. "So now I'm starting to discern which of those abilities are vampire and what is witch. It seems the more physical things are vampire."

Eric nodded. "I imagine it was upsetting to think you were so different from your friends."

"I felt like a freak. Still do, actually."

Eric extended a hand and led her into the darkness beyond the trees. He leaned against a skinny pine and pulled Alexa against him. He stroked her jawline and Alexa watched his eyes roam her face. He leaned in and kissed her softly. "I find it interesting how your scent changes."

"Are you the kid that stood in front of the fridge opening and closing the door to see the light go on and off?"

"In fact, I am," he said with a big smile. "I like knowing I have this effect on you. Thing is, I still can't identify you."

"What do you mean?"

"It's crazy how your scent changes any way, but when we kiss you definitely come forward as a vampire. There's still a essence of flowers from being a witch, roses, definitely roses, but you have a distinct vampire scent to you." He searched her face and slowly his mouth curled. He shook his head as he mulled her scent. "You're not a hunter or anything lower. Sentinel doesn't seem right. I'd almost say you're a ranger, but from the few I've encountered, I don't think that's it either. Maybe your witch scent is muddling your vampire scent? Hard to say, but ranger seems the closest I can identify."

"Exactly, how many types of vampire are there?"

"Uh, scavenger, civilian, hunter, sentinel, ranger, noble, and then in the royal families there's a destroyer and a king."

"What the hell is a destroyer?"

"A super strong vampire no one wants to cross... or can cross," he said shaking his head. "They're usually a bodyguard or something to kings."

"And each type has a different smell?"

"Scents become softer and more, um, pleasing the higher on the food chain you go."

Alexa realized there was a difference between Eric and her father, but a "food chain?" Surely he didn't mean predator and prey? "Do you mean there's a hierarchy?"

He thought about that for a second. "Yeah. Not just in scents but there's a difference in physical strength too. Hunters are pretty much middle ground."

She looked at him sideways. "So... you think I'm a ranger... and that means I'm stronger than you?"

He shrugged. "Probably."

"Is that a problem for you?"

He shook his head. "Nah. It's kinda sexy, actually."

She sighed and stepped away. "What surprises me the most is that we're just born this way. Where did the whole thing come from, the legend about turning into a vampire from a bite?"

Eric cleared his throat a little uncomfortably, "That probably comes from being tagged."

"Which is...?"

He shifted his stance. "A... uh... bite that injects your, uh, scent into another person." He shifted again. "Usually it happens..." He cleared his throat. "...during sex."

"Oh." She remembered her mother searching for a bite after her attack.

"So," he continued. "Girls would be... assaulted, walk around with bite marks, and when they came of age their teeth would drop. It was easy to presume the bite led to the teeth." He paused and his expression changed. "I assumed he tagged you. Is that not the case?"

With uncertainty she shook her head. "There's a scratch where he tried to bite me, but it's just on the surface. My mom said she didn't think I was tagged."

He assessed her for a moment and leaned into her shoulder and sniffed. "So the scent you're carrying isn't because you were tagged but because you drank his blood." He smiled and nodded. "Yeah, you're probably a ranger."

"I carry his scent?" Alexa asked, alarmed.

"You do. If scent were a flavor, the very first thing someone would notice about you is a strong robust floral, your witch scent, and then there's an after-kick that says 'hunter.' Of course now you have another hunter's scent carrying with you." He smiled. "But, mine should go away in a couple of days."

"What about the guy I killed?"

"I know the scent fades over time, but I don't think it fully goes away."

Alexa glared at Eric, displeased with this information. "Why did you just sniff me?"

"To see if you were tagged."

"How can you tell?"

"You can tag a person anywhere, but usually it's close to the neck, like shoulders... um, breasts. The scent is particularly strong in those areas, but if you only drank someone's blood it dissipates throughout your body so that guy's scent isn't in just one spot. So, no, he didn't tag you."

"So what does that *mean* to be tagged?"

"Um, well, it means possession."

Alexa's eyebrows shot up.

"No other vampire can *have* that woman. If someone does, then the guy who tagged her can kill him without repercussion. There are some guys who make a game out of it trying to tag the most women."

"That's awful," she said. "Wait!" Alexa's thoughts darted in another direction. "How old did you say you were when your teeth came in?"

"Fourteen."

She squinted her eyes. "So basically after puberty hit, but mine didn't arrive until I was twenty-five. Is that because I'm part witch?"

"No." He shook his head. "That's normal. Women are usually early to mid twenties. My sister was twenty-three."

"That doesn't make a damn lick of sense."

"No, not really," he agreed. "Women are frequently tagged as teenagers when they have no way to protect themselves. I'm not so sure about your father's methods but he has to be crazy trying to protect you." He shifted his weight again. "I can't imagine I'm a welcome arrival."

"To say the least."

"Well, your dad shouldn't worry about me too much. With one kill under your belt I'm sure you're able to keep me in line."

"I guess we're not immortal?" she asked.

"Hardly. We succumb to illness and old age just like humans. We're rather immune to viruses, but cancer and organ failure are pretty frequent. My grandfather had lung cancer, smoked like a damn train his whole life. My other grandfather fell down the stairs and that messed him up. He died about six months later from complications from his injuries."

"Damn, sorry to hear that. I guess being in sunlight isn't a problem?"

"Nope," he said. "I burn like everyone else."

"Gotta admit, if I weren't so pissed off... and scared... and overwhelmed by all of this, being a vampire could actually be very interesting." With a faint grin Eric locked eyes with her. "No!" She wagged her finger at him. "Don't you dare suggest in any way that I am very interesting."

He reached out his hand. "C'mon." Eric tilted his head toward a clearing. They walked a few steps and he leaned toward her as he said, "I definitely think you're interesting."

She stopped and turned toward him. "How did you do that?"

"What?"

"That's not a normal whisper."

"Oh, yeah." He cleared his throat and leaned in again. "It's a vampiric whisper. No one else can hear what I'm saying."

"But how?" Too late she realized how close they were standing and his scent enveloped her. She gently pushed him away and she turned her head to come up for air.

"I don't know what your abilities are," he said in a regular voice. "But it's part of a growl." Eric took her hand and placed it on his throat. She could feel more than his pulse and identified all of the parts and functions she had learned in an anatomy class - the flow of the blood up the carotid and down the jugular, the wisps of air in and out of his trachea. She also noticed how her proximity was affecting his heart rate. He cleared his throat, rattling her hand. He began with a gentle growl, ever so slight, rumbling under palm. He whispered, "I want to kiss you."

Alexa's breath caught in her throat and her pulse skyrocketed. She scrambled to bring her focus away from his kissable mouth. His eyebrows flattened as his lips curled into a sinister grin – he was well aware of the effect he was having on her. She wrestled her desire and mustered the strength to push him away as she stepped further into a clearing.

Eric continued to grin. "How am I supposed to hear you all the way over there?"

"You just keep your distance." Alexa wasn't completely sure she could avoid what felt like a magnet drawing her toward him.

She placed her hand on her throat and ran a few quiet octaves, assessing the feel of the vibration. Alexa considered the elements necessary to growl. As she thought of anger and warning, the sensation of humming came to mind. She exhaled through her nose and initiated the beginning stages of a hum. She caught the sensation, but before she made a sound her eyes widened and her mouth dropped open. "Holy crap! This is why I can't sing!" She looked into the darkness of the trees above as if the answer were lingering among the limbs. Defeated and dismayed, she exhaled. "I was accused of humming when I sang."

With new resolve, Alexa returned her hand to her throat. "I..." she said aloud. She readjusted her tones and whispered, "I never knew I could do this!" Triumph swept her face. "This is crazy!" She continued to whisper, "What purpose does this serve?"

"Besides masking an entire conversation?" he whispered in return. "I'm sure it has more malicious uses - like stirring panic in your victim."

"Why would you do that?" she wondered in a normal voice.

Eric became more serious. "Alexa, vampires feed on fear. We can walk past a witch, simply admiring her scent. But if she's scared? It won't draw just one but every vampire in the vicinity."

"What about when a vampire is scared? Does their fear draw attention too?"

"Absolutely. It's like throwing blood into a pool of sharks. It makes your teeth drop faster than anything and you're instantly ready to attack."

"But people get scared all of the time."

He glared at her. "I'm well aware." Eric drew a deep breath and eased the stern look on his face. "I avoid movie theaters for that reason." He stood quiet watching her. "Is this still our first date? Or does it qualify as a second?"

A broad smile spread across Alexa's face. "I think technically it counts as a second. What time is it?"

He pulled his left wrist into view. "Eleven forty."

"Hang out for another twenty minutes and we could argue it's a third date."

Eric laughed. "I like how you think!"

She pulled away and twirled around, her head craned back to view the canopy of trees. She took a deep breath and wondered out loud, "are humans able to appreciate how wonderful this smells?"

"I don't know."

"It's a shame if they can't." She turned around to find him watching her. She was unnerved how his stare alone made her heart pace as if he were touching her.

Chapter Sixteen

Movement on the parking lot caught their attention. Eric leaned around a tree to check the activity. Alexa followed his gaze to a black car circling the lot, nearing their vehicles. She walked up to Eric and wrapped her arms around his waist and he draped a protective arm over her shoulder.

"I think this car has been following me," she whispered.

They watched the black sedan circle the lot a second time and leave. Alexa and Eric stood quiet, surveying the empty parking lot, enjoying the closeness of their bodies. He kissed the side of her head and wrapped his other arm around her, checking his wristwatch. "Three more minutes," he whispered.

Alexa leaned her head against his shoulder, still watching the uneventful parking lot. His heartbeat thumped just inches away from her ear and his scent consumed her.

Eric looked down at her. "I think we're going to have to cut our third date short and get you home safely."

"I don't want to go."

"Trust me, I don't want you to, but I think maybe you'll be safer under your father's watch."

Alexa straightened up and faced him. Eric pulled her closer and kissed her hard and firm. His tongue twined with hers, causing her heart rate to skyrocket. Alexa jerked back and slammed her tongue to the roof of her mouth to hold her fangs in place. She turned her face and pressed her hand to her lips, struggling to control her teeth. Eric brushed his mouth along her ear to her cheek. She pulled away again. "You have to stop," she said.

She opened her eyes knowing they were still glowing yellow.

She made eye contact with Eric and he grinned devilishly.

Running her tongue along the roof of her mouth, ensuring her fangs stayed in place, Alexa shook her head. "Shit, you really are dangerous, aren't you?"

"Mmhmm." he leaned in for another kiss.

"Eric..." She pressed a finger to his lips.

He loosened his hold on her body. "When do I get to see your teeth?"

"You make that sound so dirty."

Eric raised his eyebrow. "It can be."

"Really?"

He moved close to her neck. "mmhmm."

"Yeah," she said, "I probably should go home. My father's wrath is much safer than being around you." Alexa turned and broke away. She walked out of the trees onto the lawn.

Eric caught up with her and slid his arm around her waist. When they reached her car he pushed her against the door and kissed her again.

Alexa pulled away. "Be careful," she warned, "I bite."

"I like a good challenge." He backed up to give her room. "Go home, be safe." He leaned in for a last kiss, quick and simple, then opened the door for her.

Exiting the parking lot Alexa saw him from the rearview mirror still standing in the same spot, watching her leave.

The house was dark, but she knew her father was still awake. Alexa parked in the driveway, but as she closed the car door she heard another car cruise past the end of her street and turn down the next street. She never paid attention before, but there was a familiarity to a car always a block behind her when she drove home – it would speed to the next street, make a sharp turn, and continue driving. She assumed someone with her same work schedule lived on the next street and on evenings she came home late... well it was a large subdivision, she reasoned, cars were always on the move.

But the black car she had seen at the restaurant and again at the arts building seemed familiar. She couldn't quite say how often black sedans drove past her, but she knew it was frequent. With her ears tuned-in, Alexa walked to the front door and waited on the porch. An engine rumbled down the block behind her house, but not speeding as it had done when it passed her street. She looked around the corner of the house toward the opposite end of the street and saw headlights make the turn. Crap. She pressed herself flat against the house and listened as the car came closer. Headlights illuminated the street as the car rumbled past her house, not quite coming to a stop. Alexa worried the driver saw her, but then the car sped up a bit after passing the house, came to a stop at the end of the street, and parked.

Alexa slipped in the front door. "Dad?" She sensed him nearby.

"Where were you?" he grumbled from his recliner.

Realizing his proximity in the living room, she turned to face him, panic in her voice, "Somebody is following me!"

"Where were you?"

"I said someone is following me. They are parked at the end of the street."

He sighed and got out of his chair to look out the window. When he returned to the chair he rested his arms on his knees and sighed again.

Alexa stood stunned, looking between her father and the dark window. "You're not concerned, are you?"

"Of course I am concerned," he said. "Alexa, since the day you were born I have devoted myself to your wellbeing."

"Is that car is yours? Do you have someone following me?"

Her father remained silent.

"Dad! Can you *please* talk to me like I'm an adult? Is my life in danger?"

"Yes."

"Is someone following me?"

He sat silent for a moment then admitted, "yes."

"Is the person in that car someone I can trust?"

"Yes, he is a devoted friend and would guard you with his life. The hunter's scent is stronger on you."

Unnerved, she stared at the window. Who was the driver? What was his name? How long had he been following her? She knew better than to ask, her father had already told her too much. His questions about Eric, however, were not to be left unanswered. She toyed with the idea of lying to him, but her frazzled brain couldn't formulate anything logical. "I drove up to the college," she said. "I called him and he met me there. We walked around the campus."

"Alexa, you must bring this to an end. You have no future with this man."

"You don't get a say in that."

"Yes, Alexa, I do. You can argue and stomp your feet all you wish, but now your teeth have come in you are beholden to my family's rules. Your grandfather and I have final say in the selection of your husband and a hunter will never be considered."

Dumbstruck, Alexa stood with her mouth gaping. How dare... She stopped herself before a single word dropped out of her mouth. She knew whatever her father had to say, or more likely not say, would only spurn her anger even more.

With frustration and dismay, Alexa sought refuge in her bedroom. Again tears filled her eyes. She looked around her wee little sanctuary recalling the little-girl, twin-sized, canopy bed flounced in pink pressed against the wall. How many times she had played on the once open floor with Barbies or a set of blocks? How often had she fallen asleep propped against her bed while reading and awaken mysteriously in her bed having been gently lifted there by her father? Where was that gentle man now?

Alexa leaned against the wall as she processed her scent. A strong burst of roses came forward but also another flower, vibrant and bold, she couldn't name. She also noted something woody... and then the pepper scents of hunters. Mostly she smelled Eric, and then, like he described, an aftertaste of a different scent kicked in. He and the man she killed were distinct, but not drastically so. She didn't have words to describe the differences, yet her nose dissected them easily.

What was wrong with Eric? She really liked him and her attraction to him felt genuine. Men in the past were easy to squelch, but with Eric she wanted nothing more than to be in his arms. He felt safe and comforting and she definitely liked the way he smelled. Not that she was anywhere in the realm of thinking about marriage, but to find out he's not even a contender?

She looked to the ceiling for guidance. For as much as she missed being her daddy's little girl, Alexa was ready for an adult relationship, the type Eric could offer. She held a full-time job, owned a car, and basically went through all of the moves of being an adult, except she still lived with her parents – a living arrangement that stood in the way of her romantic life.

With a strengthening resolve, she pulled out the box holding her bank statements to assess her financial situation. She began to draw up a new budget, but a name at the top of May's statement caught her eye. She never thought twice about her father on her account, but if he had someone following her, surely he monitored her financial activity as well. Alexa would have to spend her lunch one day opening a new account at a different bank – step one of independence.

Chapter Seventeen

"My mom is pissed I'm not staying at her house," Jessica said over the phone. "But it just makes sense to hang out at Clo and Simon's place while trying to put this party together. Plus I get to play auntie to little Milo."

"He is absolutely adorable, but that name belongs on a puppy, not a baby," Alexa said. "So did you get the clubhouse?"

Jessica laughed. "You're so going to Hell. Yeah I got the clubhouse, but it took some doing. They're holding some bitch's baby shower that afternoon and won't be cleared out until five p.m. I said that wasn't a big deal because no one in our group would show up until seven or eight. Well, the old hag on the phone was worried we wouldn't have time to put up our decorations."

"What decorations?"

"That's what I said! I mean it takes, what, fifteen minutes to lug the booze and snacks out of the truck? Bam! Decorations."

Alexa snickered. "Did you get Lin's brothers to help with the heavy lifting?"

"Of course I did, but you know that means they'll be sniffing around the girls all damn night."

"Yeah, I know. Hopefully you have enough women on the guest list to give the rest of us a buffer. I mean Troy and Trent are cute as hell, but I'm not letting either one of them shove their tongues down my throat."

"Dunno, Lex, might be good to blow off some steam."

"Jess, when I let down my defenses it will be on my own terms and I can guarantee it won't be with one of Lin's little brothers."

"Those boys ain't little no more."

"My eyes ain't broke."

"Don't know about that. Rumor has it you've been ducking out of a lot of shit lately. The girls are getting worried about you, maybe you're checking out convents or something."

Alexa sighed. "Doesn't sound like such a bad idea at the moment."

"Oh do tell!"

"There's nothing to tell. Just crap hitting the fan here at home."

"Then you really *do* need to blow off some steam."

"Jess..."

"You're never going to find a man if you're always hiding out with mom and pop."

"Mmm, well, maybe I'm not hiding so much as keeping myself busy."

"Oh really?"

"I lead a very hectic life."

"Alright," Jessica said, "I won't push, but I do expect details when you decide to open up. He better be hot."

Alexa huffed a loud sigh. "There's no man. I just have a lot of shit going on." She heard a dismissive grunt through the phone. She said, "I'm serious, there's nothing to tell. I'll see you Saturday. Let me know if you need anything."

"Hot. This man had better be hot," Jessica repeated.

"Good-bye Jessica."

"See ya."

Chapter Eighteen

Sitting in her cubicle, Alexa flipped through a report, the white and pale green lines on the pages of continuous-feed paper blurring in front of her. Her mind drifted to thoughts of employment – her work, her father's occupation. As an account manager he traveled a great deal, often to other countries. This sort of job typically earns a large income, yet they lived in a working class neighborhood in a modest house. For all of his traveling, their family never took vacations, not even to visit his relatives in Austria.

Was his job another lie?

How did he afford an investigator to follow her around? He said the driver of the black car was a friend, but who has time to follow her around like that without being paid?

She knew her father worked for Eppert Holdings. She hoped to request a list of their associated banks to ensure she wouldn't open an account with any of them, but when she looked through the Yellow Pages for a phone number she couldn't find a listing for the company

Alexa turned to Tamara and asked, "Hey, have you ever heard of Eppert Holdings?"

Tamara shook her head. "Can't say I have. Why?"

Alexa shrugged a shoulder. "I met someone who worked there. Just wondering."

While on her lunch break, Alexa stopped in the downtown branch of her bank where she shared an account with her father. She remembered after her sixteenth birthday coming into this building with one hundred dollars tucked into her wallet, ready to open her first checking account. Her dad coached her through the process but let her do the talking.

Having been in the bank many times since opening her account she never took much time to appreciate the size or age of the building. Alexa stopped inside the lobby as people bustled past her. The long wooden counter with six tellers had a long line of people. The tall, wood-lined ceilings insulated the room and buffered the acoustics, keeping the space quiet. She searched for someone who could answer her questions and spotted a woman sitting at a desk.

"I'm working on a project for my economics class," Alexa lied to the loan officer. "Do you have a list of your board directors and their associations?"

"Do you have an account here?" the woman asked.

After confirming Alexa's account, the loan officer, a human who would die in a screaming ambulance, smiled nicely as she left her desk and headed to a wood filing cabinet in a far corner of the bank. Alexa turned to watch the lines at the teller windows.

A petite woman completing her transaction stood at the first window. Alexa identified her as a vampire with a soft meaty scent and wondered if she was a ranger? Her death would be on a couch in front of a huge television screen nearly filling the width of the wall. Alexa stayed with the vision longer than normal - some glimpses into the future amazed her. She didn't understand the need for, or the evolution of, increased television sizes.

As she pondered the waxing and waning of television sizes, a flash of red caught her attention. A woman, a human, stood in another line wearing simple, two-inch, pointed-toe, red pumps. Matched with a black A-line skirt and blazer, the shoes were a power statement, akin to a red tie on a man. She wondered when she would sit in a management position where such a strong ensemble would be necessary? Poking numbers into a computer all day didn't require any special outfit except adhering to company policy. Maybe in her formal launch into adulthood with getting her own apartment she should look into a different job, one with advancement possibilities?

She looked back to the vampire and the vision of the giant TV. Would her future include a bigass television?

Alexa heard a chair move and she turned in time to acknowledge the loan officer carrying a blue and gold glossy folder. "Good luck on your project," the woman said handing Alexa the folder. Alexa thanked her for the information and left the bank. On the sidewalk she flipped through the pages of the annual report. In tiny print at the bottom of the first page she saw, "subsidiary of Geismar Holdings, Inc." Alexa stopped walking and stared at the page, mindless of the throngs of people forced to maneuver around her.

"Alexa?" She heard her name and scanned the moving crowd. Men and women, witches and vampires among a mass of humans, all mingled walking back and forth, entering and exiting buildings. Food. Most were seeking or returning from a meal as scents from nearby restaurants wafted through with the crowd. A man repeated her name. She turned to see Eric walking toward her. Surprised she didn't recognize his voice in the crowd or pick up his scent, Alexa slammed the folder shut and decided she would deal with its contents later.

She smiled and met him halfway, dodging three people. "Eric!" she beamed.

"Have you eaten yet?" he asked.

"No, I wasn't planning on it."

"Do you have time for a burger?" He tipped his head to the restaurant next to the bank.

"I think so," she said with a shrug.

"They're quick, come on." He grabbed her hand and nodded toward the glossy folder. "Opening a bank account?"

Alexa looked down to the folder. "Uh, yeah," she said. "I need to set up something not attached to my parents' account. I think it's time for me to..." She shrugged again. "Establish independence?"

Eric chuckled in sympathy. "I get it, and yeah, it's probably time. Can you afford it?"

"I think so," she said as they stepped into a small restaurant. They stood in line at the counter and stared at the menu board hanging from the ceiling.

She noticed Eric glanced down at their joined hands, and then looked up to her. "You okay with this?"

Alexa smiled and nodded; Eric squeezed her hand in return. They waited behind a man in a blue suit asking the cashier multiple questions. For as much as she enjoyed the time standing next to Eric, Alexa's patience was wearing with the inquisitor in front of her – she needed to return to work, hopefully having eaten first. When at last they stood at the counter, Alexa and the cashier exchanged sympathetic smiles. She and Eric ordered their burgers, Alexa choosing the "Not-Quite-Vegetarian," a burger loaded with diced tomato, avocado, alfalfa sprouts, and cilantro ranch dressing.

Alexa and Eric grabbed the last available table, a tall skinny bar-type with no chairs. He lifted a cheeseburger resting in a basket of French fries and grinned at Alexa. "Have you started looking for apartments?"

"No, just figuring out my money first," she said. "Pretty sure my attempts to leave the nest are going to be met with resistance so I've gotta do this under the radar. I know my friends will help me get through this. They've all offered a spare room several times as well as suggestions of people looking for roommates."

"High school or college friends?"

"Oh hell, junior high!" She laughed. "Two I've known since second grade, they lived down the street. The rest we met in seventh grade."

"The rest?"

"Yeah, we call ourselves the Circle of Seven – Alexa, Briella, Chloe, Jessica, Lindsay, Megan, and Tess. We use nicknames which is why a lot of people know me as Lex."

"Ooh Lex Luther," Eric said with raised eyebrows.

"Hardly." Alexa rolled her eyes. "So who do you hang out with?"

"Eh," he shrugged a shoulder, "I've got different circles. Tom from work hits happy hour with me regularly. He's itching to come to your office to check you out, maybe try to swoon you his direction."

"Some friend," Alexa said with a groan. She plucked a stray square of avocado from her basket and popped it in her mouth.

"There's way too much green shit on that burger."

"And it's overcooked," she said.

Eric turned his cheeseburger around for her to see, "Yeah, mine is too."

"Not saying it's bad, I really like it, but I definitely prefer burgers rare."

He grinned. "Me too."

Alexa winced and realized too late Eric saw her. "What's that about?" he asked.

"It's just a headache."

"Really?" he asked with an edge of challenge. "I've seen you do that before but today it's happening a lot."

"It has to do with the crowd. I, uh, get visions. There are a lot of them right now with so many people. I'm clustering them together into white noise so I can focus on what you're saying."

"Visions? Is this a witch thing?" he whispered.

Alexa nodded. "I think so."

"What type of visions?"

She stood quiet debating how much to say. At last she leaned in. "I see the last moments of someone's life from their point of view. So, their last sights, sounds, and sometimes their feelings."

"There's no rhyme or reason as to when it hits you? Or who?"

"No, I see everyone's."

"Everyone? Even me?"

"Yep, every time I see you."

"You don't like talking about this, do you?"

"Not really."

He nodded understanding.

"It's not like we can do anything about it," she said. "I've learned we can't alter our paths. I was on a field trip to the art museum in grade school and blocked a woman from stepping off the curb just seconds before a taxicab zoomed by. She thanked me profusely then turned around, looked both ways down the street... three steps out and was plowed over by a school bus. The hit by the taxicab would have been instant death, but instead the bus dragged her down the street and it was a horrible, drawn out death..." Alexa shook her head. "We can't avoid it. It's going to happen. I'm not quite sure why I get these visions. I don't know what purpose knowing any of it serves."

"I was on that school bus," Eric said.

Alexa stared at him as a chill ran through her.

Eric also appeared unnerved. "We were sent to the school counselor that afternoon," he said, breaking the uncomfortable silence. "I guess phone calls were made to our parents. It never really affected me, but some of the kids sitting at the front of the bus were upset and crying. And well, of course the bus driver too. You know, I made eye contact with a little girl standing on the sidewalk. I thought she was the woman's daughter."

Alexa continued to stare at Eric. She recalled that day, the sounds, the blur of people running to help the woman. She also remembered seeing children on the bus. "I remember that," she said in a daze. "I remember a boy on the bus looking at me."

"Huh," Eric said staring at Alexa. "That's quite a coincidence."

"Yeah," Alexa said flatly. Their eyes locked just as they had done years before.

Eric nodded and cleared his throat. "It's hard to not ask you what happens to me."

"Oh I don't know how it happens, just what you see before the lights go out." Alexa watched him restrain from asking more. She rolled her eyes and said, "It's meaningless right now. You're hit by something, but I can't tell what. Evidently that's not important to you - you're focused on the person in front of you, a woman, someone you care about, but I can't see her face. She has white hair and is lying in a pool of blood. You know you're about to die and have a sense of resignation, but are horrified by what you just witnessed, which I gotta admit is pretty awful because she's decapitated."

His eyebrows arched. "Holy crap," he said.

"Yeah."

"That does nothing but raise a bunch of questions."

"About as useful as knowing we locked eyes when your bus hit that woman."

"The woman is probably significant in our lives somehow."

"Don't say that."

"Sorry to upset you," he said with a small smile. "Come on, let's get you back to work."

After discarding their baskets and uneaten french fries, Eric and Alexa stood in front of the restaurant. "What are you doing Saturday?" he asked.

"Megan's birthday party," she said. "I'd invite you but I'm not ready to submit you to the inquisition quite yet. We are really rough on new boyfriends. In fact, I think the husbands and boyfriends are currently trying to find ways to ditch the party."

"We?"

"I'm no better than the rest of those bitches."

"I'd love to see you in your native environment."

"Hmm, no." Alexa shook her head. "I'd rather introduce you to my father than my friends, and I'm pretty sure my dad wants to kill you."

He chuckled and dropped his head in concession. "I can only imagine. Okay, I'll wait to meet your friends. Are you available next week?"

"I think I'm open."

"Okay, I'll call you."

They stood for a moment wanting to kiss each other; she saw the desire in his eyes. Instead, they squeezed hands and lingered before parting ways. Alexa broke free and crossed the street. When she reached the opposite curb, she turned to see if Eric was still watching her, but he disappeared in the crowd. Disappointed, she continued her walk to work.

Chapter Nineteen

Walking in the house after work, Alexa hoped to retreat to her bedroom, skipping dinner, as had been her recent routine. Instead she stopped in curiosity watching her mother stand in front of the television with one hand over her mouth. Her father sat perched on the edge of his chair with a studious scowl, equally engrossed. Alexa craned her neck to see the television from the entryway – a newsman stood in a wooded area interviewing a police officer. Another officer in the background walked with a dog on a leash and even further back, a bright yellow tarp strung among the trees, a crime scene.

The tagline on the TV screen showed, "3 Murdered Women."

Her mother stared at the screen shaking her head. "Hmm, three. No, that's a ritual." She turned to face her husband and said, "I don't care what the investigators find, this crime was committed by witches."

He stared back, no argument in his expression, only deliberation. He quickly glanced at Alexa and then back to her mother and nodded. "I will inquire about the murders."

"What makes three so special?" Alexa asked.

A momentary hesitation crossed her mother's face and then replaced with resolve and authority. "Three is a divine number. I'd bet the women were laid out in a triangle at some point, maybe not in their final resting ground, but a triangle for sure – three women, three points, three deaths. Triangles are a feminine symbol and feminine energy is very powerful. Someone is harvesting energy and I can only wonder why, but it's definitely not good."

"What about the couple killed near my office? Dad said it looked like a vampire had killed them?"

"And yet you saw witches approach them? With harmful intent?" Her mother asked.

Alexa nodded.

"I wouldn't be surprised if the two events were connected," her mother said. "There could have been a rogue group just murdering for sport and of course make it look like vampire activity. Or..." she paused. "Something much more sinister..." She thought for a moment. "A blood sacrifice," she said, closing her eyes in dismay. "Any blood would suffice, typically animals are used, but to use a person, even a human, that's venturing into summoning powers that are very dark. But to take a hybrid - the raw energy of a vampire, mixed with the magic of a witch, even a weak witch? Somebody is meddling with dangerous spells."

"Do you think those women are hybrids too?" Alexa nodded to the TV.

Her mother turned to her father with an arched eyebrow. He responded with a tilt of his head. He said, "You could be correct. I will investigate."

"What can be done?" Alexa asked. "Is there, like a counter spell, or something?"

Her mother shrugged a shoulder. "It's hard to say. It depends on who is behind the spell. It also depends on the purpose of the spell or spells. Honestly, the only ones I can think of are for personal gain which is really shitty witchcraft. That always comes back to bite you in the ass. Let's just hope something truly evil isn't released onto our streets in the process."

Alexa raised her eyebrows. "I can't even ask what type of evil is possible because I'm still processing that vampires are real, but, um, thank you for not giving me a bullshit answer."

"Alexa, please... I know what's happening is difficult, but please, *please* b safe. Stay in groups, especially with humans. Don't run off in the middle of the night and by all means do not tell anyone you are a hybrid." Her mother was close to tears in her pleas.

Alexa shook her head. "I have no intention of sharing that information with anyone." She made eye contact with her father. He appeared nearly as desperate as her mother for her safety. She offered a small grin and left the room.

Chapter Twenty

As Alexa prepared to walk out of the house, she stopped in the living room where her parents were watching the evening news. A report about William Geismar of New Jersey indictment for insider trading had her father's complete attention. Alexa glanced toward the TV, wondering if her father knew any of the Geismar family?

"Alexa..." her mother had a warning tone in her voice.

"Don't worry mom, I'm going straight to the party and coming directly home." She looked to her father who had finally taken interest in their conversation. "I assume there will be a black car following me there and home?"

"Yes, there will."

Unsure if she should say thank you as the thought of a bodyguard did bring her some comfort. She pressed a tight grin and headed to the door.

"Wish Megan a happy birthday for us," her mother said.

"Will do."

She arrived at the apartment complex unable to find a place to park. She drove in circles worried she would have to park on the street.

At the opposite end of the complex Alexa found a spot and walked toward the clubhouse. The black sedan openly cruised past her and stopped where the driver had a clear view of her path. The setting sun cast a variety of shadows and her attention scattered across the parking lot, noting how many places a person could hide. She chastised herself for allowing her imagination to get the better of her and remembered that help was sitting nearby. Before entering the clubhouse, Alexa took a deep breath, cleared her thoughts, and plastered a smile on her face.

Inside a sea of unknown faces passed by and she panicked - maybe she had crashed someone else's party? Chloe walked by and relief swept over her. Alexa followed her short friend through the crowd, trying to catch up.

"Clo," Alexa yelled.

Chloe turned around, hearing her familiar nickname. "Lex!" she squealed and the two embraced. Human. A vision rushed in of a similar looking woman hovering over Chloe as she suffered a clutching chest pain. The vision didn't shock Alexa, she had seen this a million times before, but it came in strong since she and Chloe hadn't seen each other for several weeks.

The crowded room flooded other visions into Alexa's head, including one where a man sees his partner's face as she is stranded under his weight during sex. Alexa jolted her head in the direction of the man somewhere in the throng of people, but she couldn't figure out who he might be. That vision would be hard to shake, but it did allow her to submerge Chloe's death. Alexa returned her attention to Chloe and beamed a broad smile.

"Where have you been hiding yourself?" Chloe demanded.

"Just a lot going on," Alexa said. "Where's Meg?"

Chloe pointed her finger over the crowd. "Over there."

"K. We'll catch up when things settle down."

She found her way to Megan - human, car accident. Ugh, Alexa hated this vision because it would be coming in the very near future. It was a strong vision and made looking at Megan difficult. Her last sight would be the steering wheel crashing toward her face with the loud sounds of crushing metal.

As Alexa moved closer to Megan, she distracted herself by focusing on the guy who dies during sex. Sex-guy didn't have any pains in his chest or down his arm, he just couldn't breathe. He felt paralyzed. Maybe he was having a stroke? Grateful to have something other than a steering wheel in her face as she looked at Megan, Alexa squealed, "Happy Birthday!" and pulled her into a bear hug.

"I'm so happy to see you," Megan said.

"Holy crap, there are a lot of people here!" Alexa said looking around the room.

"Leave it to Jess, to pull off something this huge."

"Any bets for how long it takes the cops to show up?"

"It's about damn time you got here," Jessica said from behind her. Human, gasping for air. Jessica reached past Alexa and handed Megan a drink.

"Since when do you start a party on time?" Alexa asked.

"I got in here at six o'clock and those cows from the shower were still dicking around. We had to help them tear all of their crap down."

"You should have called me!"

"Eh, it's all right," Jessica said with a flip of her hand. "Where is your drink?"

"Haven't gotten that far," Alexa said looking around. Two girls rushing toward Megan bumped into her. "Who the hell are all of these people?"

Jessica pointed around the room – Megan's coworkers, college friends, cousins, her sister's friends, and a variety of friends of friends.

Lindsay pushed forward and gave Megan a hug. She turned around and greeted Alexa - human, in the hospital.

"Hey Lin!" Alexa smiled as Lindsey pulled her into a hug.

"Ohmigod, you don't have a drink either!" Jessica pointed to the wall by the stone fireplace as she rattled-off drink suggestions.

Alexa headed to the self-serve bar. She grabbed a red cup, filling it with ice then rummaged through the bottles of cheap liquor. She poured two fingers of vodka, but before she could pick up the cranberry juice, she smelled two more witches enter the room. With a start she realized they were her two friends, Brie and Tess. Alexa poured the juice and headed their direction.

"Hey Lex," they said in unison.

Tess furrowed her brow, "What's with the look? You okay?"

"Hmm? Yeah, I'm fine."

"No, you're bothered by something," Brie said.

"Seriously," Tess said, "what's up?"

Alexa took a moment to find the right thing to say in a crowded room. "I finally understand your scents."

Brie and Tess looked at each other and then back at Alexa. Tess squinted her eyes at Alexa, and then shook her head. "Nooo..."

Alexa nodded her head with a coy grin.

Brie's eyes lit up. "Holy crap! It's about time!"

"I feel so stupid for not piecing it together," Alexa said.

"It has been impossible not saying something to you," Brie said.

"Why didn't you?"

"Lex, our moms came down hard on us to never say a thing to you," Tess said. "I guess your mom got to them early on. I don't know what the big deal was, but there were threats of banning us from playing with you."

"Geez," Alexa moaned.

"We should have told you, shouldn't we?" Brie asked.

Alexa nodded.

"Are you angry with us?" Tess asked.

"Oh God, no," Alexa said. "I'm pissed at my parents, but

never at you guys."

"How did you find out?" Tess asked.

Alexa measured for eavesdroppers and lowered her voice as quiet as possible. "Let's just say something big happened and leave it at that until we're someplace I can talk more openly."

"Was it a *bad* something?" Brie asked.

"Yeah," Alexa said.

"When did you guys show up?" Chloe wrapped her arms around Tess and Brie.

"We just got here," Brie said. The huddle broke up and they exchanged hugs with Chloe.

"Where the hell did all of these people come from?" Tess asked, looking around the room.

"Jess," Alexa said.

"Well not to be petty, but I hope all of these strangers brought Meg a present," Tess said.

Chloe snorted. "That's totally petty."

"Who the fuck throws a birthday party and invites strangers?" Tess asked.

Alexa burst out laughing. Seeing the looks on her friends' faces, knowing the joke wasn't quite *that* funny, she sighed. "I love you guys."

Tess grabbed Alexa's chin. "Poor Lex has been in a funk, hasn't she?"

Chapter Twenty-One

"Meg, do you even know all of these people?" Chloe asked.

Megan laughed and shook her head. "No, not at all. I think my family ran for the hills an hour ago. Jess, how did you pull this off?"

"I just challenged everyone to bring a friend," Jessica said innocently.

"*Darling*, you did fabulous," Megan said as she cupped Jessica's face. "I feel like the belle of the ball! Thank you!" She planted a quick kiss on Jessica's cheek and twirled in a circle.

"Are there any chairs around here?" Tess asked, trying to look beyond the crowd.

"The guys found some," Chloe said. In unison the group looked toward the four men huddled around a small cooler.

"We could bump them out of their seats," Tess suggested.

"That only helps the four of you attached to them," Alexa said. "Me, Brie, and Jess will have to fend for ourselves, I guess."

"Ohmigod, there are a ton of chairs along the wall over there." Lindsay pointed to the back wall and began walking. Tess followed Lindsay through the crowd the back wall.

Brie turned to Alexa. "I guess we have to go get chairs."

With two chairs in hand, Alexa's head snapped toward the door sensing two vampires enter. Brie stopped dead in her tracks and looked in the same direction.

With a sigh Brie said, "It's just Sidney and Tiffany."

"What are they doing here?" Alexa asked with disbelief, wondering why the biggest bullies from high school would show up to Megan's party.

"Hell if I know," Brie said, pulling Alexa toward the circle of friends.

"I'm trying to remember the last time I've seen them. I bumped into Syd at a gas station over a year ago."

"I heard Tiffany was dancing at some men's club."

Alexa stopped and stared at Brie. "You mean stripping?"

"Yeah."

Alexa scrunched her face. "Not that I would wish that job on anyone, but I bet she's good at it."

Brie giggled.

When they reached the group, Brie made the announcement. "Head's up, Sniffany is in the house."

"What?"

"Are you kidding?"

"No way!"

The friends twisted in their seats trying to find the notorious duo they nicknamed "Sniffany" in ninth grade. Alexa noticed Tess didn't act surprised with Brie's announcement and had already identified their location.

Sidney and Tiffany meandered through the crowd, likely greeting people they knew. The night almost felt like a high school reunion with the number of mutual friends present. Alexa waited for the duo to make their way to Megan's circle. Brie and Tess behaved as if they were on edge – keeping an eye on the crowd while maintaining half-hearted conversations.

Alexa noticed too late she felt equally distracted and missed Lindsay's question. She apologized when she turned to Lindsay and asked her to repeat what she had said.

"Jess says you're seeing someone," Lindsay said. Jessica grinned as Megan, Lindsay, and Chloe stared at Alexa waiting for a response.

Alexa flushed red and glared at Jessica. "You're such a bitch."

"Girl, you're the last standing virgin," Jessica said. "You owe us details."

"There are no details," Alexa said. Brie and Tess leaned in, finally aware of the conversation.

"But there is a man?" Chloe confirmed.

Alexa sighed and stared at the ceiling. "Yes." With all eyes were on her, waiting for any nugget of information about her new boyfriend, she sighed again. "His name is Eric, he's twenty-seven. We met at work, he's a copier repairman, and we've only gone out a couple of times." She looked to Brie and Tess and said, "Oh, and my father already hates him."

"Your father hates all of your boyfriends," Tess said.

"No, I mean *hates* him and has forbidden me from seeing him again," Alexa said.

Tess stared at her and raised her eyebrows. Alexa couldn't quite convey Eric was a vampire and if she kept looking at Tess she would draw attention to their silent exchange.

"What's your dad's issue?" Megan asked.

"*Very* old world," Alexa said. "I swear to God he's plotting an arranged marriage."

"You better hurry up and let someone tap that before you end up exchanging vows with Elmer Fudd," Tess said.

"You know what?" Alexa asked. "I would be a lot happier if the only person concerned with the state of my hymen was *me* and the rest of you whores back the fuck off."

"Alright, alright, fair enough," Megan said diplomatically. "We should be focusing on our two married women as I am *sure* they have plenty of advice for our resident virgin." Then she leaned back in her chair giggling.

"I hate all of you," Alexa said with a grin.

Jessica leaned forward. "You never did say what he looks like."

"The antithesis of Jack," she said in comparison to her previous boyfriend. "He's about as tall as me, light brown hair, green eyes, and a great smile."

"Oh, hey," Lindsay said, "that shithead was bugging Trent for information about you."

"What the hell is Jack talking to your brother for?" Alexa rolled her eyes. "Seriously, can't a guy take a clue?"

Megan and Chloe offered suggestions for messages to send to Jack when Alexa's attention drew back to the two vampires.

In a gathering where everyone wore blue jeans and tennis shoes, Sidney and Tiffany showed up in short, form-fitting, black dresses revealing their ample chests. Seven uninterested glares met their arrival to the circle of friends.

The duo stood side by side behind Chloe and Megan. "Hello ladies," Sidney said with false sweetness.

Jessica said, "When I was drawing up the guest list, I don't recall your names being added."

"Must have missed the bouncer at the door checking for engraved invitations," Tiffany said.

"When you spend so much time on your knees you tend to miss things like that," Jessica said. "Did you ever get your name tattooed on your shoulders so the guys could memorize your name while you're blowing them?"

Alexa snorted as she tried to subdue her grin. Tiffany stared at her.

"Whatever," Sidney said with a shrug. "We heard Meggy here was so hard up for friends you put out an all-call for everyone to bring a couple extra people. So here we are. Friend stand-ins. Feel popular yet, Meggy?"

Smirks around the circle turned into sneers.

Tiffany continued staring at Alexa. "What are you looking at, you little witch?" Years too late, Alexa understood why she,

Brie, and Tess had been regular targets of their taunts. She pressed back into her chair, upset that being a witch would be considered less than a vampire.

"Are you chewing *gum*?" Alexa asked.

"Yeah, what of it?" Tiffany asked. She intentionally smacked her gum.

"Doesn't that get tangled in your *teeth*?" Alexa asked.

"Not if you know what the fuck you're doing," Tiffany said. She and Alexa continued to glare at each other.

Sidney leaned in. "You're awfully mouthy these days. Maybe you'd like to step outside and finish this conversation properly?"

"Oh my God, please. What are we going to do, have a rumble? Be all Sharks and Jets?" Alexa raised both hands and snapped her fingers twice.

"What the fuck are you talking about?" Tiffany asked.

"West Side Story, it's a classic? Never mind." Alexa rolled her eyes and looked over to Jessica. "So anyway, what were we talking about before we were so rudely interrupted? Something about my father's plans for the future?"

"Yes, I believe so," Jess said with a large smile.

Tiffany and Sidney drifted away into the crowd and Alexa's friends burst out laughing.

"Well played, Lex," Lindsay said.

"Thank you, thank you," Alexa said from her chair, bending forward in a bow. "But damn, who acts like that? What are we, still in high school?" Alexa hadn't stopped tracking the vampires as they meandered through the crowd toward the drink table.

She shook her cup, rattling the remainder of the ice cubes. "Guess it's time for a refill."

Tess grabbed Alexa's arm and pulled her close. "Lex, what

the fuck are you doing?" she whispered.

"Getting a drink."

"You're tracking them, aren't you?" Tess asked.

"Just getting a refill."

"Alexa! They could literally kill you."

"Or it could be the other way around."

"Did your teeth come in or something?" Tess hissed. "They're full blooded, you can't fight them." Alexa stared at her friend for a moment. Tess knew she was a hybrid? Of course she did – Tess knew Alexa's parents.

"I'll be fine." Alexa broke free and walked into the crowd a bit dazed how much Tess, and likely Brie, knew about her. She redirected her frustrated energy into curiosity of the two vampires she had known most of her life. She rounded near the drink table, not quite going up to it, but close enough to catch the attention of Sidney and Tiffany and as expected, they turned their heads in Alexa's direction. Alexa made eye contact with Tiffany then rolled her eyes. Alexa turned and walked slowly, greeting a redhead she thought was named Kathy then moved through the crowd toward the restroom.

With a soft push on the door, Alexa entered. Two brunettes, humans, huddled by the sinks. One looked up, grinned at Alexa, and whispered to her friend they should go outside. She had no idea who they were but was happy when they made their exit. Alexa approached the sink and took in her reflection at the mirror. Her makeup had faded since she left home and she hadn't brought her purse with her to touch it up, not that she really cared in the first place, the clubhouse had poor lighting anyway.

Tiffany pushed into the bathroom, while Sidney remained outside the door. "You got something to say to me, Ah-Lex-Ah?" Tiffany mocked.

"What the hell are you jackasses doing here?"

"Are you still so naïve that you don't know not to mess with me?" Tiffany asked. Her expression changed as she appeared to take in Alexa's scent and she snickered. "Do you think because you've been fucked by a vampire you're impervious to what I can do to you?"

"Oh do you think you're going to *hurt* me?"

"I'd love nothing more than to wipe that stupid grin off your smug face."

Alexa rolled her eyes. "This is so high school. There's no reason to ever see each other except for reunions. Your bullying bullshit holds no..."

Tiffany growled and dropped her teeth as she stepped forward.

Alexa punched her in the mouth, breaking at least two teeth, including one of her fangs. She swirled the air around Tiffany to press her against the wall. Tiffany's lip began to swell and a small trickle of blood seeped from her mouth.

"Maybe I didn't make myself clear," Alexa said. "Stay away from my friends." She levitated Tiffany and tossed her against one of the toilet stalls. The metal rattled as Tiffany slid to the floor. Alexa turned on a heel and left the restroom. Outside the door she grabbed Sidney's arm and stood mere inches away from her face. Alexa squeezed her arm tight, but not so tight as to reveal her vampire strength. "After you finish mopping up Tiffany the two of you need to leave." She released Sidney and sauntered to the drink table.

Refilling her drink she could sense Sidney and Tiffany leaving the building. Nonchalant, Alexa resumed her seat with her friends and grinned at Brie staring at her.

Tess leaned in and whispered, "you have blood on your chin."

"Oh thanks," Alexa whispered back. "Splatter." She rubbed

her chin and grinned.

"What the hell happened?"

"Refilled my drink."

Tess glanced at Alexa's cup. "You're full of shit."

Alexa took a sip.

Tess glared at her. "Skillfully full of shit, but full of shit none the less. When things clear out tonight we need to talk."

Alexa shook her head. "Not tonight."

"Well tomorrow, then. Brie and I will be at her mom's house in the afternoon. Come down when you see our cars."

Chapter Twenty-Two

Alexa walked into the house knowing her father waited for her return. Without acknowledging his presence she headed to her parents' bedroom knowing she would find her mother asleep.

Alexa crawled into bed next to her mother where a strong scent of recent sexual activity hung in the air. Alexa labored to ignore the scent and laid her head on her father's pillow. She watched her mother stir, something Alexa learned as a child happened whenever she came near.

Her mother blinked a couple of times. "Everything okay?" she slurred.

"Tess and Brie are witches?"

Her mother grinned and stroked a strand of hair off Alexa's face. "I wanted you to find out on your own, but you kept declining their invitations to go out."

"I thought you were unusually interested in their phone calls lately."

The pale light from the hallway darkened as her father leaned against the doorjamb watching his wife and daughter talk as they frequently did when Alexa returned home from a date or night out with friends.

"I need to warn you, Alexa," her mother said, "there is a council governing the covens in the area. Brie and Tess and their families are restricted in what they are allowed to say to you. Please do not be upset with them if they don't answer your questions."

Alexa rolled to her back and stared at the ceiling. "Are you allowed to say *why* they're restricted from talking to me?"

"Yes, but you're not going to like the answer anymore than if I said nothing." Her mom propped up on an elbow. "This council does not approve of hybrids participating in witchcraft. When I married your father I was also forbidden from practicing the arts and was restricted from teaching you anything."

"But aren't these innate abilities? Like walking or talking? How can they control that?"

Her mother smiled a devilish grin. "Yes, exactly. And of course you have strong powers that won't lie latent and unused – we descend from very strong witches. While I can't teach you, that won't ever stop you from learning, now will it? But I do ask that you not jeopardize your friends' standing with the council by asking them too many questions."

"Tess asked if my teeth came in. I have to admit I'm surprised they knew I was part vampire."

Her mother sighed. "This has been so difficult for you, hasn't it? You know none of this is how we planned for you to find out. We have spent the better portion of your life arguing with our families and councils how best to present this to you. The biggest argument was that once you knew the truth you would want to be trained, which neither the witches nor the vampires felt was necessary. You've acclimated so well as a human that everyone... and let me be clear that never included your father and I, they all felt you were best left in the dark. We know you far too well that you would've stayed in the dark for much longer, even if your teeth never came in. And, quite honestly, your reaction has been exactly what we expected."

"Alexa, who is the vampire I sense on you tonight?" her father asked from the doorway.

"One of the girls at the party."

"One of your friends is a vampire?" he asked.

"Hardly," she said. "We all hate her and her idiot friend. Trust me, they were not invited - they totally crashed the party. At some point she ended up following me into the bathroom and I told her she wasn't welcome. She flashed her fangs at me and I punched her in the mouth."

Her father started laughing and shook his head. He pressed his fingers to his forehead as he continued to shake his head.

"Honestly, my first instinct was to just pop her in the face," Alexa said. "It's something I've long dreamt of doing – it just came natural. As I thought about it on the way home, though, I realized just how out of my league I was facing her."

"That was wise you understood the situation," her father said. "Alexa I have no measure of your strength, but you are untrained. One wrong move and a weaker vampire will overcome you. Please be aware of your surroundings and stay within the safe confines of humans."

With a frustrated sigh, Alexa rolled to fully face her mother. "Well, Brie and Tess are going to be in the neighborhood tomorrow so I'm going to hang out with them, probably in the afternoon."

With disapproval, Alexa's mother glared at her for dismissing her father. Alexa rolled her eyes, said "good night mom," and slid off the bed. She faced her father. "Sorry I'm such a pain in the ass, but I don't know how to talk to you without getting pissed off."

"I am aware," he said, "and I can handle your wrath. Just please, remain safe."

"Good night, Dad," she said and continued to her bedroom.

Chapter Twenty-Three

As instructed, when she saw Brie and Tess's cars in the respective driveways Alexa walked down the street. She noticed another car parked at the far end of the street, the black car. A man got out wearing blue jeans and a white t-shirt. She had seen him the night before in a suit and tie when she left the birthday party, but now in the blue jeans he looked awkward; the suit seemed more appropriate. He produced a pack of Marlboro's, Alexa could tell by the distinctive red box, and he leaned on the hood of the car as he lit a cigarette.

Tess bounded out of her parents' house and ran across the yard meeting Alexa in the next driveway. Tess hooked her arm into Alexa's and headed into Brie's childhood home. Alexa dismissed the man at the end of the street. She would have to ponder his existence at a later time.

She stood in the kitchen and opened a cabinet, helping herself to saltines and peanut butter. Her mind swirled with the death visions of the two girls who grew up only a few houses away. Tess would die of the same thing that kills her mother, hacking, coughing, gasping for air. Brie's death had always confused Alexa, but finally knowing about vampires she understood her perky, blonde friend would die from a horrible pain on one side of her neck – a bite.

Brie ate beef jerky and Tess rummaged through the refrigerator for cheese slices. With her cheese in hand, Tess grabbed five saltines out of the sleeve Alexa left on the counter. The three friends stood in the kitchen, silently snacking just as they had done for nearly twenty years.

Brie's mom walked into the kitchen and grinned.

Tess's mom stepped behind her next-door neighbor and shook her head. "My God, girls," she said. "Those aren't even proper snacks. Where is the chocolate?" Three dismissive grins greeted her.

Alexa laughed at herself for the surprise she experienced when they entered the room - of course Brie and Tess's mothers were witches!

"I'd offer you wine," Brie's mom suggested, "but I'm not sure what pairs with processed cheese."

"Something American," said Tess.

"What about peanut butter?" Tess's mom asked.

"Doesn't matter," Alexa said with a grin. "Wine is like liquid jelly."

Brie's mom rolled her eyes.

"Alexa," Tess's mom asked more seriously, "your mother finally told you about being a witch?"

"No, my mother hasn't told me shit." Alexa picked up another saltine and nibbled on the perforated edges. "In fact, what she *did* say was that I'm not supposed to threaten your standing with the council by asking too many questions."

Tess's mom rolled her eyes and dismissively waved her hand. "Honey, I have never given two shits about that stupid council." Brie's mom nodded in fervent agreement.

"Then how did you find out?" Tess asked with a wrinkled forehead.

Alexa tossed a casual shrug. "Some vampires came after me when I was jogging one morning." Concern and surprise washed across everyone's faces. "I used some sort of witchcraft to push them back, but that's also when my teeth dropped in."

"Teeth? I don't sense any vampire in you," Brie's mom said.

Alexa shook her head. "No, evidently I mask it or something, but I'm definitely a vampire." Dead silence fell over the room.

"Like a, uh, blood drinking, witch hunting vampire?" Brie asked.

Alexa sighed. "No, more like a steak eating, wine drinking vampire who already has plenty of witch blood running through her veins."

Brie's mom pulled two bottles from a wine rack. "Brie, honey, grab some glasses. This requires sitting at the table." She motioned for the girls to follow her into the dining room. "Oh, Alexa, the corkscrew is there in the window."

The women assembled around the dining room table. Alexa measured a small sense of fear, but she appreciated their willingness to continue the conversation. Glasses clinked as they poured and passed wine around the table. Conversation, however, was lacking.

Tess huffed. "This is stupid." She turned to Alexa. "Open your mouth, I want to see these vicious teeth you've sprouted." Alexa complied and tilted her head back so Tess could look inside. "You're full of shit, there's nothing in there." Alexa flexed her jaw, dropping her teeth into place. "HO-LY FUCK!"

Brie timidly stood up to see her friend's mouth. "Damn," she said in shock.

"Your scent changed too!" Tess said, surprised.

"Yeah, it's really similar to my dad's," Alexa slurred with her head tilted back.

Alexa lowered her head, displaying her mouth for The Moms to see. A small gasp slipped from across the table. She flexed her mouth again to pull her teeth in then took a sip of wine.

Tess's mom took a large gulp of wine. "Woo, darlin', that is definitelya full set, isn't it?"

"Is your father training you... how to be a vampire?" Brie's mom asked. "Lord, I don't even know what vampires do."

"No," Alexa said with an eye roll. "He just keeps telling me how much safer it is for me to be around humans. I'm not even getting handy little tips like 'hey, do this so you don't slice your tongue in half' or like how to run a toothbrush around these bastards. I'm muddling through it on my own. I'm just supposed to stick around humans. Real useful."

"Well," Tess's mom said, "humans are your best form of safety."

"What happened last night with Tiffany?" Tess asked.

"Seriously, I only punched her in the face. That's was it," Alexa said.

"Well hell, you could have done that in front of us!" Tess said. "That would have been worth watching!"

"She bared her teeth at me, so no, it wasn't something that could happen around all of those people," Alexa said. "But it did feel glorious."

"Did you... did you bare *your* teeth?" Brie asked.

"No," Alexa said, "She was trying to intimidate me and I'm so new to all of this it just seemed better to strike first and strike hard and be done with it. I actually broke one of her fangs."

With raised eyebrows Brie and Tess giggled.

"What's with the look?" Brie asked.

"I sort of feel bad for breaking her teeth," Alexa said.

"Oh, honey," Brie's mom said. "I believe vampires can regenerate their teeth."

Tess's mom nodded. "I've heard that too."

Alexa rolled her eyes. "Yet again, someone besides my family is telling me about being a vampire."

"Have you bitten anyone?" Brie asked.

"Eh, it wasn't quite 'bite' but I defended myself against those guys in the park," Alexa said.

Concern wrinkled across Brie's forehead. "Did you kill them?"

"Just one," Alexa said. Eyebrows shot up around the table. She knew they were going to ask for the details so she continued. "I used my teeth to rip most of his jaw off."

Tess whispered, "shit."

"What did the others do? Wait... how many were there?" Brie's mom asked.

"There were ten. They kinda freaked out and just picked up the dead guy and ran off," Alexa said.

Tess's mom cocked her head. "Is this the attack in the park down the street that was all over the news not too long ago?"

Brie's mom looked at Tess's mom and asked, "The one where they couldn't find the body?"

"Yes. Some were saying might have been a dog fight." Tess's mom said.

Alexa cleared her throat. "Yeah, that was me." The moms snapped their heads in unison and stared at Alexa.

"So, you've tasted blood?" Tess asked.

Alexa nodded.

"Do you like it?"

Alexa searched for words and shrugged. "I don't know. I was so freaked out by the whole thing I just puked it all up."

"Ugh, I'd puke too," Tess's mom said.

Brie's mom groaned in concern and said, "If you had enough to vomit, that means you did more than knick his neck."

"To further freak you out," Alexa said, "I can hear your heartbeats." She was met with blank stares.

"How long have you been able to do *that*?" Brie asked.

"When the sinus headaches started a couple months ago," Alexa said.

"Are you still having those?" Brie asked.

"They went away when my teeth came in."

"Well, I guess those bigass fangs sprouting in your mouth

would be a good source of a headache," Tess said. "So, onto the more important shit, tell us about the guy you're seeing."

"You're dating someone?" The moms said nearly in unison, then looked at each other and laughed.

"I told you everything last night – we went on a date... well two. We went to lunch a couple days ago. Anyway, his name is Eric and he has sandy brown hair."

"No, no, no, no, young lady," Tess wagged her finger. "You made a point to tell me how much your father hated him. What's up?"

"He's a vampire."

Tess looked at her sideways. "Uh... What? How the hell did you suddenly start dating a vampire? And what do you mean your dad hates him?"

"He's a hunter and I get the idea that my dad thinks I'm too good for a lowly hunter, or some such shit." Alexa waved her hands in frustration and changed her course of thought. "Do you know anything about vampires?" she asked the moms. "I mean no one is telling me squat. My mom said I can't ask you about witchcraft and my dad is waiting for some edict from another council. All I'm getting is radio silence, but can you tell me what you know about vampires?" As she spoke tears welled in her eyes.

Brie's mom launched out of her chair and ran around the table to pull Alexa into her arms. "Oh, honey," she soothed.

Alexa broke into a sobbing cry as her friend's mother comforted her. The other women circled, offering comforting words and stroking her back and arms. Alexa at last came up for air and apologized for breaking down.

"No, no. You ask us anything you want. Fuck the council." Tess's mom said as she planted a kiss on the top of Alexa's head. "I've never understood the need for all of the secrecy."

"They said I acclimated so well as a human no one felt the need to tell me otherwise." Alexa sniffled. "They said they were surprised I even developed fangs."

"Well, we're a little surprised as well," Tess's mom said. "But even as a hybrid you should have at least been made aware of vampires and witches." She squatted in front of Alexa. "I cannot imagine how terrifying this has been for you."

"It was horrible," Alexa said. "Ten men bearing their teeth and running at me? And in a matter of minutes I have a dead man in my arms and his blood all over me? Then I realized *I* killed him and that I have these new fucking teeth? Yeah, I was a mess... still am a mess. So whatever, everyone is surprised I turned out to be a vampire. Why couldn't they just pick up from there and start filling in all the details? The surprise was bad enough, but continuing the secrecy is just adding insult to injury." She leaned back in the chair and came up for air. "So anyway, I met Eric at work and he's been like the only person to break any of this down for me. We went out to dinner," she turned to Brie, "I totally threw you under the bus and said I was meeting you for dinner. So when I got home ready to tell them all about meeting up with you, they totally flipped out because I smelled like a vampire rubbed up against me."

"Did he?" Tess asked.

"Maybe," Alexa said. "But seriously, my dad totally flipped his shit and I stormed out of the house. Later he said that him and my grandfather will pick out my husband. I mean what the fuck is that?" She sniffled and shook her head a couple of times. "The bottom line is I need to get the hell out of that house. I need my own place."

"No kidding," Brie said. "Have you started looking for apartments?"

"Not yet," Alexa said. "I just got a new bank account set up, something not attached to my parents' name. I went to a totally different bank and the funds will be available on Monday."

"You know you're being followed, right? You have been your whole life." Tess said.

"My whole life? Geez. But yeah, the same car keeps showing up so I called my dad out on that and he admitted he had a friend following me. Dude is parked at the end of the street right now."

Everyone's heads turned toward the large dining room window facing the street as if they expected to see a vampire standing in the yard.

"Do you think this is the best idea?" Brie's mom asked. "I mean if your father has gone to such lengths to hide you that he has a friend following you around, maybe you're in danger?"

"That's the only thing that has kept me from marching out the front door," Alexa said. "There's so much I don't know. How do I stay safe? Am I jumping from the kettle into the fire? I mean, I really trust Eric, but what if he's actually a threat? I just..." She sighed with her hands in the air, exasperated and exhausted.

"Not to make things worse," Tess's mom said. "But I assume your mother hasn't talked to you about your grandmother?"

Alexa glared at her with an expression of "no" and waited for an explanation.

Tess's mom pulled a chair closer and sat down facing Alexa. "Your grandmother is on the council."

Alexa's shoulders drooped as she felt kicked in the chest.

"We don't get to attend the council's meetings, but she has been very vocal about blocking hybrids from practicing witchcraft," she said. "I always thought it odd with her having a granddaughter as a hybrid."

Alexa leaned her head back to stare at the ceiling. Tears were welling again. "So I'm fucked by both sides of my family," she said. "Why didn't they just..." Words failed her as tears ran down her face.

Chapter Twenty-Four

Hours earlier she ran down the sidewalk with the exuberance of an excited child. Now she dragged herself home, shattered and broken, with little resolve to move forward.

With her parents in the kitchen as her mother prepared dinner, Alexa stood in the doorway taking in the very normal scene of white appliances and faux wood countertops in a sea of country blue. Her father hovered over the stove, impatiently dipping a spoon in the skillet as her mother shooed him away. They both turned to greet Alexa, but their happy faces dropped when they saw her dismayed expression.

"Grandma is on the fucking council?"

"Alexa…" Her mother started to say as she moved forward.

"NO!" Alexa yelled. "My own goddamned family has caused all of this? People who are supposed to love and care about me have created these fucked up rules to keep me in the dark? I'm such a scourge on the earth that I'm not even allowed to know my own fucking identity?"

"Alexa, your language," her father said.

"FUCK YOU!" she screamed. "I don't give a shit about your stupid rules."

"Alexa, this is unbecoming of a…"

"Of a what, dad? Are there more secrets? Or am I out of line for a stupid hybrid?" Alexa turned and stormed away from the kitchen, deaf to her parents trailing behind trying to comfort her. She escaped to her bedroom, the door too light to slam shut for any satisfactory emphasis. Alexa swirled the air around the door to hold it closed as her parents approached.

Before she could get the headphones situated Alexa heard

her father try to force the door open. He rattled the doorknob and pushed heavily as if he were using his whole body. She heard her mother yell something about Alexa using witchcraft. Pearl Jam thundered into her ears erasing the sounds of her parents trying to enter her bedroom.

She yanked open the closet doors and pulled a gym bag off the floor. From the shelf she grabbed a backpack and emptied the contents on her bed. Continuing her focus on holding the air around the door to her room, Alexa shoved clothing and other essential items into the bags. She found another tote near her shoes and packed it as well.

Alexa noticed her parents had given up trying to enter her room and retreated to the dining room. She released the hold on the bedroom door and tossed her makeup in a small toiletry bag, shoving it inside her purse. She scanned the room for any last items. She bid farewell to her headphones as she pulled them from her head and unclipped the Walkman from her shorts. Without shutting off the device, she tossed the equipment on her bed next to the former contents of her backpack. She slung the backpack over her shoulders, looped the other bags and purse on her left arm, grabbed car keys off the dresser, and a faded green ball cap from the back of the door.

With years of experience, she opened her bedroom window, popped the screen and laid it against the wall in her room. Alexa climbed through the window and jumped to the yard below.

A man... a vampire, stood next to the house on the other side of the fence between her and the driveway. Alexa vaulted over the fence and stood facing the man. He looked as though he was about to say something. Alexa closed her eyes, found the sensation that accompanied dropping her teeth. She opened her eyes, knowing they glowed yellow, and she growled. The man backed away as much as he could, already pressed to the wall. She kept her eyes on the man as she walked past only to find her father standing beside her car.

"Sebastian, leave us," her father said. The vampire retreated to the backyard, the chainlink rattling in his wake.

Alexa kept her eyes yellow as she glared at her father.

"Where are you going?" he asked.

She continued to glare at her father.

"Alexa," he said as his anger built, "where are you going?"

"I'm moving out."

"That will not happen."

Alexa pushed the air, forcing him backward.

"Like the fuck I'm not," she said throwing her bags inside her car. She got in, started the ignition, and released the air holding her father. She threw the gear into reverse and backed out of the driveway. She stopped even with her father, "I'm done with this bullshit. Do *not* have anyone follow me. I'm going to Brie's apartment and I'm telling you that only so your little black car over there doesn't stalk my friends. *No following me.* Goodbye!" Alexa sped down the street, ignoring her father's pleas to come back.

She stood in front of Brie's door on the second floor and couldn't recall the drive there. Alexa looked back to the stairwell wondering if she had even bothered to lock the car. She pressed the antiquated bronze buzzer, unsure if Brie had even left her parents' house.

"Hey," Brie said with surprise when she opened the door.

"Can I take you up on that offer to crash on your couch?"

"Absolutely," Brie said as she pulled Alexa into the apartment. "You got here awfully fast, are you okay?"

Alexa gulped and shook her head. "I can't even look at them

without getting pissed off. I was barely in the house when it struck me how done I was with this whole thing."

"You're welcome to stay as long as you need."

"Thanks."

"You probably shouldn't have driven with all of that wine in your system" Brie pulled a bag off Alexa's shoulder

"Probably not, but it's not like you're that far away." Alexa dropped her other bags on the floor and followed Brie into the bedroom. Together they pulled a blanket and pillow from a trunk at the foot of the bed. "You know I never wanted to impose on anyone like this."

"You're not imposing! You've had an open door here since the day I moved in and when you get sick of me any of the other girls will gladly take you in." Brie grabbed a flat sheet and headed toward the couch. "Really, Lex, I'm glad you're here. You were so devastated at mom's house – I just feel so awful for you."

"Eh, I'll survive. I just gotta figure out how to land on my feet after all of this crap." Alexa dropped the pillow and blanket on the arm of the couch and helped Brie lay the sheet over the cushions. "I'm tired of crying about it," she said staring at the ceiling and wiping a tear away. "I don't know what the answers are. I don't even know what to hope for. If I ever had a plan for the future we can pretty much bet it's trashed now. This feels very much like my train derailed and I'm barreling down the side of a steep mountain."

"It's all we have talked about for the past couple of years, how adrift all of us feel. But I agree it does seem like your path has changed course. Maybe it's not really a steep mountain, but just a lot of trees in the way and you can't see where it's headed?"

"Maybe. Whatever it is, I'm ready for it all to stop so I can come up for air."

Brie tilted her head, her pale blue eyes boring into Alexa. "You think there's more to it."

Alexa nodded with the weakest of grins. "There's definitely more. They're both dancing around it. At bare minimum there's the real reason I wasn't told and it doesn't have to do with my grandmother hating hybrids." Her voice caught. She jerked her head to shake off the sudden emotion. "But yeah, there's more."

Chapter Twenty-Five

Alexa passed a black car as she drove away from Brie's apartment on her way to work. She assumed her father ignored her request to not be followed.

Thoughts of black cars and a general aura of being watched occupied Alexa's thoughts as she sat at her desk. Six manila folders filled with stacks of papers clipped together sat in front of her. With a yellow highlighter she marked the entry on the paper when it matched the figures on her computer screen. Back and forth she flipped through the pile. Her head snapped up and she waited as he approached.

Eric appeared at the wall of her cubicle, leaning on the ledge of the green padded wall and greeted her with a big smile.

"We thought you forgot about us," Alexa said.

"Naw," he said with a grin. "I've been covering Floyd's route."

Alexa leaned in. "Well, I hope he's better. We've missed you around here."

Eric's attention floated to something behind her, she assumed Tamara leaned out of her cubicle to watch their exchange. He looked at his watch and stiffened. "Interested in meeting up this weekend?"

"Sure, what did you have in mind?"

"Someplace quiet where we can talk."

She smiled, wondering how he managed to know what she most wanted. "I would love that."

"The Higgs Library?" he asked.

"That sounds great. What time?"

"Ten A. M.?"

"Meet you there," she said.

He nodded his head toward the copier room, "Guess I should get back to work. See ya."

The cubicle wall blocked her view, but Alexa continued to watch in the direction of the copier room. She turned around to face Tamara's inquisitive expression.

"Library doesn't sound very romantic," Tamara said.

"Dunno. In college, the third floor stacks were known to get a lot of action."

"If that's what you have in mind, you should know the librarians at Higgs have a bird's eye view of the floor."

"Not to mention all of the kids running around," Alexa said.

"Guess you'll have to get creative," Tamara said with a wink.

As Alexa turned back to her computer she caught Mary out of the corner of her eye. The woman stood against the wall, four cubicles away, glaring at Alexa, horrified. Alexa glanced over to Tamera, busy at her computer, unaware of Mary. She looked again at Mary making eye contact. Unnerved, Alexa turned her attention to her computer.

Mary marched down the aisle between the cubicles, her weekly delivery of receipts tucked under her arm. As she handed off the folder, she bent toward Alexa to say something but gasped instead.

"I guess warning you about that man is too late?" Mary said, as she stood straight.

Unsure what to say, Alexa stared at the woman. Mary seemed to have plenty more to say, but she lifted her chin and marched back to her desk.

Tamera leaned into the aisle to watch Mary saunter away. "What that hell was that?" she asked.

Alexa shrugged. "I guess she has a thing against copier repairmen."

"That woman is weird," Tamera said. "She reads her tea

leaves."

Alexa chuckled.

"No, I'm serious. I've seen her do it several times. I'm sure she thinks no one is watching but she'll chug the last of her tea and then turn the cup a million different directions, staring at it intently. Then she'll take it to the kitchen and rinse it out. That's why there's always tea particles in the sink."

"Do you think she's a witch?" Alexa whispered.

"More importantly, does *she* think she's a witch?" Tamera asked with a raised eyebrow.

Alexa grinned and returned to her computer.

Chapter Twenty-Six

Alexa strode down the sidewalk toward the Eleanor Higgs Memorial Library, stepping out of the way of a boy on a bicycle pedaling towards her. She could sense other vampires in the area, but she saw Eric before her nose identified him; the wind cast his scent in another direction. In blue jeans and an untucked green t-shirt, he sat on a cement bench watching a man pull a box out of the trunk of a 1960's baby blue Ford. Aware of her presence Eric looked up and made eye contact.

Meeting her halfway down the sidewalk, he tilted his head and said, "Let's take a walk, do you mind?"

"Not at all!" she said. "It's a beautiful day." As they walked toward the park behind the library, she could sense the electricity sparking between them.

Eric cleared his throat. "Are things better at home?"

She shook her head. "No, I moved out. I've been spending the last week on a friend's couch."

"Shit. I figured by now they would have opened up."

"Not a peep."

He snorted and shook his head as he asked, "Damn. What happened?"

"I just had my fill," she said with a shrug. Eric moved to pull Alexa close. She laid a gentle hand on his chest to stop him. "You're going to make me cry. Let's just walk."

He held her hand as they strolled along the path. "What are your plans?"

"I've looked at a couple of apartments after work and I have an appointment to look at another this afternoon." Alexa shook her head. "Nothing is really panning out. Tess knows someone with a spare room. Dunno. If I can't find anything in the next week I might move in with her."

"Don't sound so dejected. This could turn out to be a good thing, " Eric said. "You're moving up in the world."

"I don't know that 'up' is the right word. I wish I felt more sure of my actions. I just feel so... adrift."

"Did all of this happen before or after the birthday party?"

"After – on Sunday night," she said.

"So how was the party?"

"It was a good time," Alexa said with a smile. "Jess pulled off a stellar gathering and it felt good to sit with my friends. Refreshing." She looked around to ensure no one was too close to overhear. "Turns out two of my friends are witches."

"Really?" he said with surprise. "Which ones?"

"Brie and Tess. I'm staying with Brie right now. Tess offered and she has more space, but she also has a boyfriend and I don't want to be in the way." She lowered her voice and raised her eyebrows, "he has moved his toothbrush in." Alexa began to laugh before Eric had a chance to respond.

"So they're pretty serious, huh?"

"Yeah, they've been dating a couple of years and I can just see him itching to propose, but she's the skittish one. I don't have any psychic vision for it or anything but I wouldn't be surprised if she gets a ring for Christmas."

"Are these the girls that grew up down the street from you?"

"Brie and Tess? Yeah. They felt bad for keeping a secret from me, but my parents made some sort of agreement with their parents. I guess it was to keep the neighborhood peace or something. I don't know - I really didn't push for details."

Eric shook his head. "Someone sure went to a lot of effort, didn't they? Doesn't seem quite fair to ask children to keep that type of secret."

"Well, my friends were excited to know I found out."

"Did you tell them about being a vampire?" he asked.

"Of course! I mean they already knew I was a hybrid, but yeah, I told them my teeth came in. I even had to play show and tell – kinda made them nervous but they were cool about it."

He raised his eyebrows. "Be careful flashing them around. Dropping your teeth is a sign of aggression."

"Growling, fighting, dropping teeth... Vampires are basically little bundles of aggression, aren't they?"

He chuckled. "It does require a lot of self control. Yeah, we could do a lot of damage."

"And that's it? Just restrain your primal urges and live a boring human life?"

Eric slid his hand onto her waist and pulled her to face him. "Not necessarily *all* of your primal urges," he said. He pulled Alexa close and kissed her, slow and lingering over her mouth. He leaned back and looked into her eyes and shook his head. "Your scent mystifies me."

Alexa grabbed the front of his shirt and he came closer without resistance. "I don't find yours a mystery at all, but I do think it's rather alluring."

"Do you?" he said with a growl and kissed her again.

Alexa broke free and changed the subject. "Didn't you say two of your childhood friends are vampires?"

"Yeah, Justin and Ryan."

"Are they your roommates?"

"Ryan is. Todd is the other roommate. And yes, Todd is a vampire too."

"And you guys also have human friends?"

"We do," he said. "Craig and Zack. We kept it from them for a long time, but they were convinced we were shutting them out of stuff. It made life a lot easier after we revealed ourselves."

"Really? I thought you said it was bad for humans to find out?"

"It is generally, but some know the truth. It's something that has to be gauged carefully."

"I assume they took it well?" she asked.

"They did."

"So what do three vampire boys do when they hang out?"

"Beat the living shit out of each other," he said laughing. "We had to be careful around Craig and Zack because they wanted to fight too. Like I said, it was easier when we revealed. We were in high school when that happened and they just ignored our crap and started flirting with girls."

"Ah yes, the great distraction."

Eric shrugged his shoulder. "I don't know. We really liked fighting. Besides, human girls held no attraction for any of us, there weren't any vampire girls at my school, and the witches, of course, avoided us like the plague. So we pummeled the crap out of each other."

"The urge to fight," Alexa said, "that has kicked in pretty hard. I punched a girl at Meg's party. Broke one of her fangs."

"Wait, what?"

"Turns out the two meanest bitches that tormented us all through school are vampires," Alexa said. "Well they showed up to the party, started talking smack, and I don't know what I said, but they were all 'wanna take this outside?' So we ended up meeting in the bathroom. I don't know what I expected but Tiffany dropped her teeth. That's when I realized I was in over my head and just... punched her."

"You're kidding!" He laughed and shook his head then smiled at her. "I can't believe you punched her instead of biting her."

"You know, I've fantasized about punching that smug whore for so many years... it felt great."

"Bitch, whore, they really rank high in your book."

Alexa rolled her eyes. "They were total bitches to us all of the time. Non-stop comments on what we ate, what we wore, who we dated, chipped fingernail polish, it just didn't matter. And, yes, whores. Both of them, and I'm not lying."

Eric laughed as he was shaking his head. "I think I know some guys who would like to meet them."

"I'm sure they already have."

"So back up, you said dated? Did you date humans?" he asked.

"I guess I did," she said. "Oh... I guess that explains why Sniffany heckled me so much."

"Sniffany?" Eric repeated.

"Sidney and Tiffany, the two whores. It was our nickname for them."

"You're not bitter or anything."

Alexa rolled her eyes. "Who were the asshole bullies when you were in school?"

"No one messed with us," he said. "Everyone knew we fought for pleasure and just avoided us. Back to dating humans..."

"What? Are you jealous?"

"No. Just curious what attracted you?"

Alexa shrugged. "Dunno, they were nice and easy to talk to." She stared at Eric with a grin.

"Did you like kissing them?"

"That is none of your business! But, I, uh, did break up with a guy because there was something repulsive about him. I didn't tell *him* that, but it got to be almost impossible to be around him. I remember I even made him change cologne!"

"Damn."

"I stopped feeling sorry for him when he started stalking me."

"Is he still?"

"Guess so," Alexa said with a sigh. "Lin said at the party that he was asking one of her brothers about me. I don't know how to make it any more clear that it's over and I'm not coming back."

"Can't blame the guy. You were the best he was ever going to have and you just slipped through his hands."

"Yeah, whatever. Did you ever date a..." she paused as a couple jogged past.

"I took Craig's sister to homecoming. I like her and she's a lot of fun to be around, but I'm not attracted to her. I know she wanted me to kiss her at the end of the night and I just couldn't do it. I explained to her that I really like her, but just as a friend and didn't want to lead her on. She took it fairly well and today we're good friends."

"Does she know you're a vampire?"

"Not at the time, but eventually I told her," he said. "She freaked out a little and avoided me for a while. She's still not comfortable with any display or even discussion about vampires."

"I'm not sure how my human friends would take it," Alexa said.

"My advice is if witches in your circle haven't revealed themselves, then maybe it would be a good idea for you not to say anything either."

Alexa stopped walking and Eric turned to face her. "Eric, I don't know how I would have adjusted to any of this without you."

He pulled her close. "I'm sorry you're not able to rely on

your family, but I'm glad you trust me."

They stood looking at each other. She noticed his green eyes had flecks of gold. Alexa had no idea what he saw, but his heart rate was increasing. He leaned in and kissed her, soft and gentle. Her breath caught as her pulse skyrocketed.

Eric leaned back and watched her for a moment. "Your scent is lingering much longer. I think that means you're becoming stronger."

"Doesn't really matter, though, does it? I mean, I can't do anything."

Eric stroked her face and offered a sympathetic smile.

The wind shifted and Alexa snapped her head toward the edge of the park. She sensed two vampires in the line of trees ahead of her. She noticed when Eric finally caught their scents. Together they scanned the thicket of trees lining the park. Alexa noted they lacked the pepper scent of hunters, but she was otherwise unable to identify their type.

"I think they're on patrol, nothing to fear," Eric said. She caught a hint of caution in his voice. She scanned the entire line of trees – another vampire stood at the opposite corner. She turned around and faced the library to find two more vampires positioned on either side of the building. Movement on top of the building caught her eye, but she couldn't see the person nor identify any scent. She assumed a vampire, if not a few, stood on the roof.

"Why is there a patrol?" she asked.

"They ensure only Carinthian vampires come into the area."

With a blank expression Alexa looked at Eric. "What's a Carinthian vampire?"

Eric grabbed her hands and pulled them to his mouth, kissing her knuckles. "You and I are Carinthian vampires."

"How do you know I'm Carinthian?"

"All vampires living in the Brentwood suburbs are Carinthian," he said.

"But what if my family got through the lines somehow? How do you *know* if someone is Carinthian? And what else can you be?"

"Is your family American?"

Alexa hesitated in responding. His tone inferred he already knew the answer and she found that disturbing. Deflated, she shook her head no. "My dad is Austrian."

His grin never faded. "Mine too." He dropped one of her hands and pulled her back along the path they had already walked. "Carinthia is an area that includes most of Austria. There are lots of other kingdoms and most of them have colonies here in America. This happens to be a Carinthian colony and it is very closely protected."

"Colonies? Kingdoms?" Alexa sighed. "Evidently there's a witch's council that dictates hybrids can't practice witchcraft. There are even rules that because my mom married a vampire she can't practice witchcraft or teach me anything."

"Oh geez, that's severe."

"My dad said he's appealing to a council too," she said. "I guess they have similar rules about hybrids?"

He shook his head. "No, I've never heard anything like that. I've heard of people hunting down hybrids, but it's nothing sanctioned. Hell the royal family has a witch somewhere in their line."

"Really?" Alexa asked with her head cocked to the side.

"Yeah, the queen is called 'The Witch' by her detractors. I mean to some it's bad enough there's a woman in charge, but that she's part witch really riles up the haters."

"What do you mean it's bad that a woman is in charge?"

"Vampire power structure is very male dominated. I'm not

saying it's a bad thing, but a woman coming to power wasn't welcome by a lot of people."

"So your family distrusts the queen and they moved here?"

"No, the opposite! My family is very loyal to the Queen! The insurgency made it impossible to stay in our hometown."

Alexa scowled. "What insurgency?"

"People against having a witch in power. They were trying to recruit hunters like my dad, and by 'recruit' I mean coerce, threaten, or otherwise force them to join. My dad was actually in the Queen's army, but when this gang took over our town I was a baby – they would have either killed me or raised me to be one of their members. My dad said he couldn't protect any of us from them, so we left. Some of the gangs have come to America and they hunt witches and hybrids such as yourself."

"To drink my blood, of course."

Eric nodded. "Of course. That and um," he tilted his head and raised his eyebrows.

"Oh right. It's okay to rape a witch, but the bastard child conceived in that rape is an abomination."

He cleared his throat. "Something like that."

Alexa snorted in disgust. She thought of the couple murdered by her office. "So it's not uncommon for vampires to attack hybrids?"

"You know it really doesn't happen around here much, or at least I don't think it does," he said. "There are some districts where it's really bad where like they sweep the city. I think because the Queen is a hybrid that it's disrespectful."

"Did you hear about the two hybrids killed near my office?"

"Yeah, that was right around the time you and I started talking. Ryan said he heard it was made to look like a vampire attack, but that it probably wasn't."

"I have pretty good reason to think witches did it," she said.

Eric raised his eyebrows in surprise.

"My mom thinks the three women who were found over at Timber Passage were also killed by witches. She says someone is putting together a spell or something."

"Damn." He waffled for something to say, but just shook his head. "I don't understand it. I don't know what a witch has to gain from it."

"It has something to do with energy, power, I don't know. That my mom told me even that much was a miracle." She offered Eric a weak smile. "I don't know," she said with a shrug. "All this secrecy, being a hybrid, my parents telling me to continue living like a human… you know, I've never doubted my parents love me. Even with all of this secrecy, I know they're trying to protect me. And I get that with hybrids being murdered they're on high alert, but this is deeper. Clearly the rest of the family is ashamed of me."

"Well that's their loss," he said.

"No, Eric, that's not it. If the rest of the family is ashamed of me then fuck them, but somehow these councils have a hold over my mom and dad. I mean, what sort of power do they have? Is our house bugged? Then tell me in the car. Something, anything. Drag my ass down to the park where I was attacked because clearly no one is patrolling that area." Alexa let out an agitated sigh. "I'm sorry. I got all ranty and ravey there and this was supposed to be a nice date."

"Anytime I get to spend with you is nice, even when you're ranting and raving, and really, that wasn't too irate. At least it wasn't directed at me," he grinned.

Alexa shook her head and rolled her eyes.

"Babe, I wish I had answers for you. You can rant and rave, scream and yell, or even cry if you want to. I'll be here for you. Just as long as I get to see that beautiful smile."

She glared at him, finally cracking a smile. Eric beamed at his success in coaxing a grin from her.

"I don't know what it is about you," she said, "but you always manage to calm me down. It's easy to smile around you."

"I feel the same way about you."

Chapter Twenty-Seven

Alexa pulled her car into a small lot in front of a faded brick building, parking next to a yellow Lincoln from the 1970's. She stepped into an office where an ancient woman with wisps of white hair hanging to her shoulders sat behind a cluttered desk. The woman reeked of cigarette smoke, nearly masking her vampire scent. Considering her age, Alexa wasn't surprised the woman's death would be very soon, one where she would be on the floor gasping for air. More disconcerting was the woman's vampire scent - she smelled like old fish.

Lighting another cigarette while Alexa explained she had an appointment, the woman rifled through random papers scattered on the desk. She found an appointment book and slowly turned the pages. Alexa patiently stood in front of the desk waiting for the woman to find the correct page. Trying not to cough from the stench of old cigarettes piled in an ashtray teetering on the edge of the desk, Alexa took in the details of the office. The floors were clean, possibly mopped recently, but with age the linoleum squares had chipped in multiple places. The yellowed walls held a crooked picture of a dark green car with a plaque saying 1967 Galaxy, a calendar from an auto shop, and a map of the apartment grounds.

The woman stood up in a slow, arthritic movement. She grabbed her cane and hobbled around the desk with her cigarette dangling from her lip. "The unit is around the corner," she said opening a metal box on the wall. "We have another four units available, but they're two bedrooms." She ran a crooked finger along the keys inside the box, resting on one marked 33d. The woman nodded for Alexa to follow her down a short hallway to a backdoor.

The seemingly well-manicured grounds revealed to be recently mowed, but not otherwise tended. Grass had crept onto the sidewalks and wove along several cracks in the crumbling cement, weeds and bare spots displaced most of the lawn, and bushes lining the buildings needed pruning. The pale pink brick buildings, also in need of upkeep, showed their age having survived at least a half-century. Alexa recalled a long drawn out conversation one evening with Lindsay's brother, Trent, who worked with a home-repair company. He bored her with details of aluminum windows and their lack of heat efficiency. Alexa hated she was now aware of window casings and easily spotted the aluminum windows on these apartments.

Based on the condition of the grounds, Alexa had already decided viewing the apartment as a mere courtesy – she had no desire to live here. Keeping a slow pace, she walked next to the woman past one building and approached a second where a man leaned against the wall in the shade. He had a similar scent to the old woman causing Alexa to suspect they were related. Wearing blue jeans and a paint-splattered, olive green t-shirt the man appeared to be the one who mowed the lawns with dried grass on his shoes. With his shaggy hair and pudgy body, Alexa found nothing attractive about the man, especially the way he leered at her. His imminent death disturbed Alexa by how soon it would happen – within the next few hours. He had no last sights, only a panic in darkness, and that disturbed Alexa even more.

"This is my grandson, Duane," the woman introduced. "He's such a good boy." The woman patted Duane on the shoulder as she passed.

Alexa followed the old woman into the building with Duane's

stench lingering behind. He reeked of dead meat with a hint of fish, fortunately the cigarette smoke masked most of their scents. The woman progressed up the stairs at a glacial pace, trying Alexa's patience. She wanted to hop ahead of the woman, stand in the hallway, and proclaim she had seen enough. Instead, Alexa politely assisted the woman up the stairs and waited as she fumbled with the key to the door.

The death of a previous occupant flooded into Alexa's mind as the door opened – a human falling from the couch onto the floor, staring at the doorway. The decorations Alexa could see from her vision lead her to believe the dead woman to be quite elderly. A crucifix once hung above a console TV. Alexa guessed crosses weren't really a deterrent to vampires considering the current management.

Alexa raised an eyebrow at the small size of the apartment, but she considered that for one person it could be sufficient. She doubted all six of her friends could sit in the living room at the same time. She reminded herself that none of this mattered as she had no intention of living here.

An old refrigerator caught her eye; the rounded top and chrome band screamed the 1950's. She stepped closer to inspect the kitchen and snapped her mouth shut before the old woman spotted her horror. She had seen larger kitchens in RV's! The counter possibly measured a square foot, the sink couldn't handle a large skillet, and the two upper cabinets weren't tall enough for a standard bottle of vodka or a box of Fruity Pebbles. Alexa escaped the afterthought of a kitchen to find the bedroom, only to wonder where anyone could store their clothing? She didn't bother to open the closet door. The bathroom, however, would forever be etched into her memory with the tub, sink, and toilet all the same shade of blue, matching the blue tile on the wall with tiny blue tiles on the floor. Alexa wished she had a camera to prove to her friends what she had found - they would never believe her.

Ammonia had been used to mask the strong odor of cat urine. Between the ammonia, cat urine, cigarettes, stinky vampire, and death visions, Alexa couldn't wait to escape the entire building. She raised a hand to her nose with the guise of scratching her face, but was really using her own scent to drown out the other odors. She hadn't paid attention to most of what the old woman said as she extolled the virtues of the smelly shoebox of an apartment. She said something about previous occupants enjoying the view of the hillside. Alexa looked out the window, seeing nothing but trees – nice, but nothing to brag about.

"Well," Alexa said as she turned to face the old woman, "I have a couple more appointments this week and then I will make my decision."

"Without a deposit, I can't hold this apartment for you."

"Oh I understand. You have a business to run and can't wait around for some girl to make up her mind."

"Yes, dear, exactly."

Alexa followed her out of the apartment, waited again as she fumbled with the door and the lock, and assisted her down the stairs.

"Now where is Duane?" the woman asked looking around the grounds. Alexa also didn't see him but his scent lingered. The woman laid a hand on Alexa's. "He is such a good boy," she said. "He always brings treats to his old grandmother."

Alexa had the distinct impression Duane's "treats" were not boxes of chocolate, but more of the witch variety. She bid farewell to the woman at the backdoor of the office, declining the shortcut through the building.

Grateful to be away from the horrid smells, Alexa walked

around the exterior of the office trying to decide if she should even bother with a courtesy call saying she had found something else. Duane stood against her car talking to a man in a black suit - her father's friend, Sebastian. Alexa lingered at the corner of the building watching the exchange between the two men. Duane seemed dismissive and mentioned "witch" a couple of times. Sebastian kept his voice low where Alexa couldn't hear but he seemed angry and she thought he seemed ready to attack Duane.

Alexa stepped forward causing both men to look at her. "Gentlemen, do you mind? This is my car."

Duane stepped away from the door as she approached. She made eye contact with Sebastian and he too stepped back. She unlocked the door and pulled it open.

"Twelve ninety-two Billings," Duane said.

Hearing the address of her parents' home Alexa turned, grabbed Duane at the neck, and pinned him to her car. "My father would not appreciate you threatening me. You can either stay and face his friend here or get shoved in my trunk so I can deliver you to him myself." Duane's eyes widened as his nose flared. Alexa knew he was reassessing her scent – why would a witch's father have a vampire following her? With a gentle growl Alexa pushed harder onto his neck. "Or I can kill you."

From the corner of her eye, Alexa caught Sebastian waving his hand in the air. She ignored him, maintaining her focus on Duane flailing, trying to escape her grip.

Duane dropped his teeth, which were quite short, as he tried to pull her arm away without success and swatted at her face. Emitting another growl, she pinned his right arm next to his head. A black car pulled behind Alexa's vehicle. Doors opened and three men of different ages, all in matching black suits exited – they looked very much like groomsmen on their way to a wedding.

Sebastian stepped around so she could see him without breaking her hold on Duane. "We have not been able to assess if you are being watched from the surrounding apartments. I would suggest we move him to our car for proper disposal." His Austrian accent was identical to her father's.

Through gritted teeth she asked, "Can't I just strangle him?"

With an amused grin, Sebastian said, "You may, however a bite is more traditional."

"Why would I want that nasty filth in my mouth?"

Sebastian raised his eyebrows and tilted his head in agreement. "Indeed. Would you allow us to deliver him to your father? I believe he would take great pleasure disposing of this man."

After Alexa gave a quick nod Sebastian grabbed Duane's shirtfront and twisted his free arm behind his back. Alexa released her grip on Duane and Sebastian threw him into the three groomsmen who pushed him into their car.

Alexa and Sebastian watched the car speed away. She looked to Sebastian, taking in the black suit. "I asked not to be followed... but... I do appreciate you were here today."

"Your father would be proud of your quick reflexes. You also showed tremendous restraint. Rare for most, unheard-of for someone so new to her teeth."

"Are you a ranger?" she asked.

"I'm not at liberty to discuss that with you."

Alexa pursed her lips in anger. "Can you tell me about that guy? He stinks, is he a scavenger?"

He smirked and shook his head. "You have mastered your grandmother's facial expressions. Yes, that man is a scavenger. Lemon ought to remove the scent from your hands."

Without a doubt Sebastian was referring to her father's mother, which surprised Alexa. She considered, however, if he had been a longtime friend of her father then surely this man had encountered Alexandra. Her Grandmere Alexandra held sharp opinions of everything both positive and negative, communicating her feelings with a series of subtle scowls that Alexa had made great efforts in mimicking. She leveled one of Alexandra's scowls at Sebastian, unnerving the man.

"Thank you," she said and turned to get in the car. Sebastian stepped back and she drove away.

Chapter Twenty-Eight

"What the hell have you been doing?" Brie asked with disgust when Alexa arrived at her apartment.

"Wrestling a scavenger."

"A what?"

Alexa stepped closer and waved her hand in Brie's face. "That," she said. "Evidently it's a type of vampire."

Brie scrunched her face and pulled back. "That's disgusting!"

"Tell me about it. This stinky slimeball was at the apartment. He's the landlord's grandson and he was just being super creepy. When I was ready to leave he was leaning on my car. The guy my dad has following me was also there and looked like he was ready to rip the slimeball to pieces."

"Is he a bodyguard or something?"

"The guy following me? I think so."

"So why do you have the stench all over *your* hands?" Brie asked.

"I might have pinned the slimeball against my car before Sebastian, that's the bodyguard, pulled him away and threw him into another car. He was driven away and that's all I know. Do you have any lemons? It's supposed to help get the odor off my hands."

"Uh... not sure," Brie said turning toward the kitchen. "Chloe was here a couple weeks ago. She might have left a lemon in the fridge."

Alexa followed her into the kitchen, appreciating the ample counter space. "You should have seen how small the apartment was. I swear I've seen larger dorm rooms."

"Guess that explains the low price."

"Hmm, yeah, I guess. It was in dire need to be updated. It looked like it was straight out of 1955."

"Ooh Retro," Brie said as she opened the refrigerator. "I hear that's all the rage. You could get one of those red tables with the metal band around the edges. Oh, and a lava lamp. It would be so awesome for parties."

"You and one other person might be able to attend, possibly we could squeeze another person in the bathroom, which by the way is completely blue. I mean the john, sink, tub, walls, everything," Alexa said.

Brie turned and raised her eyebrows. "Everything?"

"It was horrid. It's not like it was powder blue or a nice navy blue, but hell either of those would have been just as bad. There was no accent, just... blue. And you know damn well the little old lady living there put down a blue rug and a matching fuzzy toilet cover."

Brie tipped her head in agreement.

"Oh, and a previous occupant died in the living room," Alexa said.

"Why would they tell you that?"

"Uh, no one told me. I saw it when the door opened."

Brie's eyebrows shot up. "You can see ghosts?"

"No it wasn't her ghost. I just see people's death and hers was still lingering in the apartment."

"Oh you might be a medium."

"Is that a type of witch?"

"Yep. There are several powers out there. Medium gets lumped in with psychic, but they really are different."

"I've never had anyone communicate with me," Alexa said. "Usually I just see how living people are going to die. Sometimes places or things associated with a death bring a vision."

"Okay, well, that is definitely a psychic power," Brie said. "It certainly explains your variety of emotions when you meet people."

"What do you mean?"

"I can feel people's emotions," Brie said. "I'm an empath, that's another psychic ability. You are surprised, sometimes scared, and frequently sad when people come near you. I always thought you were a recluse or something that didn't like being around people."

Alexa chuckled. "Sometimes it is easier being by myself."

"You cover it well, but the emotion lingers long after you wince and try to push past it." She turned back to the refrigerator and opened a drawer. "It's kinda old, but it should work," she said pulling out a clear bag with a lemon. Brie extended the bag to Alexa as she closed the refrigerator. "So what's the deal with Meg? You're always jittery around her."

Alexa accepted the bag as she thought how much to share with Brie about Megan's death. "Meg dies in a car crash. Her last vision is as her face hits the steering wheel."

Brie stared at Alexa. "That's horrible... do you see that every time you're around Meg?"

Alexa nodded.

"Crap," Brie said. "Do... do you see *everyone's* death?"

Alexa nodded.

"Mine?"

Again, Alexa nodded.

"But you won't tell me about it, will you?"

"No," Alexa said. "You don't need to know about it. There's nothing you can do with that knowledge, you won't be able to stop it." A knife and a cutting board were lying on the counter. Alexa ran the knife under water from the faucet and proceeded with slicing the lemon in half. "I don't understand psychic powers. Levitation makes sense, you can *do* things with that, but what purpose does it serve to know the future? It's not like you can change it."

"I'm not really sure. I guess there will come a time when all of this will make sense. Maybe what to do with these visions will also become apparent. You've always had these visions, right?"

"Yeah."

"How come you never said anything?"

"I said something to my grandpa, when I was really little. I don't remember exactly how the conversation went, but he was really emphatic that it wasn't a thing most people would understand - that people only believe what they can touch and I am *never* supposed to talk about things that haven't happened yet. I've kind of hedged around it with a few people, but... Anyway, I learned really quick that visions aren't normal."

"Well, among humans it's not normal, but witches would shrug and understand that was your power. Since your powers came from your mom, she would have these visions too."

Alexa tilted her head. "I don't think she does."

"Or she's hiding it really well."

"I guess."

Brie smiled. "I'm impressed, though. You seem to understand the implications of fate – that's some pretty heavy stuff."

"Ugh!" Alexa moaned. "Fate really has me baffled. It's like we're creatures of self-determination but then you discover those three steps you took back in eighth grade just to be a shit were actually ones you were *meant* to take. It's like this big crazy jigsaw puzzle and the pieces just come together in the most random ways, intentionally, in order, and create the most beautiful picture ever, which by the way, was not the one shown on the box."

"You're being rather philosophical tonight."

"Eh, I've wrestled with this for a long time." Alexa mashed one of the lemon halves between her hands, slathering the juice as if it were soap between her fingers and up her arms. The sharp citrus scent filled the air. "So what powers does an empath have?"

"I feel other people's emotions."

"What can you do with that?"

"Why are you worried?"

Alexa froze, unsure what to say.

"You had some trepidation after you asked that. Maybe because you said your power was useless that I might think you were saying mine was useless as well?" Brie laughed and shook her head. "Empath powers can be quite useful, they have definitely helped guide me through some tricky situations and your vision will have a purpose too, you just don't know it yet. But here's the thing, you and I are still young witches. We're like wine, we get better as we age."

"Okay, that is word for word something your mother would say."

"She says it all the damn time, but it's true. Witches get stronger as we age. So, up until a few years ago I could only sense other people's emotions, but now I'm getting a handle on how to manipulate emotions."

Alexa pulled her head back and creased her forehead. "Whoa, that could seriously screw with someone."

"My mom was trying to coax you into a different mood the night you left home, but decided to not meddle."

"What?"

Brie nodded. "She could have diffused your anger. After you

left, Tess's mom was pissed she let you go like that, but my mom said it was probably best to let you work out your emotions on your own. She said in light of all of the lies you're dealing with, a little hocus pocus would leave you feeling betrayed, not soothed."

"Yeah, that's probably true. Can you diffuse people's anger?"

"I could make you cry, that's the easiest one to do. But no, diffusing anger is the hardest and I'm not there yet. Your mood right now is lighter than when you walked in the door, so from here I could escalate you into happiness then hilarity."

"Please. You and I can do that to each other with our eyes closed."

"True."

Alexa ran her hands under water, rinsing away the remaining pulp. She waved her hand in front of Brie, "smell anything?"

"It's duller, but it's still there."

Chapter Twenty-Nine

Eric called and offered to drive her around town, but Alexa declined - she wanted to do this on her own. And on her own she went – in her car, around the familiar parts of town.

Yet, she was never alone with the black car following her everywhere. Sebastian allowed four or five cars between them, sometimes falling back the distance of a city block, but he was always there.

Signs for an open house at one apartment complex caught Alexa's eye. She parked near the office and Sebastian drove past, pulling around the corner. As Alexa entered the office she spotted Sebastian sitting on the curb, smoking a cigarette.

The apartment was perfect - clean, fairly modern, didn't smell funky, no dead people... but the rent exceeded her budget by three hundred dollars. She made eye contact with Sebastian as he stood up and she shrugged her shoulders. He offered a conciliatory grin and returned to his car.

Alexa drove down more familiar streets close to her grandparents' home. She turned onto the main thoroughfare, two blocks away from the donut shop her grandfather would take her on Sunday mornings. She pulled into the parking lot half hoping to see his car. Slightly deflated she walked inside and grinned at the glorious scent of warm donuts. She grabbed a Sunday paper from the wire rack and moved past the throng of people waiting to select donuts from the display case. At the register a frazzled teenager rang up the newspaper and belatedly asked if Alexa wanted a cup of coffee. "No, this is enough. Thanks." Alexa grinned with sympathy as she dropped two quarters in the styrofoam tip cup.

Sitting in her car with the key in the ignition, Alexa pulled the newspaper apart throwing all but the classifieds onto the passenger seat. She pulled the want ads, automobile listings, and the first pages of the real estate listings to the side, focusing on the rental listings. A couple houses were actually in her price range, but she shuddered to think of their condition. Besides, she thought, she didn't want to deal with lawns and general maintenance. No, she wanted an apartment.

After digging a pen from her purse and circling a few rental listings, Alexa started driving. As she approached the first address, something seemed familiar. The apartment complex she had visited the day before came into view. She approached from the rear, as the one she was about to visit shared common ground. Across the lawns she saw a police officer with a dog walk around the buildings and she spotted movement on the hillside.

For as curious as she was about what happened to Duane, Alexa felt maybe she shouldn't linger in the vicinity. Taking a deep breath, she backed out of the parking space and headed toward the next address. Sebastian's car stayed on her tail the entire way and she had to admit she felt relief with his presence.

The next complex gave the appearance of a forest encampment with pine trees and winding walkways. The buildings adorned with dark wood beams and open staircases further encouraged the forest aura.

A couple barely older than Alexa walked out of the office as she entered. She thanked the man for holding the door then turned to face the manager, a middle aged woman who was surely much younger than her haggard appearance. She was human who would die on a carpeted floor with a last vision of a man's dirty shoes. Alexa continued to watch the manager while explaining she wanted to see a one bedroom apartment. Terror filled the woman's emotions as she died. She suspected the woman was beaten by a boyfriend or husband and quickly spotted a wedding ring on her finger. When Alexa snapped her attention back to the manager's face the woman made no eye contact.

With a feeble excuse of bad knees, the woman slowly guided Alexa to an available apartment. As they walked across the grounds Alexa looked toward the parking lot and spotted the black car, however Sebastian was not near it. She started to scan the grounds, but trees impeded her view and also blocked her from seeing the rooftops. She knew he was close, she just couldn't figure out where.

The one-bedroom apartment at ground level didn't require Alexa to assist another apartment manager up the stairs. She sighed with relief this manager operated the keys quickly. Alexa liked this apartment and while small, she could at least envision accommodating a few people for entertaining. A functional kitchen with appliances that didn't qualify as antiques and a boring white bathroom made this apartment the best she had seen so far.

She followed the manager to the office, still unable to find Sebastian, and filled out an application. When she left the manager's office the black car had moved around the corner, with the engine running and Sebastian watching her.

With two more complexes on her list, Alexa decided to first find lunch. She returned to the street with the donut shop and drove around the corner to a café she knew to sell fabulous sandwiches. Sebastian pulled behind her car, blocking her exit.

She jumped out of the car ready to yell at him, but saw he rolled down his window and trying to get her attention.

He leaned out the window and said, "I am unable to protect

you inside that building."

She looked at the shop, then back at him. "My mom has brought me here plenty of times."

"I am aware," he said. "I cannot be of any assistance once you go inside."

"Am I safe?"

"I do not know. I am not allowed in there."

With a confused look, she turned and proceeded to the front of the building. She walked with caution, watching for anything astray. Once she stepped inside, she understood – only witches populated the space. There weren't even traces of a vampire ever being there, humans yes, but not vampires.

With wood floors and wood tables and an oversized coffee cup on the wall, she found the restaurant cozy. Warm aromas of coffee and bread filled the air further adding to the desire to curl up with a steaming cup and a book. A man in the far corner appeared to be spending his Sunday doing something similar as he held a hardcover book with his feet propped up. Alexa envied him.

The woman behind the counter with a blue kerchief holding her hair out of her face watched Alexa approach. She would die in a dark room with a sense of panic and the aftertaste of something bitter lingering in her mouth. Alexa wondered if maybe it was poison?

A man and a woman sat at a table near the window. They smelled like they had recently had sex. Alexa still found it weird how much stronger her sense of smell had become recently. In the past she only caught the most intense smells, the ones other people would point out, but now she was picking up the subtle ones. She felt intrusive knowing who had and not had sex or recently bathed.

There were more witches in the café than she could see.

They were possibly in a meeting room or second dining room behind the wall at the far end of the restaurant.

With a disapproving glare the woman at the counter accepted Alexa's order and money. Alexa wasn't sure what the glare was about and watched as the woman walked into the kitchen to pass-on the sandwich request. A scent caught her attention and Alexa walked toward the far end of the restaurant toward the room beyond the wall.

"Ma'am," the woman from the countered said loudly as she scrambled to follow Alexa. "I'm sorry, but you can't go in there."

"I know somebody in there," Alexa said.

"I'm sure you're mistaken," the woman said in a panic. "Your order is almost ready."

Alexa ignored the woman and walked around the corner. The open doorway revealed a large conference table surrounded by male and female witches... and her grandmother.

Her grandmother bolted out of her seat. "Alexa!" she said with surprise, almost scorn.

"Hi," Alexa said with an unsure voice as she looked around the table.

She knew two of the men; they were outside of the newsstand and she remembered their scents. The one scent that dominated the room, however, was the hybrid woman that was killed by her office – these people had ingested her fluids. They drank her blood. Feeling weak she looked to her grandmother, also smelling like the hybrid.

"None of your business," her grandmother scolded as she walked up to Alexa. She grabbed Alexa's arm, nearly pinching her in the process, and walked her out of the room.

In the main dining room Alexa pulled her arm away. "I'm sorry," she apologized. "I just came in for a sandwich and caught your scent."

"My scent? You're aware of scents these days?" her grandmother said sounding angry. She dropped her eyes to assess Alexa. "If that's the case then you're cavorting with the wrong type of people."

"What's going on in there? Is that coven or something?"

"Alexa, I don't know what your mother has told you, but suffice to say you are not welcome here."

The man in the corner watched her and she understood - she carried multiple vampire scents on her – dad, Eric, and the guy who attacked her. She was a witch who had been sleeping with vampires, or so these people thought. They looked at her like she was dirt, disgusting, filthy.

A bag was shoved in front of her. "Please take your sandwich and go," the woman from the counter said.

Alexa looked at the woman, to the couple at the table, to the man in the corner, and then at her grandmother. Nearly four inches shorter than Alexa, her grandmother stood with authority and, as usual, with a front of stoicism. Her grandmother's embarrassment was clear even with the façade, but was nothing in comparison to Alexa's humiliation... and fear. She didn't know what to think of those men sitting at a table with her very own grandmother, but she needed to leave. Grateful to have been trained in covering her fear, Alexa converted her energy into anger.

She turned to the woman holding the white bag. "I assume you spit on it." She shoved the bag into the woman, toppling her into an empty table. "Keep it!" Alexa marched out of the restaurant with her chin in the air.

Knowing Sebastian would follow her, Alexa drove around the corner and pulled to the side. She watched his car creep to a stop several buildings behind her. She hopped out of the car and strode down the sidewalk, keeping eye contact with him the entire time. Sebastian got out of the car and met her on the sidewalk.

"You need to go back to the sandwich shop," she said. "There's a guy in there. He has dark hair and a light green shirt, a button-down. There was another guy with him, brown hair and a grey polo shirt. They murdered the hybrids by my office."

He stood, looking unsure whether to follow her lead or to argue.

She said, "You're really good at following people undetected and dad seemed interested in who those guys were."

Sebastian tilted his head. "How do you know they are responsible?"

"I smelled the woman's scent on them. Strong, like what happens when you drink someone's blood."

His eyes narrowed.

"Trust me, they did it."

"I cannot leave you unattended," he said.

"I swear. I'm going straight to my parents' house."

Sebastian glared at her.

"Go! Before you miss them." Alexa rolled her eyes. "Oh for crying out loud, it's not like this is the first time I've ditched you. I'm not stopping anywhere, I'm going to the house."

In a sigh that bordered on a growl, Sebastian nodded. "I am not leaving until you are secure in your car."

"Okay." Alexa ran as fast as she could to her car. As she started the ignition, she watched Sebastian in her rearview mirror. The black sedan pulled into the street making a sharp U-turn, two wheels rubbing the curb on the opposite sidewalk, and sped away.

Aware she was alone without her bodyguard, Alexa looked around. No one was near; the street was abandoned except for one car in the distance heading towards her. She pressed on the gas and as she promised, drove to her parents' house.

Chapter Thirty

When Alexa pulled into the driveway her mother was trimming the hedge in front of the house. When her mom turned to see who had pulled in her face filled with worry. She rushed to Alexa's car, dropping the clippers and garden gloves to the ground.

Alexa began sobbing as she got out of the car and ran into her mom's arms. "What happened?"

"Why is your mother such a bitch?" Alexa asked with her face planted into her mom's shoulder.

With a soft laugh and a kiss on the side of Alexa's head, her mom said, "come on, let's sit down."

Alexa sniffled as she pulled back and shook her head. "No, I need to talk to dad. Is he home?" She walked toward the house wiping the tears from her face.

"What's wrong? What happened?" Her mother asked, following behind.

Alexa opened the front door and yelled, "DAD?"

Her father came forward from the dining room. "Alexa? What has happened?"

"I ran into two of the guys that killed the hybrids." Alexa turned to her mother. "I went to Brindle's for a sandwich and, ugh, it was horrible. I ran into grandma, but I'll tell you about that in a minute." She closed her eyes and shook her head trying to erase the indignity she felt at the café. She took a deep breath and turned back to her father. "Anyways, these two guys were at this big table with a group of people and grandma was there. I knew instantly who they were, they have that woman's scent on them, not like they touched her, but actually drank her blood."

Her father stepped closer to the door and looked back and forth searching for something.

Alexa said to his back, "I found Sebastian and described the men to him and told him to follow them."

Her father spun to face her. "He left you?"

"He didn't want to but I swore I was coming straight here. We went back and forth about it, but he finally agreed."

He looked over his shoulder and back at his daughter. With a tilt of his head similar to Sebastian, he said, "Possibly a wise decision. Tell me about the men."

"I wasn't there very long, just enough to catch the woman's scent on them. One guy had dark hair, the other brown."

"Ages?"

Alexa shrugged. "Thirties, maybe late twenties."

"And these were witches, not hybrids?" he asked.

She nodded. "As far as I can tell, unless they're masking their scent like I do."

"How do you mean, mask your scent?" he asked.

"I carry a second scent, a vampire scent. It's similar to yours." Seeing the confused looks on her parents' faces Alexa closed her eyes and brought the scent forward. She opened her eyes to find her father staring at her.

Her mother looked between Alexa and her father, somewhat shocked. She whispered, "oh Frederick..."

"You had this scent the night you left home," her father said.

Alexa nodded.

"I did not understand what I was smelling that night." He smiled with a soft chuckle. "You are much like your mother, I often wonder if you carried any of my traits."

Her mother closed the front door and walked toward the dining room. "The two of you have more in common than either of you cares to admit. Being vampires is the least of your similarities."

Alexa and her father followed behind. Her mother sat down at the table, motioning Alexa to join her. A plate of sausage and cheese, her father's lunch, sat at one end. He walked past his plate and took the chair next to her mother.

"Do you believe these men at the café were hybrids?" He asked.

"I have no idea. They both smell completely like witches – one's like an herb, like basil or thyme with a little bit of something floral, the other guy smelled like a fresh can of tea. But everyone at that table had that woman's blood carrying on them."

"As though they had drank her blood?" her father asked.

"Yes. It was very strong, distinct."

"I don't understand - drinking blood has a scent?" her mother asked.

"You can't tell the difference between the hunter scents on me?" Alexa asked.

Her mother shook her head no.

A quiet rumble emitted from her father across the table. "A witch would only notice a vampire scent on you, not the number of men who have touched you." He met Alexa with a disapproving glare.

Alexa grabbed her mother's hand. "You carry dad's scent because he has tagged you, and well, because you have sex. A lot. " She rolled her eyes as her mother blushed. "Oh God, don't look shocked. I've lived my entire life at the other end of the hall from your bedroom. So anyway, dad has *your* scent because he has drank your blood. It's strong on him. Dad's scent on me is light because we've only touched and it keeps fading the longer time goes by."

"Alexa carries a hunter scent from being attacked," her father said.

"But not because he had sex with me. I drank his blood. I mean I puked most of it up, but enough of it stayed in my system to carry around with me."

"Were you a man," her father said, "the scent would be a badge of honor, the sign of a warrior."

Alexa looked at her father. "You're a warrior," she said. She could tell he hadn't drank blood in a long time, other than her mother's, but the scents were numerous. "You've killed many men, haven't you?"

He nodded. "I have."

"You can tell how many?" her mom asked.

"If I focused, but it's a lot. It would take a while to sift them all apart."

Her father snorted in amused approval.

"It's kinda stupid that women aren't considered warriors," Alexa said. "It's not like we can't fight."

"Women fight to protect their young and their home. They do not join armies."

"Well that's ridiculous. So are you in an army?"

There it was – the pause Alexa came to expect - the one where her father measured how much to say... or not say. His lips thinned and the amusement left his eyes. "I have fought," he admitted, "in defense of our Queen."

"The one who insists I go through life like a human? Because I'm some sort of scourge as a hybrid?"

"No, Alexa. The Queen wishes you be kept safe and is dispatching your grandparents to come speak to you on her behalf."

"Grandfather and Grandmere know the Queen?"

"Yah, as do I. She held you as an infant, kissed your forehead, and granted us blessings to leave Austria..."

"You mean Carinthia?"

He sighed and nodded in concession. "The hunter has taught you much. I do wish this information came from me."

"You had the opportunity."

"No. No, I did not. We have rules and if the hunter's father learned of his son's transgressions there would be severe repercussions."

Alexa groaned. Worse than her father's lack of information was this new twist of condemning Eric for teaching her about being a vampire. She looked to her mother hoping for some small ounce of support. Only a weak smile was offered.

Her mother spoke up. "Alexa, I think it's time for you to come home for your safety."

"No," her father said. "Living among witches distances her from me. She is correct - my scent carries on her, but is weakening. The less contact she and I have, the safer she will be. The hunter she carries on her is common and will be overlooked. If she continues to mask as a witch, no one will question her birth."

Alexa faced her father. Did he really say it was okay to live with Brie?

"Mind, I do not condone your interactions with this hunter," he said. "He has kissed you?"

Unable to hold back the blush, Alexa squirmed. Her father growled disapproval – a genuine vampire growl, not the humanesque grumbling she had heard growing up.

She tipped her head up in defiance. "I like him and I don't care what you say about it."

"His father was a valued member of her majesty's army. He left service due to disruptions in his hometown and his family became part of a resettlement project here in Brentwood. He could be severely punished because of this relationship. Alexa, do not jeopardize this family's security for your selfish desires."

Alexa gulped. Her dad investigated Eric? She glared at him, torn between anger and dismay.

He turned to her mom. "What reason would your mother drink blood?"

"Dark magic," she said. "Summoning the dead, torture, disfigurement, coaxing a demon... manipulating a vampire."

"That stuff's real?" Alexa asked.

"It is," her mom said. "It can also be used to play with the weather but it would be much easier to find a set of witches with those powers." She shook her head. "No, she has always been intrigued by the dark arts and has surrounded herself with people of questionable intentions and dark powers. I have no idea what she has up her sleeve, but it can't be good."

"What does grandpa have to say about all of this?"

"Well..." Her mom fiddled with her hands. "I've suspected for a long time he might be under some sort of a spell. He never has spoken up against her, but more and more whenever they're together he's very zombie-like. It's gotten worse lately. I don't know if you noticed it at the Fourth of July picnic?"

"He did seem a little out of it, but I just thought his hearing was getting worse. How do you break a spell?"

"First you would have to know what spell it is, if there is one. Like I said, it's just a suspicion. I'm more concerned that she would come after you. She had made insinuations about working with *my* powers when I was younger. Fortunately, your father turned out to be the best protection we have against her. She tends to keep her distance when he's around."

"What would she do with me?"

With an evil chuckle she said, "In the wrong hands, like grandma, you would be perfect for possession or serve as a conduit. Your energy is amazing. I don't know how it's possible but you're likely as strong as any full-blooded witch. But you're untrained and don't know how to ward her off."

"So train me."

"It's not quite that easy, you don't even know the basics – you're so behind on your education. On the upside, though, most witches tend to avoid you. Even Grandma seems a little edgy when you're around. You have a dark essence that you carry, even darker than mine. I've always believed that was due to you being part vampire."

"What's a dark essence?"

"Um... people more inclined toward dark magic. Any power can be used for good or evil, but some only bring destruction. Vampires are dark beings – they kill, they're predators, they're destructive." Her mom flashed a quick look across the table to her father. "Even the peaceful ones who never lift a finger and manage to fully immerse themselves into a human lifestyle still carry the *essence* of being dark. Witches pick up on that and tend to stay away from it. But with you, when you walk into a room, you present as a full-blooded witch, a strong one, and you carry this dark vibe. You need to be careful, though, because there are witches who would love to have the type of power you carry and will try to get you to do their bidding."

"People like grandma?"

"Yes, especially now we know she had been drinking blood."

Alexa asked, "How do you carry a dark essence?"

Her mom bent closer and spoke soft. "Death and things that bring death are naturally dark, but there's also a darkness carried with those who can manipulate the elements. The night you left home, you sealed your door shut and held it closed against a *very* strong vampire." She leveled a look at Alexa. "You were manipulating air." She raised her eyebrows asking for confirmation. When Alexa nodded understanding, her mother continued, "The four elements are necessary for life. That which holds life also holds death."

"You can manipulate air as well," Alexa said remembering the stool her mother scooted across the kitchen.

"Yes," she nodded. "I've never trusted my mother around you, Alexa. I truly believe her push to restrict hybrids from learning the arts was specifically so you would not learn your capacity."

Unsure if she would get a straight answer, Alexa asked, "What is my capacity?"

"You ooze energy. The ability to manipulate air makes us stronger than most witches. I have some abilities with fire, which you may or may not have inherited. I also have some psychic abilities..."

She nodded, "Yeah, I can see things."

Her mother grinned. "I thought maybe you did." Her smile dropped and she said, "Unfortunately, we're not able to discuss any of that. Maybe one day."

"You can't even discuss it?" Alexa asked.

"No."

"What happens if you're caught?"

"I could be executed."

"Your own mother would kill you?" Alexa asked in disbelief.

"Of course not. She would have someone else do it."

Chapter Thirty-One

People were in the house, somewhere toward the back, and all of the lights were out. Alexa felt along the wall but couldn't find the light switch as she moved through the entryway.

The family room was much darker, only a small seam of light flittered from under a long curtain on the sliding glass doors. People were in the room, she could hear breathing and shuffling. Were they hiding? No, that was someone struggling.

Once her eyes adjusted to the darkness Alexa walked around the couch, past an easy chair, and stood in front of the television. By the sliding glass doors were two sets of feet where the people were laying on the floor. She moved forward and grabbed the set on top and pulled him away. He no longer held his victim's mouth and she was able to come up for air between her sobs. The man tried to punch Alexa but she swatted him away.

Men, witches, came running from the hallway and vampires came in through the front door. More people flooded into the house.

Anger.

Alexa felt anger and she wanted to hurt the man she pulled off the floor. Instead, she threw him across the room. Someone grabbed her from behind, but it was someone she knew and trusted. A woman. The woman's arms were around her and whispering something over her shoulder. Someone was coaxing her witchcraft – she felt the stir in her core.

Beams of light and smoke filled the room. She didn't know where to look and she couldn't hear through everyone's screaming and yelling. Someone was dying and people were bustling back and forth.

The room fell black, blissful silence returned, but the smoke lingered.

Alexa gasped for air, panting. She looked around the dark room and couldn't identify anything. She lied on a couch, Brie's couch, in Brie's apartment. Nightmare. That was a nightmare.

She sat up alarmed about the smoke, but there wasn't any. She sniffed to the left and then to the right. No, just the normal smells of the apartment and pizza they had for dinner. Alexa got up and opened the window. She leaned out and sniffed again, just to make sure. An overcast night and thick trees made for a very dark street even among the streetlights.

Sebastian's car was parked in his regular spot, just beyond the glow of the nearest streetlamp. There was no telling if he was in the car or prowling the street. He could have been on the roof, this building or the one across the street, or the one next door...

She breathed in the fresh air. The last sweetness of the trees in summer – leaves had already started falling.

Alexa didn't know what to think about the nightmare. She never did. This one wasn't terrifying, just confusing. She didn't know who the people were or where they came from. She didn't know what they were doing, well except the guy on top of the woman - that was pretty clear. Who was the woman that grabbed Alexa from behind and played with her witchcraft? Oh, she realized, this was feeding off the conversation with her mother back on Sunday!

What was the deal with the smoke? The smoke definitely spooked her, enough that when she closed the window she made another inspection of the apartment.

A weak voice called from Brie's room, "You okay out there?"

"Yeah, just a bad dream," Alexa yelled back.

The bedroom door swung upon and Brie padded out. "You wanna talk about it?" she asked.

"Nah. I smelled smoke but I think it was in my dream. I don't smell anything now."

Brie looked left and right, concern on her face.

"Go back to sleep," Alexa said. "I don't smell anything anymore. Just the pizza we had earlier."

"What was your dream about?"

"Some people in a house and a fight broke out – witches and vampires, screaming and yelling... and then a fire. I don't know; none of it makes sense."

"You're still upset by it," Brie said.

"Well yeah, the scent of smoke was super strong when I woke up. I'm fine now, and you know me, I'll zonk out in a matter of minutes once I lay down."

"That's for sure. I've never seen anyone pass out the way you do every night."

"Gotta get a solid eight hours," Alexa said as she pulled the blanket off the floor.

"Except that you're super busy with these nightmares," Brie said. "I mean you have them practically every night."

"Mmm... I'm pretty sure I have them every single night."

"Well, I hope you have something more peaceful dance through your head for the rest of the night."

"Thanks, me too," Alexa said. "Good night."

"See ya in the morning."

D.M. Wyatt

Chapter Thirty-Two

As Tess drove away from Lindsay's apartment, Alexa leaned forward from the backseat to better hear Brie and Tess talk.

"Do you think Lin's place will be good for you?" Tess asked over her shoulder.

"Yeah, it would be great," Alexa said. "I'll call tomorrow to find out about availability."

Brie twisted in her seat to look at Alexa. "Those apartments are kinda small. Is that going to be okay for you?"

"They fit the bill – cheap and close to work. I mean I have to start somewhere. Your couch has been an absolute blessing, but I need a place to dump my crap. Besides I know I freak you out with my nightmares."

"Yeah, there's nothing like waking up to a vampire growling in my living room."

"She growls?" Tess asked.

"She's super quiet. At first I thought it was a cat outside, but when I got up I realized the growling was coming from the living room and I could smell her vampire scent. I locked the door and hopped back into bed!"

Alexa blushed, not realizing she growled in her sleep.

"Can't you do hypnosis or something to make them stop?" Tess asked.

"She's psychic," Brie said. "She can't turn that off any more than you could that internal homing pigeon you have in your head."

"Homing Pigeon?" Alexa asked.

"Have you ever noticed she never gets lost?" Brie asked. "You could plop her in the middle of a forest and she would find her way out."

"Is that a witch thing?" Alexa asked.

"Yeah, it's categorized as divination, another type of psychic power," Brie said.

"So Lex is psychic too?" Tess asked.

"She has visions," Brie said. "And I would bet big money that those freaky nightmares she has all of the time are premonitions."

"I hope not," Alexa said. "That's some seriously gory stuff."

"Like what?" Tess asked.

"It's always blood and guts. Lots of death and just so much blood. The morning I was attacked I seriously thought it was another nightmare. I kept wondering when the hell I was going to wake up. Actually, I'm still wondering that."

"What type of visions do you have?" Tess asked.

Alexa took a deep breath, wishing she could find a way to avoid the topic. "I see death. Actually, I see what a person sees just seconds before they die."

"But not how they die?" Tess asked.

"Not usually. Whatever caused the death has already happened so it's those last moments when people take their final breath and family members are bending over saying goodbye. Some people are scared, some are resigned, most are sad." Alexa said.

"Those are kind of jacked up visions," Tess said.

"I don't understand them at all. I'd suck as a fortuneteller, 'you're going to hear beeping just before you die' or 'your lover will kiss you just before you die'. I have no idea what happens to most people to bring them to that point, so there's no warning them and I've learned the hard way there's no stopping them."

"What do you mean?"

"You remember that field trip to the museum back in fourth grade? The one where the woman was hit by the bus?" Alexa asked.

"Yeah, you had wandered off and got to see the whole thing unfold... Wait. You knew that was going to happen?" Tess flashed questioning eyes into the rearview mirror.

"We were standing in line and I knew that woman was going to get hit by a car, I think it was a taxi. So I run up to her and pull her off the curb in time for the car to whiz by. She turns around confused but when she saw the car go by and realized what happened, she was super thankful. A couple of other people saw that tragedy was averted and they were patting me on the back and everything. So she turns around, steps off the curb, looks to her right as she's walking, and bam, a school bus rolling to a stop wallops her from the left. I hadn't turned around fully so I didn't see the bus either until it collided with the woman. Then the death vision changed for her, it might have changed earlier for her but I hadn't noticed. I got to see from her vantage point getting hit by the bus, falling to the ground, knowing a set of wheels just rolled over her stomach, something catching her arm and pulling her down the street. I saw the fucking pavement pass by her eyes. There was a rip down her arm, tearing at the flesh that finally released her. She couldn't breathe and was gasping for air as she helplessly watched the rear tires come straight for her. And then there was nothing."

Brie stared at her slack-jawed. Tess was also staring but quickly returned her focus to the road.

Alexa dismissively tilted her head. "I didn't need any formal instruction on what happened. It was clear that stopping someone's death was impossible. If I meddled, the person still dies, just much more horrible than originally planned."

"Yeah, that would pretty much drive the message home," Tess said. "Shit you were like nine or ten when that happened."

"Nine," Alexa said.

"That's a lot for someone so young to figure out, especially not knowing anything about your powers," Brie said. "I mean we were taught not to play with life or death, but it took ages to appreciate it fully."

"My mom says I read as a dark witch. I'm pretty sure these visions, plus, you know being a vampire, are why."

"I just figured it was the vampire part of you that made you dark," Brie said.

"Me too," Tess agreed

Alexa spotted two police cars with their lights on pull into a gas station down the street, followed by a black car. She had seen Sebastian's car pass them a couple blocks earlier, but she didn't think the one at the gas station was him.

Tess parked in her designated spot, in front of her apartment and Alexa dismissed the police and vampire activity.

"You know," Brie said getting out of the car, "we really do deserve the family discount here."

"As if I haven't heard that before," Tess said, closing her door. "Every single one of you have tried to coax my sister for the family rate. You know damn well if she could give it to you she would."

"Okay, it makes sense for Lin, Clo, and Meg to be turned down, but me and Lex grew up with you guys. I mean we know stuff," Brie said.

"Whatever," Tess said.

"I'm not above blackmail," Alexa said.

"Fine. You go talk to Ava any damn time you wish. The management office opens at seven a.m. But leave me out of this. I've got a sweet deal here and if you fuck it up, I will never forgive you," Tess said.

Alexa draped an arm over Tess's shoulder. "I *love* these apartments, but you know damn well I would never jeopardize your arrangement here. That's not saying I won't call your sister and hassle her a little bit."

"Make sure to use a Dracula voice when you talk to her," Tess said. "She is totally freaked out that your teeth came in."

Sighing, Alexa shook her head. "I don't know when I'm going to fully process this."

"What are you talking about?" Tess asked.

"That your *whole* family, every one of them, is a witch. I mean I was a little taken back when your moms showed up and I realized, 'oh hey they smell like witches.' It never dawned on me that your dads are witches too. And I completely forgot about your sisters. I guess they're married to witches and Ava's kids are witches?"

"Yeah, Lex, that's how it works," Tess said.

"I know, but like I said, I'm still wrapping my head around it. My grandpa is a witch. I don't know, it's just really weird to me."

"That men are witches?"

"Yeah, I just never really thought about it."

"Way to be a sexist jerk," Tess said.

"Less sexist jerk and more like stupid human," Alexa said.

"You still consider yourself human?" Tess asked.

Alexa looked between her two friends. The puzzled look on their faces made her grin. She shrugged. "It's my only base of reference." Standing in the breezeway she searched the grounds. "What's that smell?"

Brie and Tess looked at each other then back to Alexa, both shaking their heads. "No clue." "No idea what you're talking about."

"It's over there." Alexa pointed toward the tennis courts. She turned away from her friends and walked in the direction she pointed. A sea of green lawns unfolded in front of her, sliced in half by a path leading to the courts. Brie and Tess followed behind.

"What is it?" Brie asked.

"I don't know." Alexa turned to face Brie, "You can't smell anything?"

Brie shook her head again. "Sorry. It's just trees and grass out here. It's probably your vampire nose picking up something the rest of us can't smell."

Alexa looked to Tess who gave the same blank expression as Brie. Tess shrugged. "After we find this barbeque or whatever is tickling your nose maybe we can dig up some tennis racquets and bounce a ball over the net?"

All three burst into giggles.

"Remember that time we tried to play tennis in junior high?" Brie asked.

"My God we were horrible," Tess said. "Lex's bionic arm kept sending the balls over the fence."

"And Clo could never get anything even *near* the net!" Brie mimicked Chloe's failed attempts at swinging a tennis racquet.

"What are you talking about, Miss Billy Jean King?" Tess said. "You were just as bad."

"No kidding," Alexa said. "You were laughing so hard at yourself, it was a miracle you didn't piss your pants!"

They approached the courts where the gate didn't completely shut and three tennis balls were caught under the curled chainlink fence. "It's over there," Alexa said. She started walking toward another path beyond the tennis courts. When they reached the jogging path Alexa stood still.

"I still don't smell anything," Tess said.

Brie shrugged her shoulders. "Neither do I. Can you describe it?"

Alexa grasped for words, but found nothing. She shook her head. "I don't know how to put it, but it's getting stronger." She crossed the path and approached the line of trees and underbrush. She continued to walk in the mowed grass, moving closer toward the scents. Death was one of the scents. She wanted to warn her friends not to approach but she also didn't want to face the people on her own. Someone was injured and someone else was definitely dead. She didn't discern any threat and continued to move forward with her friends following behind.

She pushed the trees to the side and froze. "Oh shit."

Brie yelped and backed up.

Tess leaned in. "What the fuck?"

In the clearing two women laid sprawled, naked from the waist down, their necks ripped open. One man was face down in a pool of blood. Another man sat on a boulder holding his hand to his neck as blood dripped between his fingers.

Fear. The scent was fear.

Alexa slammed her tongue to the roof of her mouth to hold her fangs in place. She breathed heavily, restraining herself from launching onto the hybrid bleeding to death.

Beyond his alluring fear were fleshy tones, not as strong as a scavenger, but not as light a hunter. He also carried a witch's scent of oregano – he was a hybrid. The three dead people were also hybrids.

He made eye contact with Alexa, pleading, nervous, and yet resigned to die. "Witches." His only word barely audible. It was then she caught the scent of the witches who had killed the couple at the magazine stand. All five had been here, including the two who were with her grandmother at Brindle's Café.

Looking over the sprawled bodies Alexa was surprised their deaths played in her head - hands over their mouths as they tried to scream for help. The women had teeth in the sides of their throats as their assailants raped them, but human... she corrected her thoughts... witch teeth, not vampire. The man on the ground drowned in his own blood as he was kicked and punched, listening to the grunting next to him. She also heard their voices as they taunted the last man.

Death was coming to him. Alexa saw his last moments – Sebastian helping him lay down.

Confused, Alexa looked back to the apartment building, trying to figure out why Sebastian played in this man's death scene. A commotion stirred from the breezeway, a bustle of men's voices. Sebastian burst forward, running towards the tennis courts and more men behind him.

Brie and Tess backed away from the clearing as the men swarmed forward. Alexa looked toward Sebastian, her yellow eyes meeting his yellow eyes. She was unsure why he and the men were rushing to the scene. She glanced to her friends huddled together then back to Sebastian.

He slowed as he approached and came to a stop when he reached Alexa. He gave a slight nod and cleared his throat as he looked to the scene beyond the trees. When he opened his mouth to speak he lost the ability to hold his fangs back and released them. "It would be best to escort your friends away from here, ideally inside a locked apartment." He nodded to the building behind him.

Alexa was transfixed on his fangs and forced herself to divert her eyes, first to the ground, then to the building, then to the men scattering into the bushes, then to Brie and Tess. She returned her focus to Sebastian and nodded in understanding, her tongue still holding her teeth in place.

He nodded again before ducking into the clearing. She moved away from the scene, noticing Brie and Tess had made their way to the tennis court, still uncomfortably close to the vampires. She noted while the vampires were on a mission to find something, or someone, they were keeping their distance from Brie and Tess. She also noticed three of the vampires were police officers, she assumed from the gas station. She wasn't sure what to make of vampires in uniforms, but it disturbed her.

Alexa looked back to the clearing in time to see Sebastian assist the man off the boulder onto the ground. She knew from the death vision the man was attempting to say "witches" again, but failed, frustrated he couldn't communicate with the vampire helping him to the ground. She could see from his vantage how kindness and pity filled Sebastian's eyes. And she could see Sebastian's fangs. While the man didn't find Sebastian terrifying, Alexa did.

Chapter Thirty-Three

Trembling as she climbed the stairs, Alexa couldn't subdue her fear. She knew she was emitting a beacon to every vampire in the area and yet she couldn't manage to scamper up the stairs quick enough to escape. Tess and Brie were equally unnerved and they kept passing jittery glances to the emptiness behind them and then to Alexa. When at last they fell into the apartment, Tess slammed the door shut, and secured the locks. Alexa fled to the window, opening it as far as possible, gasping for air.

The view over the empty lawns helped as much as the fresh air to settle her nerves. Brie leaned on the wall next to the window and watched Alexa. "What has *you* so freaked out?"

Alexa took several deep breaths without breaking her focus on the lawns below. "I wanted to sink my teeth in him."

"The guy bleeding?"

Alexa nodded. "The scent I was smelling was fear. You guys are emitting it and I'm pumping out huge doses of it right now."

"Do you want to put your teeth in us?" Brie asked in a clinical tone, although Alexa knew she was nervous.

"Not exactly." Alexa met Brie's eyes. "I'm more distracted that I can't control my own fear. But I was incredibly aware of your scents when we were outside."

Tess left the sanctuary of the door and approached Brie and Alexa. "Do you know that guy with the accent?"

Alexa nodded. "He's a bodyguard or something. He's been following me. My dad says he's a friend, somebody I can trust." She took a deep breath and closed her eyes. "I think I've finally stopped trembling." After another long exhale she opened her eyes. "This vampire gig is for the birds, I don't like it one bit."

Tess cocked a sympathetic smile. "Maybe things will be better when your vampire grandparents show up?"

"Dunno," Alexa said. "The damage is done. My first impression is carved pretty deep and it's nothing but blood and death and fear. I don't like this at all. It was a lot easier when I was a human."

"For you," Tess said. "It sucked for us."

"Did it really?"

"Watching everything we said, not able to tell you why we avoided Sniffany or other people... Lex it was hard keeping up the front. I can't tell you how many times she and I slipped," Tess said. "You're smart as hell, but you fell for some stupid excuses."

"Lin and Jess would question us long before you ever did," Brie said.

"So I'm oblivious," Alexa said throwing her hands in the air.

"No," Brie smiled. "You didn't want to know." Alexa stared at her. "You still don't want to know."

Tess sidled up to Alexa and put an arm around her. "Brie's doing her empath thing on you. She's reading you."

"Huh?"

"Do you still feel jittery from earlier?"

"I guess."

Brie stared at Alexa then closed her eyes. She slowed her breathing and softly exhaled. When she opened her eyes, she resumed her focus on Alexa. A couple times her head jerked, then her body. She blinked several times in rapid succession, and then her body relaxed. A smile spread across her face in triumph.

Tess looked at Alexa, "Feel better?"

"Yeah," Alexa said in amazement. "What did she..." she

turned to Brie. "What did you do?"

"She brought calm to herself and exchanged it for your nervousness," Tess explained.

"I thought you said you could only make people laugh," Alexa said.

"No, I said I can't dispel anger, at least not yet," Brie said. "I can only do little bits. Like when we first came in here? You were too wound up for me to expel. I could match your emotion, but not alleviate it."

"*THAT* is incredible. And useful!" Alexa turned to Tess. "And your homing pigeon divi-whatever thing? Also useful. But me? I've got visions of people getting hit by cars, but I'm not allowed to stop any of it. Useless. I'm a useless witch."

"No. You're not tapped into your powers," Tess said. "Once you figure that shit out, I'm pretty sure you'll find something useful."

"Didn't you say you used air or something to push your attackers down?" Brie asked.

"That's working with elements, and you can't tell me that's not useful," Tess said.

"I guess," Alexa said.

"Plus you're a vampire," Tess said. "A deadly one. You may not like it, but you're a force to be reckoned with. You're certainly not a typical hybrid."

Brie stroked Alexa's arm. "The problem is this is all hitting you at once, without any guidance. The vampire thing does seem daunting, and I know we're not any help. And that scene down there was..."

"Terrifying," Alexa finished for her.

"But that's not the experience of most vampires," Brie said.

"Most, but not all. I don't want to be desensitized to *that*. I don't want *that* to be my new normal. I sure as hell don't want my dreams to be real. The blood down there is nothing compared to what I see when I go to sleep. I don't want any of this." Tears welled in Alexa's eyes.

Tess pulled her closer, leaning her head on Alexa's. Brie held her hands.

Chapter Thirty-Four

Alexa looked out Brie's apartment window and saw the black car parked at the corner. She returned to the bathroom to finish touching up her makeup. Brie leaned against the doorjamb and watched Alexa apply another coat of mascara.

"You need more eyeliner," Brie said.

"I almost gouged out my eye putting this on."

"Here let me do it."

Alexa waved the mascara wand in the air in protest. "Ohmygod, he's about to pull up any minute and you want to scribble on my face?"

"Just trying to help."

"Then go check if there's a car waiting out front."

Brie left her post as instructed. From the living room she yelled, "He isn't here yet."

Alexa took a deep breath and chastised herself for being so nervous. She was behaving like this was their first date, but she wanted to be dressed up and look nice for Eric since he had only seen her in casual clothes. When they had gone to the steakhouse for their first date she tried to look as if she came directly from work, subdued, no excitement in seeing him. Now she wanted to make an effort, she wanted to look pretty and made up. She borrowed a skirt and blouse from Brie - about the only items she could find belonging to her short friend that would fit her.

She tugged at the skirt worried it was too short. She leaned into the mirror to ensure the scoop neckline of the blouse didn't reveal too much, or actually that it revealed just enough. Frustrated with herself, Alexa slammed the mascara into her makeup bag and barged out of the bathroom.

Brie turned around with a start. "Oh good, I think he just pulled up."

Alexa rushed to the window and spotted Eric's car. She looked over to Brie. "Why the hell am I so nervous?"

Brie giggled. "Because you like him. I swear, Lex, I've never seen you like this with anybody."

"I've never felt like this about anybody."

"It's about time! Get down there before he starts to sweat. You look great, but honestly, if he's worth anything you could look like shit and he would think you're the most beautiful creature on the planet." Brie pointed at the door. "Go!"

Alexa hobbled down the stairs certain she was about to stumble in her nervousness. She recomposed herself before reaching the double glass doors, smoothing out the skirt one more time. She plastered a genuine but somehow forced smile on her face and strode through the doors onto the sidewalk. Eric was leaned against the passenger door with his left eyebrow cocked. When they made eye contact her smile broadened.

Eric reached for her hand and pulled her close. He said, "Damn you look hot," and kissed her.

They parked on the street a block away from the Italian restaurant. The black car whizzed by, turning onto another street. By the time Eric and Alexa made their way to the door of the restaurant, she noticed the black car parked strategically so Sebastian could see the front entrance as well as Eric's car.

Alexa considered telling Eric about her bodyguard but she was unsure if she would jeopardize her own or anyone else's safety doing so. She wondered about her father's investigations of Eric and his statement that her selfishness could hurt Eric's family. Alexa returned her attention to Eric -

he had said something about Parmesan. She smiled sweetly and took in the scents wafting from the dining room.

As they walked to their table Alexa was surprised she didn't detect the witches and vampires sooner. Likewise, the guests were slow to take notice of Eric and Alexa, almost as if they were drugged – quite different from the diners at the steakhouse. After being seated she leaned in and asked, "What's the deal? Everyone seems drugged."

He leaned in, kissably close, and said, "garlic." Her eyes darted around the room and her nose flared. He said, "Garlic muddles the sense of smell."

"So that's where the myth comes from?"

"Yes," he said quietly as he gazed into her eyes.

Alexa grinned, knowing his intention. She put a finger on his forehead and pushed him away. She flipped the menu up, blocking his view of her. "So. Do you still think I'm a grilled chicken and salad kind of girl?" She lowered the menu to find him leering at her. "Are you going to stare at me all night or are we going to eat something?"

"I'll eat later," he said with a devilish grin. "I like watching you."

"Would you behave? The waitress is coming,"

After they gave their drink orders he said, "Actually, yes, I still think of you as a grilled chicken and salad kind of girl."

"So what are you thinking of getting?"

"Like I was telling you earlier, if I can't get a good steak then chicken Parmesan is my go-to meal."

"What are your thoughts on eggplant parmesan?"

He scrunched his face. "Dunno, sounds gross."

"Ooh, they've got an eggplant parmesan with gin marinara and basil fettuccini that sounds wonderful."

"Uh, yeah, that sounds like something a witch would order."

"What makes it a witch's meal – being vegetarian or the use of herbs?"

"Both... either... yes. Oh and garlic. It's odd how they like to use garlic in all of their dishes."

"Hmm, yes, quite odd."

Eric grinned at her rolling her eyes. "How's the apartment hunting going for you?"

She shook her head and shrugged her shoulders. "I mean, I found a place I like and put an application in, but the search hasn't been fun."

"Oh yeah?"

"I encountered a scavenger at one place," she said. "The whole place was deplorable. I knew before I toured the apartment I didn't want to live there. The scumbag at the door just sealed the deal. Ugh he was gross."

"It is a disgusting scent. It's not something you forget."

"Then the next day I ran into my grandmother. I've always known she was a bitch, but you know in a I-love-you-but-being-a-grandmother-reminds-me-I'm-old sort of way? No, she's just an outright bitch. She does not approve of mixed unions and is rather vocal about it."

"As well as the offspring?"

"Especially the offspring."

"Damn, that's harsh."

"Yeah, it was horrible." Alexa looked around the dining room, blinking back the tears.

Eric reached across the table and brushed her hand. "Hey."

She regained her composure and smiled at Eric. "It's just a lot to absorb. I'll figure it out somehow."

"You're not doing this alone."

"I know. I appreciate you helping me through this."

After the waitress took their orders Eric took a sip of wine and stared at Alexa. "You should meet my friends."

"Why do you say that?" she asked.

"You haven't been exposed to real... um... guys," he said eyeing the humans at a nearby table. "You need to see us being normal people like you're used to dealing with. I haven't told them about your full identity but they wouldn't have a problem with it, I just didn't know if you wanted that advertised or not."

"I'm not opposed to meeting them. I don't know about revealing everything though. Is it safe?"

"With them, absolutely. Actually they think it's weird you want to be around me."

She chuckled. "I guess a hybrid would make more sense?"

"It would. Anyway we're playing softball on Saturday. You should come along." -

"Are other girlfriends going to be there?"

"Uh, yeah, probably."

"Would they have a problem with me... as I am right now?"

"Ryan's girlfriend Kelly is super nice," he said. "I can't imagine she would have an issue with you. Justin said he's bringing someone, but I don't know anything about her. If it's a problem we can leave."

"I'll think about it."

Dinner arrived and Eric looked over Alexa's plate with skepticism. She cut into the eggplant, wound the fettuccini around her fork, and swirled the combination in marinara sauce, making sure to scoop up some cheese before popping the fork into her mouth. A giant grin spread across her face.

She cut another piece of eggplant and held her loaded fork inches away from his face. His nose flared before he opened his mouth.

"You're not tasting the food, are you?" she said when she realized he caught the taste of her saliva.

He shook his head no, but proceeded to chew the bite he was offered. "Actually," he said, "the flavor was quite good. I thought the eggplant would be more mushy than that."

"But you're not a convert."

"I'm a carnivore. I need meat."

Chapter Thirty-Five

As they walked to the car after dinner Eric asked, "Are you in a rush to get home?"

"Not really. I mean we both have to work tomorrow, but I think we have a little time to kill before carriages start turning into pumpkins." Before she sat down in the car, Alexa noticed the black car had already left its post.

They drove away from town and were soon following signs to the airport. He came close to the terminal but continued past. Eric evaded all of Alexa's questions as to where they were headed. He pulled onto a dirt road that skirted the airport property. She turned in her seat to see if headlights were following behind and saw nothing. She wondered where Sebastian had driven?

Chainlink fences with signs warning not to trespass stood between the road and the runways. They parked on a small hill offering a pristine view of the airport and the twinkling lights.

Alexa took in the view and thought it was pretty. When she realized where they were she turned to face Eric. "What, is this a make out point or something?"

"Or something," he said with a devilish grin. He turned off the ignition and unlatched his seatbelt. "We just haven't had any time to be together just you and me recently. I mean if you want to go back..."

"No," she said. "It's nice to be someplace where we don't have to guard what we're saying." Alexa caught that his scent was stronger. "You don't want to talk, do you?" she said leaning on the center console.

Eric met her for a kiss and lingered. She watched as he

pulled back, searching her face for permission to continue. One arm scooped around her shoulders, the other plunging next to the console releasing her seatbelt. He pulled her closer, kissing her harder.

She thought she heard his teeth release and opened her eyes. His eyes were yellow, for a moment reminding her of the morning she was attacked, but as she continued to watch him she started to find his eyes alluring. Her breath caught and her pulse speeding – he had noticed both and nuzzled into her neck.

His mouth returned to hers and his hand ran down her side. Her skirt ruffled and his warm hand slid up her thigh. She jerked back and caught his hand.

"I really want you," he murmured.

With a deep exhale, knowing her eyes were also yellow, she said, "this isn't the place and I'm not... ready. I um..."

He leaned closer, nearly crawling over the console. "Ready," he repeated as he removed his hand from her thigh. "You mean like birth control?"

"Well, yeah, and in general," she said.

"Okay," he nodded and kissed her again. "We can take care of that." Eric pushed himself up from the seat and gazed at her. "Damn you're hard to resist." He returned to his seat and took a deep breath. When he looked at her again, his eyes were normal. "Are you mad I brought you up here?"

"No. I'm sorry I wasn't..." she shrugged.

"What are you apologizing for? I only invited you out to dinner. You had no idea I wanted to bring you up here. This played out a lot differently in my head, that's all." He started the ignition.

"Well it's not like you've kept your intentions a secret. I want you to know the feeling's quite mutual. It's just that..."

Alexa gulped and her eyes darted around the dark car trying to find a way to make her confession. "I'm still a virgin."

Eric moved the gear back to park and turned to face her. He had a smirk of realization and of laughing at himself. He stroked her cheek. "Don't give it up to me, I'm not worth it."

She held his hand and kissed his knuckle. "I get to decide who's worth it, and for the record I'm very attracted to you." Her yellow eyes had faded, but she maintained her vampire scent.

He pulled her hand to his mouth taking a deep breath of the scent only he had been able to coax from her. They continued to hold hands as he drove her home.

Chapter Thirty-Six

When Alexa walked into the apartment after work, she found Brie sitting at the kitchen table carefully lining a basket with a cloth. "Did you go to work today?" Alexa asked.

"I took the afternoon off. Tess is on her way over. I thought I told you last night we were gathering stuff for our moms' party this weekend."

"You did. I just didn't know that meant you were taking part of the day off."

"Yeah, me and Tess have been tasked with getting the decorations together."

They both turned toward the door as Tess approached, where she rapped once before entering. Her face lit up seeing Alexa and pulled her into a hug, then stepped back to assess Alexa. "Girl," she said, "you reek of vampire."

"I *am* a vampire."

"Yeah, but you normally smell like a witch," Tess said. "What is he doing, rubbing all over you?"

"Maybe." Alexa grinned.

Tess raised her eyebrows and Alexa raised her eyebrows in response.

Tess turned to Brie, "What is this shit?"

"Dunno," Brie said. "But she keeps going out with him. I'm going to have to fumigate this place when she finds her own apartment."

Tess dropped a tote bag next to Brie and sat across from her at the table. Alexa joined her friends, draping her purse over the back of her chair.

"Heard anything on the apartments?" Tess asked.

"Not yet. I've got a little time tomorrow morning to look again. My dad's parents are coming to town, so I guess I'll spend the day over there on Sunday."

"Are they going to finally open up and tell you what was behind all of the secrecy?" Brie asked.

"Hell if I know. At this point I have low expectations. I'm ready for them to tell me to be happy I'm a human or some such shit." Alexa pulled the tote open revealing a bag of apples and bundles of fresh herbs. "What type of decorations are you guys putting together?"

"Well now that we can talk about it," Brie said, "they have a party for every solstice and major harvest stage."

Thinking back, Alexa didn't see the pattern. "Naw," she said, "it seems like they've just had parties every few months."

"Basically," Tess said.

"So what is this one?" Alexa asked.

"Mabon," they said in unison.

Alexa shook her head and said, "It's insane how you two do that." She watched Brie and Tess smile in unison. "Okay, so what is may-ben?"

"May-bun," Brie corrected. "It's second harvest."

Alexa tilted her head. "Like second breakfast?"

Tess scowled at her. "No, you dork. This isn't Hobbit crap."

Brie rolled her eyes. "It's the time of the year when you get the last of your harvest before things start dying and you also honor your dead relatives."

"Remind me how tipping back wine around a fire pit celebrates last harvest and dead aunts?"

"Uh *wine* and fire, that's all that's needed," Brie said in an obvious tone.

"How is that different from spring, and summer, and Halloween, and Christmas..."

"Yule," Brie corrected.

"Yule," Alexa repeated as she rolled her eyes, "and the last snow and... whatever else they gather for?" Before Brie could respond, Alexa had a thought and asked, "Wait, are their friends a coven?"

"Basically," Brie said.

"Are you two in it?"

"Mhmm."

Alexa looked to Tess. "And your sisters?" She nodded yes.

"So what does a coven *do*?"

"It really is just about parties," Tess said. "In the grand scheme of things a gathering offers combined energy. I mean even humans feed off of group energy, like you know, mob mentality. But really covens aren't really all that mysterious, nothing like you see in the movies. This group comes together because they enjoy our moms' parties."

"If something major came up and our combined skills were needed then we have established camaraderie and trust. Kinda like a, um... national guard," Brie said.

"So that's all you do, is sit around and drink?" Alexa asked.

"Not really," Tess said. "I mean from the outside it looks like that, but it's actually the communal act of being together. Don't get me wrong, some hilarious shit happens, but it's just a dinner party. At some point, we'll either hit the basement or circle around the fire out back and learn a new spell, let someone test their physical magic, maybe someone will do a reading."

"Offerings to the spirits?" Alexa asked.

Tess shook her head. "No, this isn't religion. Some Wicca groups do that, but that's not what ours is about."

"So is Wicca real?" Alexa asked.

"As a belief system, sure, but you know my Grandma Jean is a diehard Catholic," Tess said.

"But she's a witch?"

"Yeah. You'd be surprised how many witches are Catholic. Actually I think a few vampires are too."

"But..." Alexa wrinkled her forehead and stood quiet for a moment. "I don't know what to think about that." She pulled the bag of apples out of the tote bag. "Vampires in church, huh? And they don't, like incinerate, there on the spot?"

Tess shook her head no.

"Huh. So what's with the apples? Going to bob for them or something?"

"No, they're for decoration, but when we gather in the circle they'll be sliced open to look for pentagrams," Tess said.

Alexa raised her eyebrows in interest. "Very witchy."

"We need to scrounge around outside for big, full leaves and several pinecones," Brie said. "They really *are* for decoration. You want to come along?"

After changing into tennis shoes Alexa stood next to the apartment building watching Brie and Tess rummage through fallen leaves. She wandered into the trees and picked up a couple of pinecones. Tess came up behind her holding Brie's basket.

"Will these work?" Alexa asked holding out three pinecones.

"The two big ones are perfect, but toss that little one," Tess said.

Brie rushed in next to Tess. "No, keep the little ones," she said. "There's a bunch of little pinecones over there and they will work as accent pieces."

"It's like the size of an acorn," Tess said rolling the pinecone between her fingers.

"It's cute, I like it," Brie said. "A bunch of them would go great on the mantle."

"So how many do you want?" Tess asked.

"We should probably grab as many as possible?"

"That basket isn't going to hold much," Alexa said.

"Here," Brie said holding the basket toward Alexa. "I'll run upstairs and grab a few bags."

Tess and Alexa drifted further toward the back of the building, picking up pinecones and leaves as they went. Tess curled the front of her t-shirt to create a second basket as they waited for Brie to arrive with more bags.

"I wish I had changed my clothes too," Alexa said pulling at her blouse to get a better look at the smudges of dirt.

"That should come out with no problem," Tess said.

"Yeah, I know but I was hoping to wear it again before running to the laundromat. I'm sort of limited on clothing these days."

Alexa snapped her attention to the front of the building in time to see Brie escorted by her former boyfriend, Jack, and two other men. Tess was slower to catch the scents but when she did the pinecones fell to the ground and her eyes went wide with surprise.

With Jack's height and the hold he had on Brie, she hopped and jumped to keep pace. Alexa's anger flared for the way he treated her friend but the vampire in his entourage was more upsetting. He menacing glared narrowed in on Tess.

Alexa used a vampire whisper to Tess, "subdue your fear. He's honing in on your fear."

Tess looked sideways at Alexa and back to the vampire. She took a deep breath and Alexa noticed the fear subsiding, although not quick enough.

Alexa whispered again, "when Brie runs, follow her. No questions asked." Then she whispered to Brie, "Break free and run to the black car with my bodyguard. He will protect you and Tess."

Brie stared at Alexa, confused by the whisper. She looked to Tess who was also staring at Alexa.

"Jack, what the hell are you doing here?" Alexa asked.

Jack continued to march closer. "I hate when your friends lie to me. Brie has been giving me this bullshit line about not seeing you in weeks, but I've seen you coming and going from her place. Why does she need to lie about that?"

"You've been watching her apartment?" Alexa asked in disbelief.

"How else am I going to find you? Your dad damn near beat the fuck out of me and threatened to cut my nuts off if I even stepped on your street."

"So, you didn't get the message to kiss off?" Alexa asked. "Seriously, let go of her!" Alexa grabbed Brie's arm and pulled her free from Jack. She looked back to Tess and with a quick nod returned her attention to Brie. "Go!"

Brie and Tess ran the length of the building. Jack cursed and with his human friend ran after them struggling against a sudden wind Alexa stirred, swirling dust and leaves in the air. The vampire watched the humans run after the two witches and turned to face the third witch, Alexa.

Assured her friends had reached the front of the building and were in view of Sebastian, Alexa turned to run further behind the building in an attempt to escape the vampire. He followed behind and caught her, wrapping an arm around her neck, and thrust his body against hers, causing her to fall to the ground.

With the full weight of a grown man lying on her, Alexa pushed up and flipped him to the ground. He extended his teeth causing Alexa to clamp her tongue to the top of her mouth and blink rapidly to hide her vampire traits. Worse yet, he emitted a scent of arousal she found alluring.

She scrambled to get to her feet but he grabbed her arm and knocked her off balance. He rolled on top of her pinning her to the ground, this time facing each other. His hands searched for loose clothing as he ignored her attempts to break free.

A deep growl emitted from Alexa and she dropped her teeth. The vampire jerked in reaction but wasn't quick enough before Alexa sank her teeth into the side of his neck. He howled in pain, sounding very much like a wounded animal. She ripped her teeth toward his windpipe, tearing through the pulsing veins and arteries, pouring blood onto her face. He struggled against her, but she managed to keep a firm clasp on his back keeping him in place. Alexa kept her teeth submerged until she hit the tiny bones of the trachea. She jerked her head, nicking the trachea, and released the vampire.

His final wisps of air fluttered next to her ear and she knew his last vision would be of brown hair and grass. His body collapsed onto her and she wiggled to free herself.

She pushed his body off her, but he continued to float up in the air. Confused, Alexa looked to the side and saw several legs surrounding her. She tried to look up, but blood fell into her eyes. She sensed several vampires, including Sebastian to be next to her. Alexa wiped the blood away so she could see.

"Are you injured?" A voice asked.

Alexa shook her head, but she the removal of the body and the proximity of so many vampires confused her. She retracted her teeth and sat up. Four men pulled the vampire away, blood still flooding from his neck. Another man came running around the building with a blue tarp. Yet another followed with a shotgun and fired it in the air. The dead man was quickly folded and bundled in the tarp, looking like a dead animal.

A hand extended to help her up. He was younger than

Sebastian, with black hair and piercing eyes. Alexa accepted his assistance and once she was on her feet she looked around at the other men. Who were these men? They were in matching black suits like the day Duane was hauled away. Were they the same men? Then more men arrived. Two appeared to be teenagers, the others were middle aged, all in black suits, most with black hair, and their scents similar enough that Alexa was sure many of them were related – at least one teenager was the son of one of these men. Just so many vampires.

The man with the shotgun had pointed it in the air but now was aiming toward the line of trees. Nothing was in there; even the squirrels had scampered away with the arrival of so many large predators. Surely, he knew that.

Alexa couldn't process the scene and her eyes darted around wildly. She licked her lips and tasted his blood. Blood. She looked down - she was covered in blood. She wanted to lick her lips again, she liked the taste, but she was being watched. Sebastian moved closer and shooed the men away. He extended a black handkerchief. "For your face," he explained.

As if in slow motion she accepted the handkerchief. Sebastian shook his head with a smile. "Your father would scold you for taking such a risk, yet he would be amused by your unorthodox methods," he said.

What did that mean? Alexa scowled trying to figure out what was unconventional.

Brie and Tess ran around the corner. Brie appeared ready to cry; Tess stared at the blue lump on the ground and back to Alexa.

Eyes wide with horror, Tess asked, "Lex did you kill him?"

Alexa looked toward the blue tarp. Yes she had killed the guy they rolled up in there. She nodded. She looked down and the enormity of what happened struck her. She had killed. Again. She had killed a second time. Her eyes flitted around the yard and all she saw were men in black suits. Vampires, and more vampires. They were watching her. They watched her stand in the blood of the man she just killed. The man in the blue tarp. The dead man in the blue tarp that she killed.

Tears filled her eyes. What had she done? Tess stood next to her. Tess was talking. Alexa couldn't hear what was being said. Who was Tess talking to? Alexa looked beyond Tess and saw a man removing his jacket. He handed the jacket to Tess who wrapped it around Alexa's shoulders.

Brie grabbed Alexa's face. "Lex, Lex, Lex, come on, look at me." Alexa fixed her eyes on Brie. "Can you hear me?" Brie asked. Alexa nodded. "We're going to walk inside, okay? Keep your head down so no one sees the blood," Brie said. "Alexa? Can you keep your head down and just follow me and Tess?" Alexa nodded and put her head down. Tess pulled Alexa's hair forward to drape beside her face.

Tess guided Alexa with an arm around her shoulder. Alexa watched the grass as she took each step and she could hear voices and sirens. Movement near the street caught her attention but she didn't break her focus on her footsteps. As she came closer she heard her name. A man was yelling her name. The doors to the building were held open and Alexa only saw black slacks and polished men's shoes.

Brie and Tess held her arms and escorted her up the stairs. Another man stood at the top step, but his slacks were blue. Alexa tried to peak through her hair at the vampire who dared to break the dress code. To her surprise, he was in a police uniform. Alexa raised her head fully to further inspect the man.

"Put your head down," Brie hissed.

The officer scampered ahead to open Brie's apartment door.

Once they were inside he closed the door behind them and stood guard outside.

Chapter Thirty-Seven

Alexa was in her pajamas, sitting crossed legged on the couch, cupping a mug of coffee when her parents arrived. Her mom ran across the room and flung herself next to Alexa causing Brie to quickly remove the coffee from Alexa's hands. Alexa curled into her mother's embrace and began to bawl.

Her father sat next to her mom wrapping his arms around his wife and daughter. Alexa found comfort in their warmth and calmed down. Occasionally sniffing, she listened to her mother's murmurs and the rhythm of her heartbeat. Alexa listened more closely.

Alexa sat back and looked at her mother. "What are you singing?"

Her mom smiled and used her thumb to brush the moisture off Alexa's cheek. "It's a lullaby spell to sooth a troubled heart."

"A spell? I thought you weren't supposed to practice?"

"And who's here to tell my mother I was singing a lullaby to my daughter?"

Alexa looked around the room and scanned the rest of the apartment. Brie and Tess were gone. Answering Alexa's concerned look, her father said, "Their parents are downstairs."

"How did they know?" Alexa asked.

"I spoke to their fathers and they followed us here," he said.

Alexa wrinkled her forehead. Her emotions fired in several directions and she couldn't process anything. She knew how worried and scared Brie and Tess's parents would be. She wondered if she would be forced to leave Brie's apartment? Alexa couldn't deal with those issues and returned to more trivial worries. "What language were you using?" she asked her mother.

"Gaelic."

"I'd like to learn how to do that," Alexa said.

"There are books available," her mom said. "Once you master the language the spells will make more sense." She smiled again. "You are quite adept with languages, I don't imagine this will be difficult for you to master."

Alexa made eye contact with her father. "Thank you for contacting their parents," she said.

He returned a sympathetic grin and stroked the back of her head where his hand had been resting. Concern and worry crossed his face and as emotions overcame him he buried his face into his wife's hair. He pulled his little family closer and held onto them as if they were about to blow away.

He released his hold and stood up. He strode across the room and retrieved a chair from the kitchen table, bringing it back to the couch so he could sit face to face with Alexa. In a pose she had often seen him take, her father leaned forward and rested his forearms on his knees.

Alexa untangled herself from her mother's embrace and sat up. She noticed traces of red in his eyes betraying his earlier tears.

He cleared his throat. "Alexa, you must tell me what happened."

Nervously Alexa recounted how she, Brie, and Tess came to be at the back of the building and the arrival of Jack and his two friends. She watched her father as she spoke and saw he was keeping track of the details, surely each step would be called into question and she would have to account for her reasoning. Alexa struggled explaining the man's attack and her counter-attack. Their movements were quick and Alexa operated out of instinct – attack and escape. She remembered the blood and how freely it flowed into her mouth. She remembered the taste and the weight of the man lying on top of her, but she couldn't remember where she bit him or her logic behind her bite. She recalled a large number of vampires appearing, seemingly out of nowhere, and the slow realization that she had killed someone.

Tears filled Alexa's eyes. Two kills. She was so ashamed of herself.

Her father made a sound deep in his throat and shook his head. "Alexa, your methods are unconventional. My concern is how you used yourself as bait to lure the man away from your friends."

"What else was I supposed to do?" she asked. "If I pulled Brie to safety that would have left Tess unprotected. I was the only of us who had a fighting chance against him."

"And yet you do not know how to measure his strength against your own. You could have been killed."

"His intent was to rape a witch, which one of us didn't matter," Alexa said. "He wouldn't kill the witch until he was done with her so there was a window of opportunity to fight back. It may have been a small window..." She stopped short upon seeing her father's perplexed look.

"You knowingly risked being raped in order to fight this man?"

"Rape isn't death. I mean it's horrible, but lots of women lay there and take it whether it's forced or not. The fact is men are most vulnerable when aroused. Why more women don't take advantage of that is beyond me."

"Alexa," he said frustrated, "you used yourself as *bait*!"

"What was I supposed to do? Let him rape and kill Brie?" Alexa yelled back.

"You are alive only as a matter of luck," he said, his anger building. "You are not a skilled fighter."

"Then teach me!"

"I am *not* teaching my daughter how to be a fighter! You must learn to keep yourself safe at all times to avoid these encounters."

"Why can't you teach me how to fight?" She screamed. "Is it because I'm a weak little hybrid or is it because I'm a *girl*?"

"Alexa, it is not appropriate for you to fight," he said with forced calmness.

She crossed her arms and said, "That's not a reason."

"It is a reason and it is sufficient reason," he said. "Please simply do as I instruct."

Alexa scowled at her father as her anger increased. She sat in silence stewing over his latest round of vagueness and could only hear her heart thumping. She continued to scowl at her father and he scowled back. At some point her mother moved off the couch and stood near a window. Alexa was aware of the movement but never looked to see why her mother moved; Alexa fixated on her father.

A low deep sound reverberated through the room; her father was growling at her. She realized the entire time she had been scowling she was also growling.

She watched as her father held his fangs in place. With even words he said, "Do not growl at me, it is a sign of aggression."

"Then teach me how to fight," Alexa said in the same measured tones.

Exhaling heavily through his nose and narrowing his eyes at her, he grabbed Alexa off the couch and carried her across the room, pressing her at arm's length against the wall. Her feet dangled inches above the floor and she was incapable of wiggling loose from his hold. Unable to contain her anger any further, Alexa dropped her teeth. Her father's shock of seeing her fangs was enough of an opportunity for her to shake out of his grip. Once on the floor she plowed into him, pressing him against the opposite wall at which point he dropped his fangs. Her arms were shorter and he was easily able to get a grip on her and again lift her off the floor.

Alexa pulled up and expanded the air between them, thrusting herself out of his hold. "Fuck this shit," she screamed. She turned, grabbed her purse off the chair, and marched out of the apartment.

Once outside, she swirled the air to press the doors closed as her father was mere steps behind her. Ignoring the cries from Brie and Tess asking what happened, she strode past Sebastian and sneered, "Don't fucking follow me!" She got in the car, released the hold on the door causing her father to fall onto the walkway, started the ignition, and peeled away from the apartment complex.

Alexa drove down random streets constantly checking the rearview mirror. She never saw evidence of being followed, but she didn't trust that her request was being honored. The donut shop her grandfather frequented whizzed by as she followed a red Pontiac. She turned on the next street then into an alley, onto the next street and pulled in behind the sandwich shop she had visited just days before. The vacant lot gave her ample room to back into a space. Alexa cut off the lights and the ignition and leaned her head back, contemplating her next move.

"Not here," she said aloud. That was all she knew. She didn't want to be here, behind the sandwich shop where she wasn't welcome. She didn't want to be here in Brentwood with the lies and cover-ups and spies on every corner. An apartment to herself wasn't going to be sufficient distance; she needed to be further away.

As a plan began to formulate, she looked down to her lap and saw the pink flannel pajamas with white floral print. After a quick scan of the area and noting she was truly alone, Alexa crawled into the backseat and changed into the jogging clothes she kept in a gym bag. Grateful she had the insight to stash a bra, socks, and shoes in the bag, she shoved her nightclothes in their place and returned to the driver's seat.

Her regular haunts were off limits. Sebastian had proven he knew where she liked to frequent and easily anticipated her moves. She had to go someplace unexpected, outside of her routine, someplace she had never been before. Alexa thought about finding a payphone to call Eric, but no, he would surely be under surveillance, possibly his line bugged. She had no idea to what lengths her father and Sebastian were capable of tracking her down.

She had not yet committed to watching him play softball, but if she wanted to see Eric at all, the softball game would be her only chance.

Chapter Thirty-Eight

With a jolt, Alexa awoke to a squirrel chipping an acorn apart. He sat at the end of the hood of the car, blissfully digging into the nut. She scanned for scents around her car – only the squirrel and the dog registered.

She had heard the coyotes in the distance not long after she parked the night before. She never checked to see if the dog that circled her car was in fact a coyote or just a stray, but whatever he was he brought her comfort. Through the night she would drift in and out of sleep and the dog was always there. Occasionally he would circle the car as if walking sentry and then return to his resting spot next to the driver's door.

The pale beginnings of sunrise glowed in the distance and she hoped daylight would bring some reprieve. She especially hoped for a large number of humans to populate the fields, but she wasn't sure how long she would have to wait or even if waiting was a good idea. As if the dog sensed her need for continued protection he walked around the car again, scaring off the squirrel. Instead of resuming his resting spot next to her door, he went into the wooded area behind the car. The dog began barking, startling Alexa. She turned in her seat half expecting a vampire to emerge from the trees. Instead the medium sized brown dog stood in a clearing barking at her. He casually walked back to the car and jumped up, resting his paws on the door and looked at Alexa through the glass. This startled her too. The dog barked once and looked back to the clearing.

Alexa raised her eyebrows in confusion. "Do you want me to go in the woods?" she asked the dog.

The dog barked once and wagged his tail.

"Am I supposed to get out of the car and follow you?"

The dog growled.

"I need to stay in the car?"

The dog barked again.

"Am I really talking to a *dog*?"

Again the dog barked.

"Oookay..." she said. "I should move my car into the woods?"

The dog barked and dropped back to the ground. He ran far enough away so she could see him further out in the lot. She turned around and assessed the clearing. The space would easily fit her car and provide enough cover to hide her from Sebastian and the other vampires in black suits. She looked back to the dog watching her. Alexa shrugged her shoulders; the dog's plan was better than anything she could come up with. She started the engine and put the car into reverse, easing it into the dark cavern of trees. Once she was off the asphalt, the dog began barking and running toward the car. Alexa put the car in park and watched the dog – he headed to the dumpster. He jumped along the side of the dumpster then ran to the car and jumped in front of the hood. He repeated the action two more times before Alexa understood.

She pushed the air next to the dumpster scooting it across the parking lot coming to rest in front of her car, hiding her from view. The dog leapt onto the hood of her car and curled into a knot.

Hidden behind a dumpster and surrounded by trees brought a darkness not even the burgeoning sunrise could break. She found the area more than a little spooky. Alexa took comfort from the ball of fur on her hood and nestled down in her seat, laying her head on the gym bag.

Hours later the need to relieve her bladder forced Alexa out of the car. The dog had long since moved away from her and the dumpster, but she sensed he was still in the area.

After fishing a couple of napkins from a discarded Wendy's bag in the backseat, Alexa communed with nature in relative privacy next to her car. Hunger was her next issue. She argued with herself what to do with her possessions. Already dressed for jogging, she had an easy cover to move in and around the park, but holding her wallet would look stupid. Trotting around with a handbag would be even more ridiculous. She opted to shove her purse inside the gym bag with her pajamas and casually walk to the concession stand.

Over the next six hours Alexa drifted from field to field, watching baseball and soccer games while on constant alert and struggling to appear casual. In random conversations she explained how she arrived at the wrong time or was looking for a certain person, all the while keeping her eye on the parking lots.

Much to her frustration, vampires were all over the place. Alexa had no idea if one of her father's cronies was undercover either as a player, coach, or parent. Several witches were also in attendance and Alexa watched with fascination as witch and vampire children played side by side. The parents, however, sat separate, politely conversing only as necessary in front of the humans.

Ah the humans... those poor oblivious creatures. They sat blissfully unaware of the tension brewing between their neighbors, gleefully cheering their children to hit harder and run faster.

From the main entrance a wave of tension swept through the crowd. Black cars buzzed in, circling the lots. Several men in suits poured from the cars and began sweeping through the sidelines of the games. Alexa assumed Eric had arrived, leading the patrols directly to her. She watched both vampire and witch monitor the commotion. Several humans also picked up on the activity and their questioning looks received shrugged shoulders in return.

Alexa left her seat watching middle-schoolers swing bats with impressive dexterity. As she moved closer to a different game she changed her scent to reveal as a hybrid, hoping the men in suits were looking for a full-blooded witch and ignore her. She walked with her face averted from the suits; they may not know her vampire scent but she assumed her face would be easily recognized. Whenever one approached she turned as if someone was talking to her or would drop to tie her shoe. Alexa sidled up to a group of vampires awaiting information from their scout talking to a suit.

"They're looking for a witch and believe she followed someone here today," the man said.

"Really!" one of the women said.

The man made eye contact with Alexa and her obvious attempt at eavesdropping. She casually looked after the suit meandering near the next set of stands. "Sure seems like a whole lot of effort to find one person," she said. Alexa returned her attention to the man.

"Yeah, I don't get it," he shrugged. "I don't think we've ever had a sanctioned witch hunt in Brentwood, well at least not in my lifetime." The statement would have had more impact if the man were old, however he looked to only be in his thirties.

"Hmm, well, I wish them luck," Alexa said. She put her hands on her hips and looked past the man. "I get such a kick out of watching those kids play! Well... I have got to find my group. This place is a freaking maze and if anyone told me the field number I wasn't paying attention, that's for sure."

"You don't know what field you're going to?" the man asked

in disbelief.

"No idea," Alexa said with a grin. "I guess I'm going to stand in the most central location possible and hope he can find my scent."

The man burst out laughing. "You're going to be left standing for a long time. There are far too many scents in this park to single out one person." He nodded toward the next suit milling through the stands. "Hell they're even having a hard time."

Alexa smiled again and made her way toward the concession stand where she had a better view of the field the suits were circling. She was certain Eric was there but she had no way to get to him without being seen. Sitting on a park bench she tried to watch the game on the field. Distractions abounded as people filed past to get to the restrooms or concessions. She made the painful decision to leave the gym bag under the bench. First she did stretches then jogged in place. She broke past the people milling around the bench and loped toward the field. She made her way to join other joggers on the path surrounding the park.

At last Alexa spotted Eric. She slowed her pace and hoped a vampire whisper could reach him from such a distance.

"Eric," she whispered, "I don't know if you can hear me, but I'm in the park. The patrol followed you here and they are looking for me."

He never responded, but from the outfield he changed his stance and was looking from side to side.

"Touch the grass if you can hear me," she said.

Eric bent side to side as if he were stretching and then touched his mitt to the grass. He stood up and returned his focus to the batter.

"I'm on the jogging path wearing black shorts and a yellow

shirt," she said.

Hitting a fist into the mitt, Eric nodded several times, his eyes still on the batter. The ball hurled over the third baseman's head and fouled. Eric took the opportunity to scan the crowd.

"I see you," he whispered. "I couldn't respond until I saw you. We have two more innings."

"I can wait," she said. "I don't know how to meet up with you and not be seen." She watched Eric jog toward the bench – his team was up to bat.

"We'll figure it out," he said.

Alexa jogged along the path surrounding the park. Vampires dressed in dark suits continued to mill through the crowd stirring confusion and suspicion among the players and spectators. Alexa counted eighteen men on patrol and realized she had encountered most of them the night before when she killed Jack's friend.

She hadn't taken time to think about the big vampire accompanying Jack. How long had Jack known him? Where did they meet? She could only imagine the variety of Jack's possessions that carried her scent. Her hair. She had given him a small braided lock of hair only days before they broke up.

The breakup was fierce. She knew he had slept with someone although he denied it. She remembered the look on Jack's face when she said she *smelled* the other woman on him. Jack's anger and accusations, his pleas for her to return... His relentless calls to her house. If she ever thought she loved him, and she did believe she loved him at one time, his response after their breakup showed only selfishness. Alexa had no regrets in leaving Jack, only that she had wasted nearly a year of her life and affections focused on him.

The lock of hair had to be the link that attracted the vampire.

She could still taste his blood and it carried several witches – twenty, thirty, maybe more. The man may not have been a "hunter" but he hunted witches. A human toting around a witch's lock of hair had to capture his attention. What an intrigue to find a woman willing to date a human, a woman with low standards? He probably stalked all of Alexa's friends and everywhere Jack knew her to visit, likely with a story of trying to help him win her back.

That Sebastian didn't encounter him lurking was interesting. Maybe evading Sebastian was why he took so long to find her? What a deadly encounter that was.

She couldn't believe she had killed a second man. Alexa held no remorse for a rapist to be off the streets, only that the execution was by her hand, or rather her teeth. She felt filthy, not just for having another person's blood pour over her, but for causing it to pour in the first place. She thought it sickening to sink her teeth into another person, and yet only days earlier she wanted nothing more than to rip into the dying hybrid by the tennis courts.

Ripping flesh and cracking bones haunted her memory like one of her grotesque nightmares. She could see it, feel it, hear it now. Worse, she could still taste it. Alexa stopped jogging to wipe the tears from her face. Was she the monster in all of her dreams?

Chapter Thirty-Nine

As she approached the main entrance, Alexa slowed to a stop. She darted to the grass and dropped to retie her shoe – she saw Sebastian lean on a car while watching the joggers.

Taking another glance toward Eric's game, which was still in play, she decided to grab her gym bag. An elderly man and a little boy were sat on the bench, eating hot dogs. Alexa felt a small burst of relief seeing her bag behind their feet.

"I'm sorry," Alexa said, "but my gym bag is behind your feet."

They stood up allowing Alexa to retrieve her gym bag. While she squatted to grab the bag, four vampires passed behind her. She quickly unzipped the bag and checked the contents, but the vampires lingered. With a heavy sigh and a quick prayer, Alexa stood up and faced the vampires. "Can I help you gentlemen?"

They weren't looking at her face.

"I'm going to assume if you're overdressed like that, maybe you're supposed to be working or something? Is your boss going to be happy you're wasting your time staring at my ass?"

The man on the right met her eyes and seemed surprised to be called out for leering at a woman's body. He then looked over his shoulder towards the main entrance causing the other three vampires to glance in the same direction.

"Yeah, that's what I thought," she said. "So for your final thrill you can watch my tight little ass walk back to my car. Bye guys." Alexa flashed a big smile and waved as she sauntered toward the parking lot. She overheard them talk among themselves in German. Frustrated she didn't have as firm of an understanding of her father's native language as she had of French; Alexa did catch enough to know they were astonished at her bold confrontation and that someone was indeed tracking their movements.

When she was far enough away from the vampires, Alexa exhaled heavily, unloading the false bravado. She continued walking but slowed enough to assess her surroundings and relocate Eric. The patrol members had exhausted their search of the crowd and moved toward the woods.

"They're getting close to finding my car," she whispered to Eric.

"Me and my roommate are going to swap cars," he whispered back. "His girlfriend has unlocked the car so you can get in there and hide in the backseat – brunette hunter at the silver Aurora, three cars down from mine."

Alexa had no idea what an Aurora looked like, but she knew Eric's car. She scanned the parking lot spotting three different brunettes when at last she found the vampire standing next to a silver car. The woman appeared to search for something in the car as she walked to the passenger side and ruffled through the contents of the seat. Alexa whispered, "I see her," then noticed when the woman got the message she could return to the field. The woman acted as if she found the lost item and proudly strutted back to the softball diamond with something in her hand.

"Once you're in the car we will figure out a diversion to rush off the field– Justin will drive my car back to our apartment and you and I can go a different direction," Eric said.

"I think I can create a diversion, just tell me when you're ready."

"Two more outs and the game is over."

"When the dust kicks up, run like hell to the car."

Grateful the car was parked close to the sidewalk, Alexa trotted toward it keeping pace with another jogger who blocked Sebastian's view of her. As she neared the car she slowed and again dropped to the grass to tie her shoe. She tossed the gym bag to the pavement between the silver car and the black pickup next to it. Acting as if something fell out of the bag, Alexa hunched over and pretended to pick pieces up from the ground, grabbed her bag, and slid into the backseat of the silver car. She stayed as low as possible, but kept an eye on the game. The player stood on first base with another batter at the plate.

Commotion across the park caught Alexa's attention. A man stood on top of the dumpster... her car had been found. She returned her focus to the softball game in time to see the ball leave the bat, shooting over the pitcher's head. Impatient for the game to be over, Alexa caused the ball to drop into the unsuspecting second baseman's glove. He tossed the ball to first base and the game ended.

A black car buzzed through the parking lot passing behind Alexa. She turned in time to see the players leaving the outfield and shake hands with their opponents.

The time for her diversion had arrived. Alexa hadn't played with her powers enough to know how much wind she could manipulate. She took a deep breath and thought of the doll on her bookcase. Focusing on the trees behind the dumpster, she pulled the air toward her. She saw small movement among the boughs. She continued the momentum, bit by bit, they moved more until there was a full sway. She continued to watch the swaying branches as more energy swirled. A small breeze tumbled down the hill and across the park. With all of her attention honed in on the swaying trees Alexa mustered more energy, summoning the wind to dance in the open fields. Another small puff of breeze passed the car. She remained focused, nearly hypnotized, pulling more energy, picturing in her mind a large, dense cloud of dirt and debris swirling across the ball fields.

The trees bent in submission and a howling wind rumbled down the hillside and across the distant parking lot. Leaves and pine needles and pieces of trash tumbled onto the lawns as spectators covered their faces. Alexa continued to coax the wind forward and it answered her call barreling onto the baseball diamonds blasting dirt twenty, thirty feet into the air.

Wind billowed through the parked cars bringing dirt and paper plundering toward the cornfield beyond the entrance. The driver door opened and slammed shut – Eric was in the car. With the keys already in the ignition he started the engine and turned in his seat and grinned in disbelief at Alexa, leaning on the passenger seat. "That is definitely one hell of a distraction," he said laughing. "Get down," he said as he backed the car in reverse.

Alexa crammed herself onto the floor of the backseat, pulling the gym bag and someone's T-shirt on top of her. She hoped the shirt smelling like another hunter would be sufficient to cover her scent.

They were in a long line of cars crawling forward. Alexa heard another car rumble past, several men yelling, then more cars speeding. "They're checking cars," Eric whispered.

"I'm hidden," she said.

He rolled down the driver-side window and Alexa sensed when a vampire approached. No words were exchanged but Alexa imagined the vampire was sniffing the car. When the vampire walked toward the next car, Eric began driving forward. As they exited the parking lot there was commotion. Eric's window was still down and Alexa could hear walkie-talkies crackle. She distinctly heard the words "woods" and "dumpster" – her car had definitely been found.

They pulled onto the street and more cars sped toward the ball fields as Eric and Alexa drove away. After several turns and a long stretch of road, Eric told Alexa she could come out of hiding. She managed to pop herself out from the crevasse behind the driver's seat, sitting up and looking around — they were driving on a narrow road between a yellowing field of corn on one side and a harvested field on the other. Beyond the brown dirt littered with bits of corn stalk laid a house and barn. No other vehicles were on the road.

Eric stopped the car and turned to Alexa. "Who's the guy?"

"What?" She asked confused. "Oh," she said realizing he was referring to her scent. "Some guy was trying to attack Brie last night." She sighed. "Damn, that feels like a million years ago."

"You killed him?"

Alexa couldn't decipher whether the strange look on his face was disapproval, anger, or maybe humor. Timid, she replied, "yes."

"Is that why you're being followed?"

"No... well, I mean not exactly. It has more to do with my father."

Before Eric could ask any more questions, Alexa stood up as much as possible and wiggled a leg between the front seats and moved into the passenger seat, nearly bashing her head into Eric's face. He grabbed her, holding her in place above him and firmly kissed her.

"Eric, I smell like crap."

"No, you smell like another man. That fresh kill is all over your face and down your neck," he said with his eyes trailing to her breasts. "You must have really ripped him apart."

Alexa pulled free and settled into her seat. "He was laying on top of me so it was hard to avoid getting drenched."

"I thought he was attacking Brie?"

"That was his intention, but he ended up coming after me."

"Poor guy thought he had caught a witch, huh?" Eric smiled.

"Yeah, basically," she mumbled. She leaned into the headrest, staring up. "Eric, I think my dad works for the Geismars." Alexa rolled her head to face Eric, "In fact, I'm like ninety-nine percent sure."

Eric wrinkled his forehead. "Why do you say that?"

"Well for starters," she said pointing over her shoulder, "that. I'm not sure how many black suits are part of her Majesty's patrol, but this little hybrid doesn't warrant that type of turnout."

Eric grunted.

Closing her eyes and taking a deep breath, hoping she wasn't endangering Eric or her father by revealing her speculations. "Do you remember that car that was following me? The black car we saw at the college?"

Eric nodded.

"The driver's name is Sebastian. When I confronted my dad about being followed he wasn't upset and when I pressed that maybe he had someone following me he admitted it was true and said the driver was someone I could trust, that the man was a close friend. I learned his name the night I left home and moved in with Brie. I asked that no one follow me but he's always there, that damn black car of his is always somewhere in my rearview mirror. When you and I were at the library, I'm pretty sure he was standing on the roof."

Eric's eyebrows shot up in surprise.

"He's been watching us, you and me. He knows my patterns and tendencies, of course I would reach out to you somehow. Eric, I'm endangering you, but I needed to give you a head's up before you're cornered. I mean you can tell them everything I've said, I'm not going to tell you where I'm going."

"You're leaving?"

"I have to. I need to get away from all of this madness and clear my head. I need to get some space away from my family, and don't take this wrong, but from you... I just need to come up for air."

He nodded, acted as if he was going to say something and nodded again. "We should probably get moving before Farmer in the Dell over there reports an abandoned car." Eric tilted his head toward the farmhouse in the distance then put the car into drive. As the car rolled forward he looked over to Alexa and asked, "So why do you think your dad's with the Geismars?"

"Besides my dad's buddy is part of the patrol? Well, that day we went to lunch? I had just come from my bank, the one my parents use. I had been researching the company my dad works for and couldn't find anything. On a lark I asked to see the bank's annual report, said I was doing something for school. I didn't recognize any of the names but it happens to be affiliated with Geismar Holdings. Why would my dad bank someplace held by the competition? You know unless of course he has been lying to me the whole time and told me some bogus name for his employer? My dad flies to Austria and New York all the fucking time for business. What if the little suburban house is just a cover? What if he's actually one of their managers or something?"

"That's really a loose argument, Alexa. But..." Eric paused as he formulated his thoughts. "I don't know. The area where you live is almost impenetrable; there are checkpoints even on walking paths. I know that a lot of people connected to the Geismars live out that direction, but I think most of them are up near Vinewood. Anyways most of us just avoid all of that because it's such a pain in the ass. How you were ever attacked is beyond me."

"Vinewood? The school?" Alexa asked.

"Yeah, it's a private school for vampire girls," Eric said. "It's why there were so few vampires in public school. Remington is the boy's school."

"Vampires only?"

"Yeah."

"Huh!" Alexa pondered the admission criteria for the schools.

"Well, like I said, it's a loose argument, but plausible," he said. "I still don't get all of the secrecy."

Alexa shrugged her shoulders. "It really doesn't matter at this point. I'm fed up with it all. I just need to get out of town and clear my head."

"Where do you want to go?"

"Dunno. I kinda think I want to do an Underground Railroad thing – hit up a friend of a friend of a friend and hopefully drift far enough away no one can find me."

"I don't like the sounds of that."

"I'll find ways to communicate," she said. "I can't really do anything until later tonight, so if you don't mind just driving in random circles..."

"Actually, we can go to my parents' house. They're out of town visiting my sister until tomorrow. So we could park away from the house and get you something to eat."

Chapter Forty

Radio commercials played while Alexa watched the blur of houses pass as they wound through different neighborhoods. They parked in front of a non-descript ranch style home with red shutters, a cookie cutter duplicate of every other house on the street varying only in color and landscaping.

Alexa grabbed her gym bag and joined Eric on the sidewalk. He held her hand as he led her past several houses then cut through someone's yard to the rear where Eric jumped over the back fence. He assisted Alexa with the bag as she made her way over the fence.

She looked to the house and around the yard. "Is this where you grew up?"

"Yep, since fifth grade."

"Great trees!"

Eric glanced up to the giant birch with large branches extending across the yard and smiled. "Only a vampire could admire a tree like that for the reasons you do."

"So you've jumped out of it?"

"All of the damn time," he said with a laugh. "The neighbors were terrified I was going to break my neck until the time my dad got up there with me and started jumping out too."

"That had to be a sight."

"My mom said she should do it to just for good measure."

Alexa laughed.

"We should test your strength," he said.

"What?"

"Toss your bag over there and stand out in the opening. I'll come at you and try to knock you down."

"Um okay."

"The only rules are no killing each other - going for the neck is a kill shot. So hit me with everything you've got. Just remember, stay away from the neck." Eric winked at her and walked away.

She winced. Yeah, she knew all about the neck being a kill shot. Evidently she was expert at it. Alexa tipped her head up, putting the blood and guts thoughts to the back of her mind. She at last had someone willing to show her how to fight like a proper vampire.

He went to the corner near the house, next to another big tree and a barbeque pit. Alexa tossed her bag to the side and watched, unsure what to expect. As he began to run toward her she was reminded of the morning she was attacked at the park.

He was off-center, she noticed, like he planned on running past her. Once he was beside her he reached out with an arm across her chest then kicked a leg behind her, knocking her off balance. Alexa fell onto her back, the wind knocked out of her. She coughed and rolled over to get up. Eric was on one knee glaring at her with his teeth dropped.

His fangs looked like every Dracula movie poster she had ever seen. She recalled her father's warning - a vampire showing his teeth was provocation. Eric was definitely provoking her.

Keeping their eyes locked on each other, Alexa got to her feet and as she stood up Eric rose at the same time. He stepped to the side and she followed suit, measuring his next move. As he stepped, she stepped. Alexa sensed his heartbeat easing and she was ready for him to lunge. She caught him, flipped him to the side, slid her foot behind his leg as he had just done to her, and successfully dropped him to the ground. The shock of being knocked down sent a jolt that came across as fear. The scent filled her nose and her teeth dropped as she hovered over him.

Eric's face filled with shock as he scrambled to get out of her way. Alexa crouched and grabbed his foot, flipping him onto his back. She jumped on top of him, pinning him in place.

As she moved closer, running her nose along his cheek, Eric embraced her, moving a hand up her back and another to her hip. She paused at his jaw. Eric turned his mouth to meet hers. When their teeth rubbed together she gasped, shock waves rippling the length of her body.

Eric wedged a foot to the ground and flipped Alexa to her back. He returned his mouth to hers, kissing her hard. He ran his teeth along her jaw and down her neck, pausing. He continued down her neck to her collarbone, his nose pushing her t-shirt from her shoulder. Alexa's mouth rested on the back of his neck where she could take in all of his scent. Her eyes were closed, savoring the sensations.

Eric returned to her mouth where she eagerly received his attack. He was no longer gentle and pressed his body onto her. As she raised her knees to bring him closer, they both froze at the same time. Humans.

Eric jolted to his feet, extending a hand to Alexa. She looked up from the ground, trying to catch her breath, seeing Eric had already drawn up his teeth. Alexa snapped her teeth back into her mouth but she could feel her eyes still glowing yellow. She closed her eyes and Eric pulled her into an embrace. She laid her head on Eric's shoulder and he stroked her hair. He whispered into her ear, "Let's go inside."

A dog ran to the fence from the neighbor's yard and barked in ferocious alarm of the two predators standing in Eric's yard. A man yelled at the dog, ignoring Eric and Alexa, as he tossed a large white bag into one of the trashcans standing behind his garage.

Eric led Alexa to the house. At the door he took her face in his hands and kissed her. She wrapped her arms around his torso pulling her body against him. He responded, sliding his hands down her back pressing their bodies together.

Eric pulled back, his eyes searching her face. "I'm taking advantage of you."

"No, you're not. Eric, I want to be with you." He tried to step away, but Alexa didn't let go. "Open the damn door and take me inside."

A slow smile crept across his face then he kissed her, slamming her against the wall. Eric stepped back and fished his hand along the top of the doorjamb producing a key. He fumbled with the lock, finally opening the door. Alexa stepped inside and he followed her, locking the door behind them. As he ushered her through the house, Alexa didn't take time to observe her surroundings except to assess if they were alone.

He pulled her into a bedroom, closed the door, and pressed her to the wall. He ran his hand the length of her body, pulling her closer, pushing himself harder into her. Alexa rested her hands on his hips as they each kicked off their shoes. When his mouth brushed down her neck, her hands moved under his shirt and up his back.

She released a breathless exhale triggering his teeth to drop. He rested the front of his teeth on her shoulder, inhaling her scent. He brushed his mouth up her neck, along her cheek, and to her mouth. Pressing his teeth on her lips sent a quiver through her body causing her teeth to drop.

They stood still, teeth rubbing against each other, smelling the mingling of their scents, their gold eyes glaring at each other. Again Eric was giving her a chance to escape but Alexa had no plans to leave. She understood what he wanted and pulled him closer to encourage him to continue.

She leaned back and shimmied out of her shorts and pulled her t-shirt over her head. His nostrils flared, as he looked over her bare skin. Alexa grabbed his shirt and pulled it over his head as he wiggled out of his shorts. Like a magnet her mouth was drawn to the pulse at his collarbone.

Eric grabbed Alexa away from the wall and tossed her onto the bed. Eric paused, standing at the edge of the bed, his eyes roaming her body. She extended her legs, pulling him forward. He fell onto her, nuzzling into her neck and with a soft groan shook his head. He stood up again, dropping his underwear then pulling hers off. Before Alexa could release her bra his face was between her breasts, pushing her back onto the bed, crawling between her legs.

With frantic fumbling he plunged into her. She jolted back at the tear of membranes but quickly relaxed, summoning him to continue.

She ran her knee along his leg and rested her teeth against his neck, sparking him back into action. She held on with her nose firmly planted against his shoulder, sweat swirling between them as their momentum built.

He released a deep groan into her hair when he reached climax. Alexa ran her mouth along his shoulder, pausing at his neck to lick the drops of sweat. This was the first time she had truly tasted him.

Waves of energy surged through her. This wasn't a vampire thing, she sensed — something stirred her witch powers. She couldn't identify what triggered her but she focused on a spot deep in her abdomen that seemed to house her powers.

As Eric became more slack as he breathed heavily into her hair. He seemed content, but Alexa was becoming more energized. Her heartbeat increased, her breathing more rapid.

Alexa rolled him to his back and landed on top of him with her teeth extended, nuzzling the base of his neck, but she couldn't get enough of his scent. With a jerk she sat up, straddling him with her hands running over his chest and abdomen. She unconsciously rocked as she moved but once she became aware how much she enjoyed the movement she knew where to focus her activity.

Alexa's rocking and grinding didn't last long before Eric's arousal returned. She lifted to allow entry, but her inexperience didn't bring the two together gracefully. Once he was in place Alexa paused to appreciate how perfectly male and female fit together. She moved slow, learning how to bring pleasure to herself. She saw him watching and he seemed enjoy her exploration, as if he was holding back his own urges.

Her pace increased, but she curled forward, running her mouth along his shoulder muscle. He seemed to know she was searching for blood and relaxed his shoulder and arm to accommodate her. Her teeth, Alexa discovered, were sensitive not because they were newly formed but to allow her to locate veins and arteries. Fortunately she also understood enough anatomy to know where to avoid injuring vital organs. Despite its incredible lure, she also remembered his warning to avoid his neck.

Alexa found a soft area below the collarbone and above the thoracic artery near his shoulder joint. Her teeth sank easily into his skin, blood pooling in her mouth. His flavor was deep, not quite earthy, with overtones of pepper. As she swallowed she plunged a little harder forcing another gush into her mouth. Slowly Alexa withdrew her teeth drinking more blood. She ran her tongue over the two punctures, capturing the escaping blood. Bitterness alarmed her and she realized her teeth had leaked a fluid. Eric slid his hand under her mouth and began rubbing the small puddle over his wounds. "It's a sealant," he explained.

She pulled back enough to see the coagulant do its job. Alexa ran her tongue along Eric's finger, removing the traces of blood. She sat up, vigorously resuming her rocking. Climax rippled through her body, a flush spreading across her chest and up her neck.

Eric sat up and grabbed Alexa, pulling her to his chest. He flipped her on her back, slid his legs to the edge of the bed, pulling her with him. When he got his footing, Eric pulled Alexa off the bed, swung her around, and pinned her against the wall. His mouth sought the same soft spot on her shoulder. She didn't remember retracting her fangs, but when he bit her the pain released her teeth. She leaned her head back trying to relax and taking in the smell of her own blood, floral and meaty. Extracting his teeth from her flesh was nearly as painful as when he broke the skin. The coagulant may have stopped the bleeding, but it did not reduce the pain.

He seemed rejuvenated and with increased strength, he reached down to her thighs, lifting her even with his waist. He easily guided himself into her and proceeded to take her forcefully. Alexa locked her legs and arms around him, leaning her head to the wall. She moaned with each thrust, encouraging him to go faster and harder.

At his conclusion he turned Alexa around and dropped her onto the bed. He laid down next to her, uttering a mystified, "shit." Exhausted she turned her head to face him. He grinned and rubbed something off her chin, she assumed blood. "Damn, I've never met anyone like you," he whispered.

Alexa loved the way he looked at her, like no one else mattered. For the moment she didn't want to think about his past, who he had been with, or that he was only drawn to her for smelling like a witch. Instead, she focused on the moment, the exhilaration of what they had shared, and the amazing way he made her feel.

A chill woke Alexa from a deep sleep. She rolled over seeking a blanket, the movement stirring Eric. He reached over her, yanking the blanket free from the foot of the bed and pulled it over her. His arms wrapped around her and he nudged his nose into the back of her neck.

Afternoon sun peeked through the curtain, casting a play of light on the opposite wall. Alexa watched the swirl of dust in the ray of light. She felt Eric behind her, brushing his lips along her spine. A shiver ran through her body and she leaned back into him.

"Alexa, I don't want to let go of you," he said in a gruff voice.

She stiffened and rolled over to face him, curiosity wrinkling her forehead. She searched his eyes. "I know who you are," she whispered in disbelief.

"What?"

She flinched, fluttering her eyes open and closed. She looked past him and fluttered her eyes again. The experience exhausted her and she was breathing heavily when she at last made eye contact with him.

"You're the man in my visions," she said. "I've heard your voice. I know who you are." She stroked his cheek, her eyes inventorying his face. "It all makes sense now."

"What makes sense?"

"When I die, I hear *your* voice."

His worried expression went blank.

"I'm trying to protect someone and all I have ever known was he sounds like an old man behind me, and it's someone I care for very much." She paused as tears filled her eyes. "He cries my name in agony, it's very gravely," she said with a gulp.

"Eric, that was your voice." She sniffled. "Then I drop and that's it. In your death, the last thing you see is an old woman lying on the ground in a pool of blood."

"And that's you?" he asked. "The woman I'm distraught over?"

She nodded

Eric tilted his head and softly wiped a tear off her cheek. "We die together?"

She nodded.

Eric stared at her. "I love you Alexa," he said.

Alexa threw her arms around him and shoved her face into his shoulder. A different force surged through her, a different type of passion. Eric pulled her face to his and he kissed her soft and sure. He rolled her on her back and gently lowered himself onto her. No teeth, no raw passion, just genuine love bringing two souls together. Their lovemaking ended with them in an embrace, refusing to let go.

Chapter Forty-One

Alexa snuggled into the warmth next to her. The room had long since lost the beams of sun and dancing dust particles. She looked up to find Eric watching her in the pale glow of a distant streetlight.

"How long have you been awake?" she asked.

"I never went to sleep."

She propped onto one elbow to better face him. "I thought guys always fell asleep afterwards?"

"Humans maybe," he said. "But I'm a vampire and we don't sleep more than an hour or two."

"I sleep. I sleep a lot."

"That must be the witch in you," he said. "Does your dad sleep?"

"Yeah... well... I guess. I mean he stays up and does a lot of business at night. Honestly, I don't know."

"You talk in your sleep," he said. "And twitch your nose, you're kinda fun to watch."

"What did I say?"

"Nothing I understood. When you made any sound it was mumbles, mostly your lips were moving. Something scared you but you managed to subdue the fear pretty quick and then you kicked me."

"Sorry about that."

"You're definitely feisty in bed," he said with a teasing grin.

"I really am sorry," she said. "I should have warned you about my nightmares. Brie said I freaked her out a little – I guess I've dropped my teeth a couple of times in my sleep."

Eric took a deep breath and said, "Yeah those teeth were

meant to do some damage. You're strong as hell too. Whoever is crossing you in your dreams is not coming out alive, that's for sure."

Alexa rolled her eyes and shrugged. "That's all my dreams are – death and dying and destruction, screaming and crying and blood everywhere. It would be nice to have a happy dream just once. You know, fields of flowers with skipping and singing and... I don't know. Chances are I would be so freaked out I would wake up screaming."

Eric grinned. "Do you often wake up screaming?"

"Sometimes. That's how I know my dad sleeps at least a little. He would pick me up and carry me to my mom. I would wake up slammed against her and he's snoring away next to me."

"That still happens? Him carrying you into their bed?"

"No, it got weird somewhere in my teens. But my mom has crawled in bed with me and soothes me back to sleep."

"How are you coping with it not living with them anymore?"

"It's actually pretty hard. I've got to grow up some time and figure this out. And if that means waking up drenched in sweat and bawling my eyes out by myself, then I'll just have to cope."

"Crying?"

"Lately, that's been my reaction, not as much screaming. It's just some of those dreams are so vivid and painful. The heartache is just..." she shook her head. "Isn't it bad enough that I witness death and dying every moment I'm awake? But then I also have to dream it so vividly and so... viscerally? It's like there's no escape."

"Do they have any meaning?"

"I don't know. The ones I remember are like snapshots from a horror movie, like you would see in movie previews – just a lot of blood and guts with no meaning. I don't understand their context. Why am I chained to a tree or why am I being pulled through the halls of a dungeon? And seriously, *who* is the kid screaming? Oh my God, that one has been constant. Most of them I forget though. My mom will get me to describe what I saw, then in the morning when she tells me about it? I have no idea what she's talking about."

"That's not very useful. It does sound like you shouldn't be alone when you sleep, though."

"Like a babysitter?" she teased.

"No." Eric watched her for a long time, then said, "Let's run off and get married."

Alexa sat up and faced him directly. She saw he was serious and offered a weak smile in return.

"I take it, that's a no," he said.

She shook her head. "Eric, I'm not ready for you. I have a lot of shit to sort out and come to terms with before I could ever make that commitment. What we've got going on here is a student-teacher relationship and when the time comes for us to be together I want to stand next to you as an equal, not as some little girl who just discovered that vampires don't sleep."

"Alexa..."

"Eric I would love nothing more than to be your wife and..." Alexa choked back the tears. "...And to have a family with you, but none of that can happen."

"What are you talking about?"

She grabbed his hand as she gazed to the black ceiling for guidance. In fits and starts, she grappled to find the right words. "Eric, there's um, there's a uh another woman in your future."

"You know how I'm going to die, you know there's another woman in my future. Is one of your abilities to be a fortune-teller? Do you also know how many kids I'm going to have?"

"Actually I do know, but I'm not going to tell you how many."

"You... you know how many children I'm going to have?" he asked in a voice teetering between disbelief and fear.

"It's actually because I know you're going to have children that I know another woman comes into your life."

"What?"

"You have children in your future, I don't. I'm not the mother of your children. I know there's lots of children around me – my friends' kids and kids I'm related to, so I assume they're my cousins', but none of them are mine."

"You can't have children?"

"I don't know if it's a matter of *can't*, but I know it won't happen."

"Then why were you worried about birth control?"

"I said I wasn't ready. You inferred birth control."

"But you were ready today? I mean that was just a couple days ago," he said.

"The car was kinda awkward and you did catch me off-guard, but today, trying to tell you I was leaving... I really did want it to be you," she said. "I do love you Eric and yes, I want to marry you."

"But you won't."

"Not right now."

"But if we did get married..."

"That doesn't change our realities," she said. "I mean we can get married, but you're still going to end up fucking some other woman and she's going to have your babies and then I'm going to get all pissed off and possessive and have to kill her and then you're going to be resentful and then it's going to be this big ass bloody mess..."

He laughed. "You'd kill the mother of my children?"

"If we were married I would have to. I mean, come on, no

one screws around on me."

Eric narrowed his eyes. "You're sure you need to go away? I mean if you're able to joke about killing people maybe you're already coming to terms with things?"

"No, I'm just not cool with guys screwing around on me. If I knew I could rip people apart earlier, this town would be minus a few assholes."

"But you wouldn't kill me?"

"Well no, I love you too much. Besides, that's not how you die."

He laughed again and pulled her face to his. "You are the most amazing... curious creature on the planet." After the lightest of kisses, Eric leaned back and watched her again. "You tagged me, I can't marry anyone else."

"Exactly what are the rules to being tagged?"

He pulled her on top of his chest and then gently pushed her hair away from her face. "In its most basic terms it's ownership, saying nobody else can touch my girl unless I give them permission. With that comes my protection that if anyone tries to hurt you I can kill them without any sort of inquiry. It's like a get-out-of-jail-free card. You're mine and I'm yours, although I think maybe you're better equipped to protect me than I can you."

"Ownership," she repeated.

"Yeah, it's archaic," he said as he rolled his eyes, "but it's generally respected across the board."

"Well, I release you. Go find her, marry her, make her *this* happy, as happy as you've made me. Have children. Then one day we will find each other, because I get you in the end. She doesn't die with you, I do."

"I don't like this plan."

"Not right now you don't, but one day this will all make

sense. We're young and we have a whole long life ahead of us to live. Make the most of it. Repopulate the earth. Then you can come back to your first love... wait... am I your first love?"

"You're my only love."

Chapter Forty-Two

Movement in the bed stirred Alexa. Groggy and unsure where she was, Alexa had difficulty opening her eyes and considered maybe she was still dreaming. Adjusting to the darkness she spotted Eric scrambling to find his shorts.

Fear and anger rushed down the hall. The door burst open and with a blast of light from the hallway, a panicked man entered, scanning the room. His nose followed a scent as he darted wildly around the room without finding a satisfactory answer. He approached the bed and Alexa sensed danger. As he drew closer she growled.

Eric yelled something indistinguishable and startled Alexa by throwing his body on top of her. "Alexa, he's my father. He's trying to protect me."

Alexa looked over Eric's shoulder to the man and registered his scent. The two were nearly identical except Eric carried another essence, a scent belonging to the woman standing near the door. The woman, her eyes wide in confusion and concern, stepped closer to Eric's dad. "Your mother?"

"Yes, that is my mother and this is my father and neither one of them are a threat to you," Eric said releasing his grip. Alexa pulled the sheet around her again without taking her eyes off his father. She sat up watching his nose flare.

"Who are you?" his father demanded in a thick German accent. "You smell like a vitch and growl like a vampire. Is it you who carries the scent of Edvard the Destroyer?"

"What the hell is he talking about?" Alexa asked under her breath.

"Martin!" Eric's mother scolded, also in a German accent.

"Eric is safe. Come. Let them dress and we will discuss at the table." She grabbed her husband's sleeve and ushered him out of the room.

After getting dressed, Alexa followed Eric to the kitchen where his parents were seated. She felt embarrassed for having sex in their house and being caught like errant teenagers.

Alexa looked between his parents and decided Eric most resembled his mother. She was average height and average build and had light brown hair and a sweet face. His father, on the other hand, had darker hair with heavy doses of gray. He was a bulky man, not fat, but filled the chair. But his eyebrows... Eric had his father's eyebrows.

Their deaths filled Alexa's head, both would die from bites on their necks. His mother's death was difficult to submerge – a baby cried from her arms and she was terrified for its safety as a man and woman hovered behind her each trying to reach the baby.

"Father, this is Alexa, we met at work and have been dating for a while. She is a hybrid."

Alexa broke free from the visions, but the baby's cries continued to echo in her head. Her face flushed red as she flinched.

His father eyed her up and down, sighing heavy disapproval.

The man scared her. Alexa's eyes darted from Eric, to his father, over to his mother, to his father, around the kitchen, and back to his father. She tried to grin as she tipped her head in respect, muttering, "How do you do?"

She sheepishly slid into a chair placing her between Eric and his mother and facing his father.

Eric's father narrowed his eyes at her. "You smell like a vitch."

"It's my normal scent," she said melting into her chair. "I didn't know I had another scent... until... until I met Eric."

His father looked at her exasperated. "You did not know you are a vampire?"

"I didn't even know I was a witch." Her attention darted between Eric and his father.

Confusion crossed his father's face. "How can you *not* know you are a vitch?"

Alexa shrugged her shoulders. "No one told me. I was raised as a human."

"Are you an orphan?" he asked.

"No," Alexa said, shaking her head. "I grew up with both of my parents here in Brentwood. My mother is a witch and my father is a vampire, but I didn't know that until my teeth came in."

"You have teeth?" his mother asked with surprise.

"Ach, you heard her growl," his father said. "She is a vampire."

Eric's mother gently cleared her throat. "Your parents are hiding you," she said.

"They told me they were protecting me."

His mother shook her head. "A witch from a noble family would be in extreme danger. They are hiding you."

Alexa brought her nervous focus to Eric's mom. "Noble family?" she repeated.

"There is no doubt, you carry the scent of a noble," his mother said.

Alexa's eyes darted to Eric. He thought she was a ranger; no one said anything about her being a noble. What the hell did that mean? Eric appeared as surprised as she was. Alexa struggled to keep her panic at bay before it broke into outright fear.

"No, to be exact," his father said with authority, "you carry Edvard's scent."

"Who's Edvard?" Alexa asked.

"Prince Edward," Eric said.

"You are not related to an Edvard?" his father asked.

Feeling as though her heart dropped into her stomach, Alexa said, "My, my grandfather's name is Edward."

"Is Vilhelm your father?" his father asked.

She shook her head, wooziness washing over her. "Wilhelm is my uncle," she said quietly.

"Philippe is your father?" his father asked.

"No," she said as she shook her head. "I don't know a Philippe"

"But your mother is a witch." Eric's mom said. She turned to his dad and said, "Remember the rumors of Philippe and a witch? He is using a different name to hide his family." She turned back to Alexa. "My dear, you are not simply a noble vampire, you are a Von Geismar!" She pronounced the name "geese-mar" but Alexa understood.

Alexa's eyebrows shot up. "How is that?" she asked out of breath.

"Remember?" Eric said, looking equally shaken as Alexa. "The Geismars, or Von Geismar, are the ruling family of the Carinthian vampires. Edward the Destroyer is the Queen's son,"

She began trembling, tears welling in her eyes. "What?" she asked. "My... dad doesn't *work* for the Geismars? He *is* a Geismar?"

"Sounds like it," Eric said.

His father wagged his finger in the air. "Yah," he said with resolve, "Philippe's son... that is the scent... *THAT* is the scent you carry."

"Son?" Alexa repeated moving her eyes from his father back to Eric. "My, my father... he has a son? I... I... have a b...b...brother?"

Eric nodded. "Prince Philippe has a son," he said softly. "He is a destroyer like his grandfather... *Your* grandfather."

A soft hand rubbed her shoulder. Alexa turned to Eric's mother who looked at her sympathetically. "You knew none of this?" his mother asked.

Alexa shook her head. "Who... who is he?" she asked. "My, my mother's son died at, at, at birth."

"Philippe's son is from his first wife," Eric's mother explained. "She was a princess, a vampire. She died after giving birth."

Alexa stood up, blindly scanning the kitchen, gasping for air as if she were suffocating. She leaned against a wall for support. Her eyes landed on Eric. He was watching her, his eyebrows wrinkled with concern. She nodded and said, "This is why I have to go. I don't even know... how or where... to begin to start to process this. Any of this." She tipped her head against the wall. "I doubt the moon is far enough away for me to deal with this."

Standing up, his father gripped Eric's shoulder and leaned to his ear. "You just slept with a Von Geismar - they are going to kill you." He opened the refrigerator and removed a beer.

Alexa stepped away from the wall and glared at Eric. "Who's going to kill you?" she demanded. "Nobody can kill you. I would never give my permission for that."

His father leaned down to Eric again and sniffed. "She tagged you?"

Eric cleared his throat and nodded. "Yah."

His father glared at her. Eric's mom glared at her. Eric was glaring at her. "What?" she asked.

"Ah, uh," Eric stuttered. "Women don't typically tag men."

"What!" Alexa screeched. "Why the hell didn't you tell me?"

Eric chuckled. "I couldn't exactly stop you, not like I minded, I mean I'll catch hell for it from my friends, but you're totally worth it."

Alexa blushed as she looked between his parents.

"But you're right," he said. "Nobody is allowed to kill me without your permission."

His father snorted.

Eric turned to face his father. "She's the granddaughter of a destroyer and she is very strong. She also has two kills and her teeth have only just come in."

His father's eyebrows shot up as he reassessed Alexa. "You are but a hybrid," he said.

"A noble hybrid," Eric corrected. "Her teeth are huge."

"Eric," Alexa said with resolve. "I need to leave. I think I left my bag in the backyard." She looked towards the backdoor. A fog built in her head and she had to get out of the house; she couldn't breathe. She looked back to his parents. In other circumstances she would have thought them to be nice people. Alexa forced the words out of her mouth, "I have to go."

Eric grabbed her hand and pulled her toward the back door.

Chapter Forty-Three

Eric's parents jumped from their seats and rushed to the front door. Eric stopped to watch the commotion. Alexa didn't understand the movement and wanted to retrieve her bag, but Eric wouldn't move.

She heard the front door open, but she didn't care. She wanted her bag in the backyard. Familiar scents caught her nose and she turned in time to see her father barreling toward her and Eric. Her dad's teeth were extended and his intention was destruction. He wanted to kill Eric.

Instinct snapped, her teeth dropped, and she tackled her father to the floor.

She was lifted into the air and tossed across the room.

Alexa scrambled to her feet and turned to see her grandfather. Beyond him her father had Eric pinned to the floor.

"DAD!" Alexa screamed as she ran toward them. She reached around her father's head, shoving her hand in front of his mouth. With her other hand she pulled on his collar, but she couldn't release his hold. She growled in his ear. "He's tagged. You can't kill him. He's *mine*."

"Let go," she repeated moving her teeth to his neck. When he released his hold, Alexa grabbed his arms and pulled him off Eric. She landed on the floor with her father on her lap. He stood up, ready to lunge at Eric a second time. She summoned energy and thrust him across the room. Alexa rushed after her father, pressing him to the wall.

Before she could turn him to reach vital organs, an arm came around her waist from behind - her grandfather lifted her off the ground.

Her grandmother rushed to block her dad from attacking Eric again. She reprimanded him in French and her father responded in growls.

Alexa was swung away from the scene - the backdoor, a wall, and dining table all a blur. She pulled and twisted enough to break her grandfather's grip and fell to the ground.

She was yanked off the floor and carried toward the front of the house. Alexa wiggled her legs between his and tripped him, causing him to fall to the ground. Her grandfather braced himself to not land fully on top of her, giving Alexa enough room to crawl out of his hold. He grabbed her feet and pulled her closer.

All Alexa wanted was to ensure Eric was safe, but her grandfather kept pulling her further and further away. The noise and commotion agitated her - Eric and his father were arguing in German. Her father and grandmother were also yelling at each other, but in French. She would have found the exchange funny if she weren't so pissed off - her father's French was horrendous. Other vampires loomed nearby, not inside the house but close.

As she moved to check on Eric she was pulled closer to the front door. She tried to slide past her grandfather but he blocked her. She tried again and he picked her up. He was strong, tall, and had long arms. Wiggling free drained her. They slammed against the wall and a picture fell, shattering nearby. She was pulled away from the shards of glass, hitting a different wall.

She knocked him to the ground a second time. Again, he caught her foot, then her other one. She pressed for release, emitting a growl.

Her grandfather growled in return. His eyes turned yellow

as he craned his mouth open, dropping his teeth. Crap his teeth were long. They were nothing like the other vampires she had seen, even longer than her father's.

She stared at him, measuring for his next move. Her teeth had dropped again but she pressed them to the roof of her mouth. She didn't want to challenge her grandfather, she already felt guilty for the hits they had exchanged. No, she just wanted to get past him. She wanted to talk to Eric.

Her grandfather remained still, assessing her. She glanced to the scene behind him – Eric's mother holding onto her son for dear life, his father standing guard between him and her father. Alexa's grandmother had coaxed her father away from Eric and his family, but like Eric's dad stood as a barricade, in case her father changed his mind. All five were watching her – a tenuous peace, if only for a moment.

She returned her focus to her grandfather. They both panted, geared for a fight, but not yet exhausted.

He stood straight, dropped his arms to his side, and retracted his teeth. His left cheek rose in a grin. "You should have been tested long ago. You are no witch, Alexa. You are a vampire."

"Trust me, I'm a witch," she grumbled.

"Ha, yes of course you are. Just as *my* grandfather, his mother was a witch and his father was a king. You are every bit as strong." Pride danced in his eyes.

Alexa's father left his post and walked towards her. "It is time we left," he said.

She looked again to Eric and his parents, all three now huddled - fear bubbling, but restrained. Alexa began to understand the implications of her presence – no one was supposed to know of her existence. Now she was revealed, not only in identity, but also in strength. Worse yet, the son of this family had committed a crime, he had slept with the daughter of a very powerful man, the granddaughter of an even more powerful man, the great-granddaughter of the Queen. Tagging Eric wasn't enough to keep him alive.

Alexa shook her head. "No, no. Nothing can happen to this family." Tears started rolling down her cheeks. "We've made a shambles of their home. None of this is their fault. You should have told me. They had no idea Eric and I were even seeing each other and Eric had no idea who I was. *I* had no idea who I was. You cannot punish them for some stupid secret you've been keeping. This is not their fault."

"ALEXA!" her grandfather shouted.

She fluttered her attention back and forth between her father and grandfather. Her fear rose and she had difficulty tampering it.

"Nothing will happen to the family," he said. "Reparations will be made and the family will be safe. Allow me time to talk with them, but you must go to the car at this moment."

She stood still.

"You have my word, they will be safe."

She looked over to Eric. He whispered, "I love you. Go."

She whispered back, "I love you too."

Alexa turned feeling as if the life had been sucked from her chest. She couldn't see through the tears and she couldn't breathe. She took a step and lost her balance, reaching out for the wall.

An arm pulled her up from the waist. She turned to see her grandmother, her beloved Grandmere Alexandra, holding her up. Alexa leaned into her and together they hobbled toward the car.

Chapter Forty-Four

Riding in the backseat slammed against her grandmother, Alexa sniffled and shook as she struggled to control her sobbing. Not until they reached her parents' house did she realize she had at last ridden in one of the notorious black sedans that had been following her. She couldn't recall any details of the ride or the interior of the car or, well, anything.

She only remembered the look on Eric's face – his fear of her grandfather, the pain of farewell. Regret.

Her mother came out of the house grinning as she greeted the car carrying her in-laws but was taken back when she saw Alexa. Her mom pulled the car door open with a panicked look on her face. "Alexa, what happened?"

Alexa tumbled out of the car and shooed her mom away. "I don't want to talk about it. I hate my life, I hate being a vampire, and I don't want to be around anybody right now."

Her mom looked to the others for information and back to Alexa. More cars arrived – five in total, all lined in front of her house. Vampires poured out, each wearing a sleek black suit.

She looked back to her mom. "I can't do this right now. I need to take a walk or something." Without waiting for a reply she started walking down the sidewalk clutching her gym bag that had been on her lap in the car – her grandfather had brought it out of Eric's house when he departed.

Alexa didn't have a destination, she just headed where her feet took her. Standing in front of Brie's parents' house she sighed. Of course this was where her autopilot took her, where else would she go?

She looked next door to Tess's parents' house, they were

hosting a party, the one for which she, Tess, and Brie had been collecting pinecones as decorations. Was that only the day before? It seemed a lifetime ago. Alexa had no desire to crash the party, not that she had been invited. She merely wanted her friends, *needed* her friends.

Without any thought of how long these parties took, Alexa decided to wait. She sat down on the front porch and hoped to keep a low profile until Brie came to retrieve her car. She leaned against the wall, her mind a blur. Four houses down she saw her parents' house with all of the cars out front - they looked like they were hosting a party too. She glanced down the street at the various houses, her neighbors. No one would think anything out of place. Who would ever suspect a coven having a rollicking party at one house and vampires sitting around brooding at another? She assumed they were brooding; she had no idea.

Somebody was inside the house. Maybe Brie was home? Alexa focused, discerning more than one person in there. Unsure if she would be interrupting, Alexa approached the door. She turned the knob and the door was unlocked. She thought maybe she should leave, but curiosity pushed her forward. She nudged the door open, ever so slightly. The house was dark as it would be if no one were home, but she still sensed several bodies inside and she heard shuffling.

She pressed the door open, enough for her to slide inside. Six people were in the house besides her – a man and woman in the family room and four men in the bedrooms. The woman was Brie's mom, but she was pretty sure the man was not Brie's dad. Curiosity turned into suspicion something was awry.

Alexa ran her hand along the wall for guidance. She bumped the light switch and decided to leave the lights off until she had a better understanding of what was going on. The more she zoned in on Brie's mom and the man, the more Alexa suspected the man's intentions were malicious.

She heard more shuffling, like feet scraping on the floor, and grunts. Then she heard a squeal, a cry for help.

Alexa ran back to the door, out to the yard, and screamed, "SEBASTIAN! SEBASTIAN!" She saw she had his attention and he was running her direction with other men behind him.

She ran back into the house, her hand fumbled along the wall trying to find the light switch again. No luck. She plundered forward into the dark family room, hoping the furniture hadn't been rearranged.

Hands extended she found the couch as expected, offset away from the wall. With her leg pressed to the couch as a guide she walked in the direction of Brie's mom and the man. Tiny beams of pale light blipped as someone was hitting the curtains on the sliding glass doors.

Alexa startled as she realized she was in a dream. No, this was reality but she had seen this in a dream, chaos was about to erupt.

She strode to the sliding glass doors and just like in her dream were two people on the ground, Brie's mom and a man on top of her. She grabbed the man's feet and pulled him toward the couch, Brie's mom scrambled away into the kitchen. Vampires flooded into the house and the other witches from the rear of the house came into the family room.

The man on the floor struggled to crawl away. Alexa caught his waist and pulled him upright. He had blood on him, Brie's mom's blood. Stirred by the scent of witch's blood and her anger, Alexa's teeth dropped. With a deep growl she thrust him into the crowd of vampires. Upon catching a whiff of the witch's blood, they too dropped their teeth.

A blast popped from the hallway. Alexa turned to see three of the witches with their arms clasped together, chanting a spell toward the men holding their friend.

Alexa's grandfather stepped forward and commanded the vampires to drop the man that this was an issue for the witches to address.

One of the vampires that had been holding the witch dropped to his knees, clasping his throat and coughing.

Her mother wiggled through the line of vampires with her hand outstretched. "Alexa, give me your hand!"

Alexa reached for her mother who then moved behind her, wrapping an arm around her waist.

"Just relax," her mother whispered, "and trust me." Her mother grabbed Alexa's left hand and placed it over her own on Alexa's waist. Then she grabbed Alexa's right arm and waved it back and forth in front of her. "Just lean into me," she said. She continued to wave Alexa's arm.

The witches in the hall turned their focus onto Alexa and her mother. Her mother began chanting, softly, rhythmically. Alexa didn't understand the words; she assumed them to be Gaelic.

Fervor built among the witches in the hall and Alexa sensed their energy building. Her mother however remained calm and focused.

Alexa's core began to burn and vibration ran through her body. The energy needed to stir air built and small bursts popped from her fingers. The men's hair waved in little puffs.

As her core continued to warm, Alexa's vision faded. A cloud swirled, blurring the faces in front of her. Her head tilted back onto her mother while her arm felt detached as it was waved to and fro.

She was mildly aware of the addition of more people to the house, witches. People were talking – stern orders issued in

German, women chanting in Gaelic, men chanting in English. Furniture was scooted across the floor and the sliding doors were opened.

Smoke. Alexa smelled smoke. And her fingers felt hot.

Screaming. Men were screaming in pain.

Her clouded vision dimmed to black, the screams faded. Smoke was her last memory.

Chapter Forty-Five

Waking, but eyes still closed, Alexa was aware people were nearby. They were quiet but moving about. Someone crawled next to her, the bed dipped from the weight.

Mom. Mom was next to her.

One eye peeked into the world and she found her mother watching her. Alexa felt woozy like after a bad night of tequila. She slammed her eye shut and groaned.

Her mother stroked her face and pushed a strand of hair behind her ear.

"I feel hung-over," Alexa slurred, her eyes still closed.

"I'm sure you do," her mother said. "You exhausted a lot of energy."

"Was that a dream?"

"No, honey, it really happened."

"Men were in Brie's house? They attacked her mom?" Alexa fluttered her eyes open, mere slits allowing minimal light through.

"Yes."

"I dreamed that a few days ago."

"I'm not surprised."

Alexa wrinkled her forehead. "What?"

"I said I'm not surprised. I imagine many of your dreams are premonitions."

"I hope not," Alexa groaned. "They're all awful and bloody and gross." Her eyes finally adjusted and she could look at her mother directly. She was in her parents' bedroom. "Is Brie's mom okay?"

"Yes. Lynn is a little banged up and extremely upset, but

she'll be fine. Brie is going to stay there for a few days."

"The guys in the house, they weren't burglars were they?"

"No, they were the men that had been attacking hybrids. Your father confirmed what you had reported – each one carried the scents of drinking hybrid blood."

"So were they arrested?"

"No, they were executed."

"What? Did the vampires take them out?"

"No, this was considered a witch problem and it was up to us witches to resolve." Her mother paused with a serious look on her face. "The reason you're so exhausted is that I used you as a conduit like I told you about the other day. Using you, we were able to break the curses three of them were constructing. And, man, you're strong, so much untapped potential."

"Did we kill them?"

"No. We only disarmed them. The vampires ensured no one ran away, but witches that were gathered next door came over and dealt the executions. It was handy having the vampires there, though. They know how to dispose of bodies rather quickly."

"I probably don't want to hear how that's done."

Her mother shrugged. "Not nearly as gruesome as you would imagine. I think they have a connection with a crematorium."

"What about Grandma? What happens to her?"

"That's a bit dicier. Unless we put your nose up to her and all of the council members we really don't have any proof, but I'm pretty sure they're all involved. Your father and I agree you cannot be around her until you get more training. She's dangerous and underhanded. That said enough people were present at the Mabon gathering to understand the severity of what these men were doing and who they are associated with.

I imagine there will be an uprising against the council – either they'll be replaced or the whole thing dismantled. Hard to say, but you and I need to stay out of it."

"Yeah, I don't need any more drama in my life."

Her mother offered a sympathetic grin.

"I don't want to be a vampire," Alexa whispered.

Her mother stroked her face again.

"I'm serious, Mom. I can't do this."

"You've been through a lot. You just need time to adjust."

"That's exactly what I need. The only reason I was with Eric yesterday was to tell him I needed to step away from everything and come up for air."

"You were breaking up with him?"

"No... not exactly. I just want to leave..."

"You were running away?"

She shrugged and said, "yeah."

"Was he going with you?"

"No. He did propose..." Alexa's eyes filled with tears. "Mom, I love him so much."

"Oh honey." Her mom planted a kiss on her forehead and watched as Alexa sniffled and came up for air. She asked, "Is that why you had sex?"

"Dunno. Maybe. I don't regret it. It was wonderful."

A slow smile spread across her mother's face. "Good. I'm glad it was wonderful. It should always be wonderful."

Alexa nodded. "I agree. It should always be like that."

They both laughed and Alexa sniffled.

"Did Dad..." Alexa took a deep breath, afraid of the answer. "Did Dad say what is going to happen to Eric?"

"Yes. Your grandfather made an agreement with his family. As long as no one mentions your identity, or well your existence, they will be allowed to stay in Brentwood. And I'm sure they will be watched to make sure they comply. Eric is being conscripted into the Queen's army and according to your grandfather, Eric's father agreed it would be a good way for a young man to, um, 'temper' his emotions."

"The army," Alexa repeated.

"Yes. And you should know that your grandfather is the head of the Queen's army, so I'm sure he will be particularly interested in Eric's progress."

"So he's not in trouble?"

"Well, he's being forced to join the army, so that's definitely punishment." Her mother giggled then said, "Your father is so upset, but he did start to laugh when he told me you tagged Eric."

"I had no idea what I was doing."

"It is sort of funny"

"Why the hell can't women tag men?" Alexa shook her head in exasperation. "Vampires are archaic."

"Yes, that is true. You know your father isn't going to approve of you marrying Eric," her mother said.

"It doesn't matter. I told him I wasn't ready to get married. I also told him that I knew he would marry someone else." Her mother's eyebrows arched in curiosity. "I said I knew he would have children and that meant another woman was in his future because I don't have children in my future."

Her mother dipped closer. "You see orbs?"

Alexa smiled. "Yeah, orbs. That explains them. You see them too?"

She nodded.

"You don't see any orbs around me, do you?"

Multiple times her mouth opened to say something, her eyes sorry. Her mother shook her head. "No. No I don't."

"Well, that confirms it," Alexa said. "I had sort of hoped

maybe I just couldn't see my own."

"I'm so sorry."

"I made peace with it a long time ago. So, the little boy orb that bounces around you all of the time, he's the baby that died?"

"Donovan. Yes." Her mother chuckled. "I wondered if you could see him. He used to play with you when you were a little girl."

"I remember."

"Do you?"

Alexa nodded. "Didn't you say you wanted to make my first name Marie? That would have made us Donny and Marie."

Her mother burst out laughing. "I never made the connection with the Osmond's!"

"Mom, you can be such a dork at times." Alexa flashed an ornery smile. "So who's this other brother I have?"

"You really need to know how your father and I met, but since you're in a fragile state, we'll hold that story for another time. And please don't think I'm hiding anything from you, now is just not the time with everything else on your plate."

"It's pretty bad, huh?"

Her mother nodded her head - her expression said everything. She searched Alexa's face and softly smiled. "His name is Radimir. He is the son of your father's first wife, but she died when he was only a few days old. I've considered him my son since then – I've held him, nursed him... It breaks my heart to be away from him, but I get to see him a couple times a year. We would send you off with my parents or make other arrangements. This was the worst part of keeping secrets from you, especially since you so desperately wanted a brother or a sister. But you should know Radimir adores you and is angry you two weren't raised together. *I'm* angry you weren't raised together, but it was my decision to leave Austria and come here. I wasn't forced to leave, in fact I was begged to stay, but I had to get out of there. The vampire life was a bit much for me, enough that I was willing to leave behind my little boy."

Alexa saw the sadness in her mother's eyes. She grabbed her mother's hand and they pressed their foreheads together.

Her mother sighed. "I really do understand the need to step away from the vampires. We did you such a disservice by raising you as a human. I wish we could go back and find a better way to deal with all of this."

"Yeah, well, it's all in the open now - that's all I ever wanted. Now I just want to hide away from it all. I've got a lot of emotions to work through."

"I'm sure you do."

"I don't want to break your heart, but I need to leave. I need to get so far away from all of this..."

Her mother nodded. She got off the bed and headed to the dresser. She brought back a small wooden box, mumbling a few quiet words. The lid popped open revealing a Bible.

Alexa's eyes brightened. "Do you know how many times I tried to open that thing?"

"Mhmm, your father too."

"You had a spell on it? You would have gotten in trouble for that!" Alexa wrinkled her forehead.

"The spell was cast long before I ever met your father." Her mother opened the Bible where a four-leaf clover had been pressed. She flipped the pages until a photograph fluttered to the bed. Handing the photograph to Alexa, she said, "It's my father and his two sisters."

Alexa recognized the young man in linen pants and Hawaiian print shirt. His big, bold smile shined even in black and white. Two girls, probably junior high aged, stood on either side with their brother's arms draped over their shoulders. A lake was behind them, likely a family vacation. She flipped the picture over, "Corinne, Conrad & Catherine – Lake Mohawksin June 1938." At the bottom, in a different handwriting, "218-723-3259". Alexa looked up to her mother for explanation.

"Aunt Corinne gave me this picture and said if I ever needed refuge to come find her. I was probably fifteen at the time. She never did like my mother. But it was funny because after I came home married to your father, my dad pulled me to the side and suggested if I needed to escape I should find my way to Minnesota and find one of his sisters." Glaring straight into Alexa's eyes and clasping her hand, she said, "You should keep this. I won't ever leave your father."

Alexa bent forward. "Are you saying what I think you're saying?"

Her mother straightened with feigned innocence. "I merely handed you an old family picture. What you do with it is up to you." She leaned forward and kissed Alexa's forehead. With her lips still pressed to Alexa, she whispered, "I love you very much and want you to be happy. Please find peace with yourself."

Chapter Forty-Six

Shimmying out of a window had never been difficult, but Alexa had never tried to escape from her parent's bedroom. The drop to the ground didn't bother her nor did the row of hedges lining the front of the house. No, the large number of people, vampires in particular, milling about was her biggest hurdle.

She landed with a thump catching the attention of a young man of similar same age, smoking on the front porch. She turned and closed the window and flashed him a smile. "I'm just going to visit my friends down the street. I'll be back in a few minutes."

He looked at her blankly. What could he say? It wasn't as if she were a prisoner. Alexa pushed through the hedges and headed toward Brie's parents' house. She sensed behind her the man left his post and went inside, likely to report her departure. No one followed her and she kept walking.

She stood in front of the DuBourg's home staring at the front door. Her sense of time was distorted; she wasn't even sure what day it was. How long had it been since Alexa walked into this house suspecting foul play? Twelve hours?

Brie flung the door open and pulled Alexa into a hard embrace. "Oh my God I don't know what would have happened if you weren't here last night!"

Alexa pulled Brie's arms away and stepped inside. "How's your mom doing?"

"She's fine. A little weirded out by everything. That guy was trying to bite her neck like he was a vampire! She has a horrible bruise right here." Brie pointed to the base of her neck.

"My mom said it was something about a blood offering and black magic."

"Oh dude, it was totally black magic. They were summoning some weird shit. They almost asphyxiated one of the vampires."

Tess came around the corner from the family room and rushed to Alexa and Brie. She wrapped her arms around Alexa and they squeezed each other.

"What are you doing here?" Alexa asked.

Tess pointed over her shoulder. "My mom is making sure Lynn takes it easy and is pampering her left and right." She turned to Brie. "I think your dad ducked out and is with my dad next door."

"I don't doubt it, your mom is being ridiculous which is of course stirring up my mom."

"Can I see her?" Alexa asked.

"Sure, c'mon." Brie pulled Alexa by the arm into the family room toward the bedrooms.

Alexa stopped in the family room and assessed the damage. The stench of smoke hung in the air, flashing memories of the previous night intertwined with her corresponding nightmare.

The furniture was missing, as was the family portrait over the fireplace. Through the glass doors she could see the couch and armchairs sitting in the backyard, charred from fire. On the ceiling were grey streaks, she assumed from flames. As she continued to stare at the smoke designs on the ceiling she asked, "What the hell happened? I don't remember anything after my mom showed up."

"Dude, it was the most amazing thing I have ever seen," Tess said, her eyes wide as saucers. "Your mom had your arms waving every which way. She had men pinned to the ceiling and then slamming them to the ground. One guy was trying to crawl to the back of the house and she whipped up a tornado thing and pulled his ass back in here. And then Brie's dad – I didn't know he could jolt electricity but he zapped the fuck out of the guy that tried to bite her mom. The guy would try to stand up and Tom would zing him down again. And then Magda steps forward."

Brie giggled and said, "Magda is the quietest person on the planet. She has been coming to these parties for as long as I can remember and just sips tea. Never has a glass of wine, never says a word. She just watches."

"Yeah!" Tess nodded. "I think she gets a kick out of watching everyone. But anyways, she steps forward, and again still not saying a thing and then POOF. Flames shoot out of her fingers."

"What?" Alexa stared at Tess. She wasn't sure if she heard correctly.

"Flames," Tess repeated.

"It was like little lighters at the tips of her fingers," Brie explained as she wiggled her fingers.

Tess shook her head while grinning with amazement. "But then your mom swung you around to Magda and whatever she was channeling through you she funneled into Magda. She put your hands on Magda's shoulders and suddenly those little sparks turned into flamethrowers. You guys *incinerated* two of them."

Alexa's attention bounced back and forth between Tess and Brie with a weak smile. "I guess that explains the couch." She nodded toward the backyard. The acrid smell lingered throughout the house.

"It was amazing," Tess said. "I've never seen anything like that."

"Me neither," Tess's mom said as she pushed off from the

wall in the hallway, startling Alexa. "I knew Magda was a pyromancer, but she keeps that under wraps and just sticks to reading tea leaves. I was surprised to see her step forward, to be quite honest. But holy crap, you and your mom pumped some serious energy into her and she just ran with it. She directed those flames like an expert."

Alexa looked between her two friends and Tess's mom. She had killed again. Something in her lent to the death of another person. She felt weak and wobbly and searched for a place to sit down. Without any furniture in the family room she sank to the floor.

The women joined Alexa on the floor, squatting beside her - furrowed brows of concern hovering over her.

Struggling for air, Alexa looked between them. "I've killed again?"

Tess's mom held her face. "No. You did not kill anyone last night. Magda directed the fire and she shoulders the responsibility. Alexa, honey, you were passed out and had no conscious effort in this. Your mother was pumping your energy and Magda aimed it."

"But it was my energy."

"No. You hold no responsibility here. You were merely a conduit and conduits are not responsible for the damage others unleash."

Alexa sat still, guilt filling every pore. She closed her eyes hoping for clarity; instead she only smelled the smoke. She opened her eyes again, roaming the room where she had spent so many hours playing with her friends. "I need out of here."

"Okay we can help you home," Tess's mom said.

Brie's mom arrived wrapped in a pale blue bathrobe, devoid of any makeup, and her hair unkempt.

"No," Alexa said, calm and resolve building in her. "I want to escape."

"You mean leave Brentwood?" Tess's mom asked.

Alexa nodded her head.

"Did your mom finally tell you what's going on?" Brie's mom asked.

Alexa looked at her and smiled. She looked like hell and had a big, white bandage on her neck. "Not exactly. I've been told enough. We were supposed to have a bigass family meeting today with the big reveal, but I kinda shot that to shit last night and um, I really don't care what they have to say anymore. I just want to leave, get as far away from here as I can."

"That's sort of hard with the vampire mafia milling around at the end of the street," Tess said.

Alexa huffed. "You have no idea." She looked Tess straight in the eye. "I need your help. Just toss me in the trunk of your car and drive me the fuck out of here. Don't stop until you hit Chicago or Memphis, or someplace far away from here."

Chapter Forty-Seven

Sitting at the dining room table in Brie's house, Tess's mom set a plate of cheese and sausage in front of her. Alexa couldn't remember the last time she had eaten. She wondered how many hours had passed since seeing Eric... since killing the vampire next to Brie's apartment... since quietly typing numbers into her computer at work?

Tess and Brie took seats on either side of her, each grabbing a slice of cheese from her plate. The Moms sat across the table, encouraging her to eat.

Alexa nibbled on a piece of sausage, waiting for the lecture. Seeking distraction she turned to Brie. "Does anyone know what happened to Jack? I mean, not that I particularly care about him, but what did they tell him about how his friend died?"

Tess chuckled a fake laugh. "Yeah, the news is going ape shit over that one. Evidently, a *bear* attacked a man and woman behind the apartments. The man died at the scene and the woman, *you*, suffered minor injuries."

"A bear? Who the hell believes that shit?" Alexa asked in wide-eyed wonder.

"Everyone who heard an animal growl and a man shrieking as he was torn to pieces," Tess said. "Then there was a rifle shot, but they said it just scared the bear away... I assume they shot the guy attacking you?"

"Well, no," Alexa said. "I killed him before anyone got to us. He was dead and dripping blood all over me when he was pulled off. Some guy just randomly fired the gun into the air. Speaking of which, where did all of the vampires come from?"

"Three jumped down from the buildings across the street and then your bodyguard came bolting from his car," Brie said. "He was yelling into a walkie-talkie and then, like seconds later, cars filled with vampires came from all directions. Some cops showed up..."

"Vampires," Tess added.

"...And yelled at me and Tess to go inside. My neighbors were in the stairwell wondering what the hell was going on. But I saw them pull Jack and his other friend to the car for questioning. Eventually, one of the cops came inside and directed everyone back to their apartments, then asked us to step out for questioning, but he really wanted us to help escort you inside."

"It was crazy, absolute mayhem," Tess said. "When my parents showed up there were vampires dressed like guys from animal control marching around in the neighboring lots 'looking for tracks.' Three news trucks were out front and Brie's neighbors were giving interviews. I heard one of them talk about the menacing growls."

"Now there's suspicion the dog attack in Fenton Park was actually from the bear and people are freaking out," Tess's mom said.

Alexa wrinkled her forehead. "What dog attack? Oh, the morning I was attacked in the park?" Everyone nodded their heads. Alexa closed her eyes and sought peace somewhere in the darkness, not that darkness ever brought her peace. She shook her head and with her eyes still closed she mumbled, "This is why I have to leave." She opened her eyes and looked around the table. "I don't care where I go, but I have to get out of this town."

Tess's mom stared at her and shook her head. "You can't go where you don't know anyone. You're so inexperienced, you have no idea who to trust."

"And if you had a problem who would you turn to?" Brie's mom asked.

"You can't escape vampires," Tess's mom said. "They're everywhere. I mean you can continue to present as a witch or even as a hybrid, if you prefer, but that doesn't keep you away from vampires."

"I don't know what to do," Alexa said. "I just... I just can't stay here."

Brie's mom offered a sympathetic grin. "I hear you, but you also need to consider your safety. If anything happens to you, Alexa, your father would rain down on us like hellfire. It's a shame you can't turn to your grandparents."

"Oh, my mom is adamant that I keep my distance from Grandma."

Tess's mom leaned forward. "If your mother didn't say it, I would have. That woman has never been up to any good – and what she was doing with those men attacking hybrids cannot be trusted. Getting far away from Beverly Meyers is reason enough to leave town." She drummed her fingers on the table.

"Do you remember my college roommate, Abbey?" Tess asked.

"The weirdo pig farmer from Iowa?" Alexa asked.

"No, that was Claire. Abbey was the one where we got busted for having alcohol on campus," Tess said.

"Okay, yeah," Alexa said.

"You know she's a witch?" Tess asked.

"No."

"Well, maybe we could go visit her." Tess and Alexa watched each other. Alexa considered the possibility, the opportunity to delve further into the world of witches. She thought about the photograph shoved in her pocket. Why involve her friends any more than necessary? Abbey could be the key to a new world. Far away. She wanted to be far, far away.

"Can we go now?" Alexa asked.

"Yeah, but..." Tess hesitated.

"I just need someplace safe to make a phone call," Alexa said.

"You have someone to call?" Brie's mom asked.

"It's not that vampire you've been seeing?" Tess's mom asked.

"No," Alexa said. "Someone in my mom's family. Don't worry, it's someone who doesn't like my grandmother. I just can't make the call from here. It's too likely the mafia down the street has your lines tapped."

Tess's mom rolled her eyes. Brie's mom tilted her head in resignation.

Tess looked over to her mother. A silent exchange of raised eyebrows and shrugs ensued. Her mother said to Tess, "You should go talk to your father. His car probably has a full tank."

Ignited with possibility, the conversation turned into excited chatter. A plan came together to smuggle Alexa out of the house and then out of Brentwood. She sat in stunned silence as the idea became action - Brie ran to the basement, Tess went next door to her parents' house, and their mothers dug through their purses. In a matter of minutes a ride was arranged, spare clothing loaded into Alexa's gym bag that she had left on their porch, food and drink into a second bag, and cash shoved into her hands. Then, she and Tess's mom swapped clothing.

When Tess's mom emerged from the bedroom, the women erupted into laughter. The two never could pass as the other, but from a distance with her hair in a ponytail and carrying Alexa's scent, Tess's mom could walk down the street with Brie and Tess as a decoy allowing Alexa to slide away.

Overwhelmed by their generosity, she hugged each woman

with fierce love and gratitude.

Together they watched the clock. At 4:50 Brie, Tess, and Alexa's decoy would walk to the park. At 5:00 Tess's father would drive to his aunt's house as he did most Sunday nights.

It was 4:45 and Alexa hugged her friends again, not knowing if this plan would work or when she would see them again. They tried not to cry and no one dared to say good-bye.

Alexa stepped back as Brie and Tess recomposed themselves. They locked arms with Tess's mom and launched out the front door like they had with Alexa had so many times in the past.

Brie's mom held onto Alexa tightly as she shook. Everything was happening so fast, she wasn't ready. She took several deep breaths and said, "I need to get a drink of water."

Alexa went to the sink and looked out the window but didn't find any revelation in the yellowing grass in the backyard where she had spent her childhood. She could almost see her younger self running with Brie and Tess. Echoes of laughter and squeals bubbled from her memory.

Wiping her face she thought back to the day before her teeth had come in when she knew nothing of witches and vampires, before she knew the name of the copier repairman who visited her office. Despite her determination to not cry, another tear rolled down her cheek as she bid farewell to a life and world she would never see again. Somewhere between grief and hope Alexa understood she had just begun a new chapter in her life.

Made in the USA
Monee, IL
01 August 2021